A Little Justice

Catriona King

This is a work of fiction. Names, characters, places and incidents are used fictitiously and any resemblance to persons living or dead, business establishments, events, locations or areas, is entirely coincidental.

No part of this book may be used or reproduced in any manner without written permission of the author, except for brief quotations and segments used for promotion or in reviews.

ISBN: 978-1533494504

First published in 2012
Copyright © 2016 by Catriona King
Photography: Ken Tannenbaum
Artwork: Jonathan Temples:
creative@jonathantemples.co.uk
Editors: Maureen Vincent-Northam and Sue Caskill
Formatting: Rebecca Emin
All rights reserved.

Hamilton-Crean Publishing Ltd. 2016

Discover us online:
www.hamiltoncreanpublishing.com

For my mother.

About the Author

Catriona King is a medical doctor and trained as a police Forensic Medical Examiner in London, where she worked for some years. She has worked with the police on many occasions. She returned to live in Belfast in recent years.

She has written since childhood and has been published in many formats: non-fiction, journalistic and fiction.

'A Limited Justice' is the first in the Craig Crime Series and is being re-released in June 2016.

The other novels in the Craig Crime Series are

- The Grass Tattoo
- The Visitor
- The Waiting Room
- The Broken Shore
- The Slowest Cut
- The Coercion Key
- The Careless Word
- The History Suite
- The Sixth Estate
- The Sect
- The Keeper
- The Talion Code

A new Craig Crime Novel will be released in autumn 2016

Acknowledgements

My thanks to Northern Ireland for providing the inspiration for my books.

My thanks also to: Maureen Vincent-Northam and Sue Caskill as my editors, Jonathan Temples for his cover design and Rebecca Emin for formatting this book.

I would like to thank all of the police officers that I have ever worked with for their professionalism, wit and compassion.

Catriona King
Belfast, June 2016

Discover the author's books at:
www.catrionakingbooks.com

To engage with the author about her books, email:
Catriona_books@yahoo.co.uk

The author can be found on Facebook and Twitter:
@CatrionaKing1

A Limited Justice

Chapter One

The Lower Bann River. Portglenone, Northern Ireland. Wednesday, 17th October 2012. 9 a.m.

The river ran clear and fast past Maria Burton's feet, and the morning sun made the day feel more like June than October. She pulled off her jacket and rolled-up her T-shirt sleeves as she walked, shaking her long hair loose from its braid.

The houses on the bank opposite were quiet but they would soon be awake, and she dreamed of living there someday, laughing aloud at the fantasy. She loved her job but it certainly wasn't for the money.

She gazed dreamily at the water as she strolled on, free to ignore her surroundings for one more work-free day. It would be her last day ever.

****

Belfast. Wednesday afternoon.

Detective Chief Inspector Marc Craig considered the man at his feet. There was no question about it, he was dead. His shocked face was bloated and pale, and a ring of fresh black bruising etched out his mouth. Golden oil covered every part of him, soaking into his hair like some exotic pomade. More of it ran across the petrol-station's concourse filling the gutter by their feet, the fumes stinging Craig's eyes.

"Rough way to go, boss. Even by my standards."

Inspector Liam Cullen stood so close to his boss that his loud voice vibrated Craig's ears painfully and he moved away, motioning the crime scene investigators to start their work. If Liam had noticed the shift he didn't comment; they'd known each other too long to be offended now.

The dead man lay face-up, staring at the sky in the Belfast terraced street, a petrol pump projecting vertically from his mouth. It had been rammed between his tonsils so hard that the uvula's inch-thick projection acted as a deadlock and a young C.S.I. was feverishly trying to extract it, without destroying evidence. Around them the petrol's fumes combined with the smell of burnt flesh to make a perfume that would never find a market.

The dead man was somewhere in middle age, strong but overweight, his skin showing the wear from an outdoor life. His hands lay open in supplication, their palms torn from small pieces of gravel embedded in the worn fat. His lower limbs had already contracted into the boxer's pose so typical of burns and his half-open green eyes held a look of complete surprise.

"Do we have a name yet?"

Before Liam could answer, a C.S.I. handed him something.

"These might help."

It was the contents of the man's unburnt jacket pocket, but there was little to tell his story. Just a laminated driving licence curling up from the heat and a basic model Nokia, several years old. Ian McCandless, fifty-six and a resident of the Rogreen Council estate in East Belfast. Not a resident anywhere now.

Liam read aloud, adding. "I wonder who he'd annoyed enough to warrant this. Hardly accidental was it?"

Craig didn't answer, just squinted up at the dimming winter sky, shielding his dark eyes with a hand.

"Who's the medical examiner?"

"The Doc."

They both smiled. No matter how many doctors there were, 'the Doc' only ever meant one man. Doctor John Winter, Northern Ireland's Director of Pathology. He was brilliant and strange and Craig remembered him being the same at twelve, thirty years before, at their boys' integrated grammar. John would give them quick answers.

Craig gazed around the petrol station where they stood. It was so derelict that there were imaginary tumbleweeds blowing across the forecourt. Even the 'closed' sign looked tired, as if it wasn't a new state of affairs. A bin half-full of rubbish lay overturned by the door of a one-storied shop, its contents scattered and drifting across their view.

He lifted a slim, brown envelope from the ground, turning it over in his sterile hand. It bore yesterday's postmark and its single sheet of contents was hanging half-out. He scanned the bin thoughtfully.

"Liam, call the Met office and check what the wind has been like. This bin went over today and I don't think it blew over. It's far too mild."

"How do you know it was today?"

Craig pointed to a 'Belfast Chronicle' lying on the ground, its pages strewn across the shop's entrance. "That's yesterday's newspaper." He looked down at the envelope as he spoke.

"And this has yesterday's postmark and this address, so it arrived here this morning. I'm betting McCandless came into the shop, lifted the post, and was opening it when he was attacked. He didn't even get the letter out of the envelope. The bin fell over in the struggle."

Liam nodded slowly, not fully understanding but waiting for the rest. Craig continued evenly. "If the bin had been over when McCandless had arrived, he'd have lifted it on the way into the shop rather than let rubbish blow all over the forecourt."

"Unless he was a real slob?"

Craig shook his head.

"Not even you're that bad. The bin's weighted, so it would take a hell of a wind to topple it, or a very sharp push. My money's on the push. Either McCandless knocked it over or whoever killed him did, so get it printed, please."

Suddenly Liam jumped; the Nokia in his hand was vibrating and its screen showed an incoming number. He glanced at Craig and answered on his nod, keeping his deep voice neutral.

"Hello. Can I help you?"

A hesitant female voice came down the line, slightly slurred, as if she was very tired. It was a middle-class accent from somewhere out of town, and Liam narrowed it to west of the Bann.

"Oh yes...thank you. Can I speak to Mr McCandless please?"

"Who's calling?"

The woman hesitated, and for one moment Liam thought she was going to hang up; all sorts of nefarious reasons flashing through his head if she did. After a moment's silence she continued, speaking so softly that he strained to hear her words.

"My name's Monica Gibson. I'm calling about the car that's for sale."

"Car?"

Liam shot a look around and spotted a row of old cars with lurid green price stickers, half-hidden behind the shop's wall. He walked across quickly, peering at the cars as he talked. They were battered and scraped and the youngest was at least five years old, although the prices didn't reflect it half as much as they should have done. McCandless had obviously been a bit of a Del-Boy.

They supported her reason for ringing but he kept her talking anyway, while he thought of ways to extract more information.

"Which car were you interested in?"

"I was told there's a red Ford Focus in good condition?"

Her voice rose hopefully and Liam stared at the only red car sceptically. 'Good' wouldn't have been his word for it, but it gave him an opening.

"Have you viewed it yet?"

"Oh...no. Not yet."

He noticed that her voice got quieter at the end of every sentence, no matter how short. It was as if she ran out of breath, or energy, and he felt vaguely sorry for her. As much as his suspicious 'new-case' mind allowed him to feel sorry for anyone.

"That's why I was calling. I was hoping to arrange a

viewing?"

Her voice rose so hopefully that he thought it was fairer to reveal himself. If she hung-up they had her details for a trace anyway.

"I'm sorry Ms Gibson, but that won't be possible. I'm afraid there's been an accident at the garage. I'm a member of the emergency services helping out. Mr McCandless can't get to the phone at the moment." It was the understatement of the year.

The woman gave a sharp intake of breath, reacting as all nice people would when they heard 'emergency'. Her next comment belonged to a script that Liam had heard often.

"Oh dear, I hope no-one's hurt. I'm sorry; I'll ring him back another time."

Good luck with that; it'll be a quiet conversation. But he didn't need to upset a stranger, so instead he acquiesced kindly. "You do that, Madam. Goodbye."

Craig watched the exchange comfortably, knowing that Liam would prise every grain of information from the encounter. It was his forte, that and being politically incorrect. Just then, a liveried Skoda pulled up to the kerb, and the small, brown-haired figure of Detective Sergeant Annette McElroy got out.

She walked briskly across the forecourt, joining Craig outside the shop. One glance at the smoldering corpse convinced her that once was quite enough; she'd catch the movie later. Liam loped his six-feet-six frame across from the cars, and the three of them walked past a kneeling C.S.I. into the shop's neon-lit interior. Craig nodded at the Nokia.

"What was the call about, Liam?"

"Some wee woman who's just had a narrow escape. She almost bought the worst car this side of the Bann, and he was asking four grand for the heap of crap as well. Her miss was her mercy." He smiled, pleased with himself, like a man who had just done his good deed for the decade.

"McCandless did a side-line in used cars then? How many are there?"

"Five. We'd better impound them or they won't

have wheels tomorrow. I'll check her out, but she just sounded like the usual nice Northern Ireland lady. Probably thought she'd slum it and get a bargain." He snorted cynically. "McCandless would have seen her coming a mile off. She didn't sound too healthy either. I felt quite sorry for her."

It was Annette's turn to snort. Liam feigned hurt, but he conceded that he wasn't usually known for his sympathy. Just then, a shiny blue Chrysler Crossfire pulled up and Liam whistled loudly.

"Now *there's* a lovely motor. I wouldn't mind that for four grand."

Craig recognised the number plate and smiled. The familiar lanky frame of John Winter unfolded itself from the car's interior and he beckoned him over to join them.

"Are those the Doc's new wheels? Bit of an improvement on that crappy old Beamer he used to drive."

John raised an eyebrow. "I heard that, Liam! Show some respect for the dead. I had that car for ten years."

Annette shook her head. "And now you've chucked her out for scrap... just like a man."

The pathologist turned to her in mock dismay, charm in every gesture.

"Now, Annette...you know I wouldn't. In fact, she's parked in my garage right now, awaiting tender loving restoration. I always respect a lady." Then he winked at her so obviously that she blushed and turned away, flustered.

"OK, Marc. What've you got for me?"

"Nice car, John."

Winter nodded regally, and was just about to launch into the details of its AMG engine when Craig headed him off at the pass.

"Right. Our victim was a Mr Ian McCandless. We think he's the garage owner. The place is pretty run down but he was still selling used cars. We've just had a call from a woman trying to buy one. The victim was found at about two-thirty by a passer-by and she gave her statement to uniform. She didn't see anything useful, was just walking her dog when it ran over to a pile of smoldering rags that wasn't.

There's a lot of loose petrol out there, but I didn't want to sand it and ruin your scene. But quick as you can please, John. Don't light any matches and switch off your mobile. There's a fire engine waiting at Sydenham when you're done."

Liam suddenly remembered the Nokia, turning it off quickly. Craig caught the move and smiled.

"Just your quick first impression, John, please."

Winter nodded and grabbed a white jumpsuit from the pile by the door, joining the C.S.I.s outside. They would get his first thoughts; he wasn't like a lot of pathologists, refusing to comment at all until the post-mortem.

Craig still had the envelope in his hand and he turned it over, studying the frank. It had been sent from the High Court the day before, so their victim had probably been in trouble for something. He struggled with the temptation to rip it open but knew that Des Marsham, the Head of Forensic Science, would roast him if he did. He suddenly realised what he'd thought, substituted 'beat' for 'roast' and felt instantly better. Strange the niceties people cared about at murder scenes.

Liam was wandering noisily through the aisles in the cold shop. It had darkened fridges and half-empty shelves but he'd managed to find a packet of Kit-Kats. He distributed them with largess, until Annette's disapproving voice cut through his feel-good factor.

"I hope you're paying for those."

She was the office conscience and occasional pain in the ass, but Craig took the hint. Looking pointedly at the Kit-Kat hanging from Liam's mouth, he reached into his pocket for some coins and was just checking what he'd found when something else caught his eye. He bent down urgently to stare at one side of the doorjamb, about twelve inches from the ground.

A bright new nail was protruding from the weathered wood, as if it had only been hammered half-in. Either a botch job or a hurried one. A length of needle-sharp wire had been wound several times around its head, the cut edge protruding vertically. Its sheen hinted at a recent cut, about as old as the nail.

Craig looked instinctively at the opposite side of the door. No nail. Damn. He leaned in, peering more closely while the others watched, well used to his hawk-eye. After a few seconds, he rested back with a triumphant look, pointing at the jamb. Liam hunkered down to have a look at the invisible clue. There was a small, fresh hole in the wood, exactly opposite the nail.

"You must be a detective, boss."

"Very witty. Right, Annette, get a C.S.I. in here, please. There's a nail with wire on it and a hole on the other side matching its level exactly. Someone had a tripwire across this doorway and not that long ago. That edge is too bright to be old."

"What are you thinking, sir?"

"I'll tell you in a minute. I just need to check something."

He crossed the forecourt quickly to a kneeling John Winter, who was peering through his black-wire glasses at Ian McCandless' corpse. To anyone else it would have looked like a pile of burnt clothes, but the body would tell him more than any textbook.

"Can you check something for me, John?"

"Sure. What is it? I'm almost finished."

"Is there any impression on his shins, say from something sharp?"

Craig held his breath as the pathologist stared hard at the dead man's shins. There should have been two of them, but the heat had melted his lower extremities so badly that they formed one broad, flexed shank, with nothing to say where one leg ended and the other began.

John took a bright, needle-sharp probe from his instrument pouch and touched the area so lightly that only the thinnest crust flaked off, revealing a livid horizontal cut beneath. It was narrow, red and deep, and ran the full breadth of the single limb. He stared at the area from every angle, until finally he nodded and Craig exhaled.

"It looks like he's been cut with a cheese wire. How did you know?"

"Measure its position, then come into the shop and I'll show you. Liam found some Kit-Kats and the coffee's on."

Ten minutes later, they were fed and coffee-ed and John gave his brief summary. "Right. Looking at what Marc saw first; there's a sharp cut across both of our victim's shins, approximately eleven to thirteen inches from his feet. I can't be more accurate until the post-mortem because of skin contraction, but that's my best estimate." He took a sip of coffee before carrying on.

"The cut's new, quite deep and it definitely happened before he died. The instrument must have been razor-sharp and the pain would have been excruciating, so he probably had only brief contact with whatever caused it. That would be consistent with the limited depth of the wound. Des can get us more details on the type of instrument, but I know you already have a view on that."

Craig nodded quickly. "I think it was razor-wire, tied at shin height across the doorway. The likeliest scenario is that McCandless walked into it as he was leaving the shop, then he tripped and fell forward onto the forecourt outside the door."

John nodded slowly. "That could fit with the abrasions on both his palms. There's gravel embedded in them and it looks the same as the type outside the door. But I can't be sure until..."

"Until you do the post-mortem...We know."

Craig moved quickly to the door and hunkered down, pointing out the nail. The C.S.I.s' dust had dulled the wire's sheen slightly, but its sharp edge was still clearly visible.

"This was definitely a tripwire. The nail and some wire have been left here, they probably didn't have time to get rid of it, and there's a matching hole on the other side. The cuts on his shins fit with the height of the nail."

John nodded. "In addition to the abrasions on his hands, I'm sure we'll find cuts on his knees."

He looked thoughtful for a moment and then continued. "Unfortunately there were more than just those injuries. Your victim also received a blow to the back of his head."

They looked shocked as he continued. "It depressed the skull completely. Beside the Foramen Magnum where the bone's thin."

Craig nodded, understanding.

"The what, Doctor Winter?"

"It's a big hole at the base of the skull, Annette. Where the spinal cord runs through. The point is, it's nearly impossible to hit that area by accident."

He raised a hand to stop Liam's looming question, knowing that his next words would complicate things even further.

"The blow fractured the skull and went right through to the brain. Its diameter would fit with some sort of narrow implement, maybe a hammer. And I'd say they knew exactly what they were aiming for; there are no hesitation marks."

Craig interrupted. "Would one blow have killed him?"

"Probably, although not definitely. But it would have knocked him out immediately."

Craig sat down and poured another coffee, looking satisfied with himself, and Annette knew that he'd already worked out the scene.

"OK, so we know that Ian McCandless was tripped by a wire and then fell forward, onto his hands and probably knees. He was then hit on the back of the head when he was down, in an area of the skull that would either concuss him or kill him immediately. Then he was dragged over to the petrol pump. I'm sure you'll find abrasions on his thighs and shins to back that up, John."

"If I can remove the burnt material without destroying what's behind it."

"Then he was turned onto his back, either already dead or unconscious, and possibly drowned in petrol. But..." Craig gave the pathologist a wry nod. "We'll know more about that after the post-mortem. OK, then, as if that wasn't enough, the killer set fire to the body. Probably trying to hide any clues, or perhaps even erase the victim's identity completely. But we were lucky, the fire burnt out before it could destroy everything."

Liam couldn't resist a quip. "Unleaded wasn't very healthy for him, was it, boss?"

Annette whacked him so hard on the arm that he jumped. "God, Liam, that's a terrible thing to say. That's a human being out there."

For a moment, they all looked shame-faced. Their logic and dark humour helped them cope with the things they saw, but Annette knew to call time when they'd gone far enough.

"Quite right, Annette. That's us told off."

She blushed, not knowing whether Craig was being sarcastic until his softly delivered next sentence.

"We need you to remind us sometimes, when we really need civilizing." He smiled kindly at her and then turned immediately back to the case, all sentiment forgotten.

"OK, thanks John. That tells me one thing loud and clear."

Everyone looked at him, puzzled.

"What?"

"McCandless' attacker was a small man. Or maybe even a woman."

"Where did you get that one from?"

Liam's face screwed up in doubt and Annette stared blankly at Craig.

"I don't mean to be rude, sir. But where *did* you get that from?"

Craig smiled. "Now I know how Sherlock felt. OK, I think Ian McCandless came in here about two p.m., lifted the mail and made himself a coffee. The kettle was still slightly warm when uniform arrived at two-forty-five and there's an open carton of new-dated milk on the counter. The fridge is off in here so he must have brought it with him. Maybe he made a few phone calls or did a few things in here as well."

Liam flicked on the Nokia and checked the calls.

There'd been three that day. "You're right; his last outgoing call was made at two-fifteen. That times death between two-fifteen and two-thirty, when the dog-walker found him."

Craig nodded, continuing.

"The wire wasn't across the door when McCandless entered or he'd have tripped on the way in. So it must've been set quickly while he was in here making his calls. That's why the nail was only hammered half-in; it was done while he was here. So, either the attacker hid themselves very well, or they were small and less visible."

Liam leaned forward urgently. "And they must have muffled the hammer or he'd have heard the noise, another reason the nail was only half-in. Loud blows would've attracted his attention."

"Correct. Plus..." Craig pointed to a small portable radio sitting beside the milk.

"My money's on the radio being on, masking any noise even further. Liam, check if the lads turned it off when they arrived."

Liam nipped outside and came back a few seconds later, nodding. Luck had been on the killer's side, or they'd known Ian McCandless' routine very well. Annette was about to ask something but Craig continued.

"I'll come to your question in a second, Annette; just let me explain a bit further. This shop is so small that McCandless would have had clear sight of the entrance at all times, unless his back was turned to the door. Which it might have been when he was making the coffee or phone calls. Agreed?"

They nodded, seeing where he was going. The killer had needed to be virtually invisible, much easier if they were small.

"By the time he went outside, maybe to check on the cars, the tripwire was in place and the killer was ready. McCandless tripped and fell. The wire cut his shins and he put his hands out to stop himself falling, hence the shin cuts and palm abrasions. He was still conscious then.

I think he pulled the bin down as he fell, and dropped the envelope he was opening onto the ground. That's why the paper was half-out of the envelope and only some of the bin's contents were on the ground. Then McCandless was hit on the head, dragged across to the pumps, drowned in petrol and set alight."

John made a face. "OK, that would explain the injuries I've found so far, and why he didn't finish opening the letter? But why couldn't the assailant have been large and strong?"

Craig sipped his coffee before answering.

"Well...they could have been, but then why would they have needed the tripwire? If murder was their intention, which it obviously was, a large assailant could have just waited until McCandless was leaving the shop and hit him from behind.

But McCandless was a strong man, so unless the assailant was equally confident of their strength, why take that risk? The hammer might have glanced off, and McCandless certainly wouldn't have gone down without a fight. And, tell me if I'm wrong, John, but there are no signs of a fight on the unburnt portion of his hands or arms, are there?"

John nodded his agreement slowly. "No, but..."

Craig kept going.

"And there are no signs of a struggle in here, or outside. Just the bin tipped over, and it's still beside its base so it probably only fell once. It didn't roll or change direction, which it might have done in a lengthy fight, or there would have been far more rubbish around. And the rubbish wouldn't only have been lying at the front of the bin. Yes?"

Annette nodded quickly, seeing now where he was heading.

"So even without the forensics, that tells me it's very unlikely that the killer tackled McCandless head-on. And it's unlikely that they had a gun or a knife, or they would have just shot or stabbed him." Liam looked increasingly puzzled but Craig forged on.

"And all that tells me that our killer wasn't certain that they were strong enough to kill Ian McCandless in a direct fight. They didn't bring a gun or knife for whatever reason. Lack of access, or they aren't a professional criminal, or..."

"Or what?"

"Or they had a more personal motive so they *wanted* to kill McCandless bare-handed, and in the particularly vicious way they did." He paused. "OK. Annette, you wanted to say something?"

She leaned forward eagerly. "The till wasn't lying open so it doesn't look as if robbery was a motive, sir. In fact McCandless hadn't been trading much at all recently. The last receipt was two weeks ago."

Craig nodded. "Theft's not our motive and it's unlikely to be a sexual attack either on a man, especially in broad daylight. So that probably leaves us with a personal agenda and an assailant not fully confident of their own strength. A small man or possibly even a woman."

Liam shook his head.

"You've lost me now. I get the bit about lack of strength from there being no struggle, but why a woman?"

"It could have been a small man, Liam, but most men of any size would still usually go for a punch, a gun or a knife. Our killer didn't. They tripped McCandless up and sneaked up behind him when he was down. Why go to all that trouble? Why so elaborate? To me that says that they were *very* unsure of their own strength, and that they had a personal motive. They had some strength, enough to drag him, but not enough to fight him. And they were small enough to set the tripwire and not be seen."

John was cleaning his glasses thoughtfully. "So you're saying our attacker was most likely a small man or lad, or a woman, and they knew the victim?"

Craig nodded.

"I think that's the likeliest. Unless anyone can think of another scenario?"

John took a punt. "OK...maybe there were two people. One to act as lookout and one to kill. Then they both dragged him over to the pump?"

"OK. That could work. But at least one of them was small, whoever set the tripwire must have been."

There was silence as they searched further for inspiration. None appeared so Craig concluded.

"So... cherchez la femme."

"Or the lad?"

Craig shrugged. "Or both. They would all work with the forensics. OK... Now, let's just bear in mind that I could be completely wrong. But either way we've got as far as we can here.

Liam, you call the fire brigade, and Annette, ask the C.S.I.s to finish up please, then John can take his patient to the lab. I'll drop in tomorrow after the postmortem, John. Meanwhile, let's see if we can find out why someone hated Ian McCandless so much."

****

The thin woman watched them from the alley opposite. She watched the fire-engine and mortuary-van arrive, and the trail of multi-coloured cars finally leave, one by one.

She laughed quietly to herself as she watched. Until hot tears streamed down her cheeks and her small nose started to bleed bright red droplets. She wiped them away with a torn hand and smiled.

It would take the police a long time to work out what had happened here, and they would never find her in time to prevent the next.

Chapter Two

Thursday morning. Lough Neagh.

The early morning was cool and quiet and the mist lifted slowly from Lough Neagh, to reveal hundreds of frost-tipped trees at its edges. The day's soundtrack had already started. Birdsong was mixing with the sound of small craft jetting across the lake's glass surface, while their occupants' murmured voices provided a light harmony.

Jessie's head ached this morning. It always ached, but on a good day it simply siphoned off her energy to feed her misbehaving brain's needs, making every action laboured. On a bad day the pain drilled through her, until she banged her head off the wall for relief and vomited up everything, mentally and physically. Today was a very bad day. Today it was a grinding, bone-deep pain, piercing her wide brown eyes and making every image double.

She stared through the picture-window at the small hillock on the Lough's west shore. Fixing on the famous Celtic cross, with some vague attempt at belief in God, a belief that had left her years before. Nowadays, her eyes moved to the graveyard beside it instead.

She stood completely still, watching. Unconsciously rubbing her forehead so hard that the frayed skin broke, and small splashes of red streaked carelessly across her clean T-shirt. She sighed at the mess, a sigh deep with feeling that made only a thin, tired sound; half-smiling at the contrast. Time was when her voice shouted her soul, now it only whispered it.

Reaching across the bed for the small bottle of tablets, her numb fingers screwed the lid down hard, breaking the plastic child-lock, and she marveled again at her newfound strength. She tipped out the day's red pills and they acted almost instantly, making the fog that she always lived in warmer and less painful. Then she lay down on the bed and drifted slowly back to sleep, the sound of young children laughing in the next room making her smile.

Fiona was gently chiding them to be quiet, but their laughs were a lullaby, carrying her into a dream where her mind was as clear as last year. Then deeper into the shadows, where she planned her next steps.

****

Docklands Coordinated Crime Unit. Pilot Street, Belfast. 9 a.m.

The tall glass building that housed the Docklands' C.C.U. shone in the winter morning sunshine. It lit up the narrow street at its entrance, closed in for years by tall churches and brick apartment blocks.

Craig's tenth floor office was full of the natural light that showed every speck of dust on its charcoal carpet, and each prismed smear that the window-cleaners had left. It was some architect's dream and every cleaner's nightmare. The occupants froze in winter and boiled in summer and he would have happily stuck with the Victorian headquarters they'd left, but higher powers than he had decreed the move.

Craig threw his sports kit into the corner and stood for a moment gazing out over Belfast's dockland sprawl. In the far distance lay Stormont's white edifice, pale and grand, too grand for the ideas it produced. Harland and Wolff's gritty cranes were much closer, in every sense. Their size and familiarity created the illusion that he could almost touch them. That everyone in Belfast could.

In the other direction a tugboat was leading some eager rowers back up-river, like a naughty school crocodile; the tug's frustrating slowness part of their punishment for straying off-piste. They'd rowed past the weir somehow, their youthful enthusiasm almost pulling them into Belfast Lough and onwards to the Irish Sea. Their team shirts said that they were visitors, explaining their expedition, and he could imagine local counterparts waiting impatiently for their guests' return.

Suddenly the Cox caught sight of him and waved, prompting a cheer from her rowdy horde. Craig waved back casually, thinking about yesterday's murder, until their fit enthusiasm prompted a guilty glance at his sports kit abandoned in the corner.

His guilt was disturbed by a soft knock at the door and he threw "come in Nicky" over his shoulder, his guess confirmed by the familiar click of her high heels. He turned, already grateful for the coffee that he knew would be in her hand, and beckoned her to sit. His own percolator took ten minutes to warm up, and ten minutes without coffee was ten minutes of his life wasted.

Nicky Morris sat down and pushed a steaming mug towards her boss, lifting her pen and notepad ostentatiously, to remind him of the management part of a D.C.I.'s job.

She was small and slim, with the year-round mahogany tan of the Belfast working class, her frequent trips to Turkey keeping it just this side of black. Her quirky prettiness and Madonna-like fashion sense always made Craig smile, in an almost paternal way, although there was only five years between them.

She was the best secretary in the C.C.U and he thanked God every day that the Chief Superintendent had been made part-time in Limavady, releasing her full time to him. She bossed him in a mothering way, tolerating his frequent silences and occasional moods and blaming them kindly on the pressures of 'the job'. He in turn tried never to aim them at his team. There were things, past and present, which almost justified his moods.

"Morning, sir. Do you want my list now?"

Craig sighed in mock-despair. Nicky's 'list' was infamous, the D.C.S. had sworn about it for years and now he understood why. But without it there'd be chaos in the murder squad, so he sat down heavily, taking a swig of the sweet black coffee that he would mainline if possible. It helped him think all day and buggered-up his sleep at night - even his Italian half couldn't tolerate the amount he drank.

Nicky looked across the desk at him, concerned. The shadows under his eyes got deeper by the week, although he was still too handsome for his own good. But he didn't even notice the trail of mooning females who found excuses to visit the squad every week, leaving Liam to chat them up instead.

Craig sighed dramatically. "OK then. What do I have to do that I haven't done? And what's new for me to do?"

She laughed. It was a loud, Belfast laugh that belonged to a six-foot man. Its sheer incongruity made others laugh, so that the whole place cheered up with her. Craig knew Liam would already be joining in outside.

"And good morning to you too, sir. It's a lovely day, don't you think?"

He nodded wryly, conceding that he'd missed the niceties yet again.

She continued brightly. "Well, apart from the fact I haven't had expense forms from either Liam or you for three months and the D.C.S. is going grey because of it, well, that's *his* excuse anyway, I also haven't had your crime returns for last month!"

She pursed her lips, attempting disapproval, and then instantly produced two spread-sheets from the large pile in her arms. She slid them across the desk with one red fingernail and continued talking without missing a beat.

"I've filled in the returns and your expenses, and all I need is a signature on both." She pointed at the paper. "Just there, where X marks the spot."

Craig could have hugged her. He should have completed the forms weeks before, but Nicky understood that when there was a murder to solve he barely remembered to eat, never mind fill in spread-sheets. And there was always a murder to solve.

He signed them with a grateful smile that somehow accentuated his tiredness, and not for the first time Nicky thought that he needed a wife, wondering how he had escaped this long. But she belonged to the 'not my place to ask' school of personal assistants, or at least until Craig gave the sign that he was willing to talk.

Occasionally she'd catch him looking out his window so sadly that she'd guessed there'd been a love story somewhere. Probably in London. He could hardly have lived there for fifteen years without meeting someone. Craig's next comment surprised her, as if he'd read her thoughts.

"Nicky, remind me to propose to you sometime. You're a goddess."

She smiled, trying to cover her immediate blush. "I tell Gary that all the time, but he just ignores me."

The detective decided to test something out. "Have you done Liam's expenses for him as well?"

It wasn't her job to do admin for the team, although he would never stop her. She shrugged, blushing even deeper. "I might have. But he'll have to ask me for them."

Craig had long recognised the underlying frisson between her and Liam; at times the air between them crackled with possibility. They controlled it because they were both married, and he really hoped that would continue while he worked there. He liked them both too much to choose sides if things went wrong.

The moment passed and they shifted into a routine 'list session', with Nicky telling him what needed to be done and then suggesting who he should delegate it to. She had it all sorted out before he even needed to think; the mark of a brilliant P.A.

The meeting was drawn to a halt twenty minutes later by the ringing of Nicky's desk phone, and he nodded her out with a smile, only to have her boomerang back a minute later.

"That's the lab, sir. Can I put them through?"

Craig nodded and picked it up on one ring, expecting John. He was wrong; it was Des Marsham. He and John worked in shiny new facilities at a science park on the Saintfield Road - it was his main coffee stop after Nicky's desk.

He hadn't spoken to Des for weeks and greeted him cheerfully. "Hello there. It's not often you call."

"Hi Marc. Are you seeing John later?"

"That's the plan."

"Well, nip down here as well, please; I want to show you something. This wire is proving very interesting; it's not something I've ever seen before, or the hammer indent for that matter. John said he'll have finished the P.M. by three, so I'll see you about four?"

"Sure. See you then."

Craig's curiosity was piqued, and he opened the office door, waving Liam in.

"Where's Annette?"

"She's gone to see McCandless' wife to arrange the formal identification, then she's bringing her back here for a chat. I've Davy looking at the murder to see if there's been anything like it on the mainland, and I've just spoken to the Irish police; they'll check their records and get back to us."

Craig nodded him to the desk-chair opposite. He had a 'comfy area' in one corner of his office, but his six-feet-two and Liam's six-six made it so difficult to fold themselves into the low chairs, that watching them get out again was standard office entertainment. The high desk-chairs suited them both much better.

The D.I. talked on as Craig poured him a coffee from his now-bubbling percolator.

"Seems that McCandless was in a bit of financial bother. The garage went under about two months ago, about the time of that last till receipt. The courts were chasing him for a couple of smaller debts as well, so that's probably what the letter was about."

"I'm seeing Des later so I'll get a copy."

"Grand. Anyway, he had a wife, thirty-two years married, and two sons. One's a bricky working in England, and the younger one's at the Tech doing media studies. Here, what exactly are media studies?"

"It's where you get a degree for studying Kylie Minogue."

"Half the force deserves that one."

They laughed loudly and Craig could see Nicky turn

round at her desk, smiling at Liam as she eavesdropped.

"Des says he has something on the wire and hammer, and if we're very lucky the C.S.I.s will have found some prints. Anything on the close circuit TV?"

"There are some shop cameras on the Belmont Road but nothing up Harkinson Street, and we're out of luck on patrols. I've checked and there were no car or foot patrols around there all day yesterday. But the good news is..." Liam played a drum roll on the desk. "The garage is overlooked front and back, so I've some of the lads from Richard Street Station starting a house-to-house. I know John Ellis, the sergeant down there, pretty well; his wee lad plays football with my nephew. So I'll nip down when Annette gets back and see what I can find out."

Liam had been a detective in Belfast during most of 'The Troubles' so there was hardly anyone that he didn't know. Or who didn't owe him a favour.

"Good. We need to find out why someone wanted McCandless dead badly enough to kill him in such a nasty way. So far, we have no theft or sexual motive, or any motive at all in fact. When the formal I.D. is done, check if anything might have been taken from the shop or cars. Ask his wife; but be sensitive please, Liam."

The D.I. pretended to be offended, but nodded, conceding the point; 'people skills' weren't one of his strengths. It was something he'd never quite mastered, like doing his expenses. He was old time police, when they'd been too busy with the bombs and bullets to worry about the smiles and glad-handing. He'd been on every sensitivity course ever invented, and he knew what he *should* do, but all his good intentions went out the window once he had his eye on a perp.

"Aye well, Annette will keep me right there; she has the old people skills in spades. Nurse or nature?"

"Nature. Nursing just topped it up. And thank God we have her or you'd have the political correctness brigade lining up to hang you." Craig relented, adding. "And me too, when I'm busy."

They lapsed into silence while they both thought.

Finally Craig spoke again.

"Of course, McCandless could just have hacked someone off, but somehow I doubt it's as simple as that. If he'd just got on the wrong side of a creditor or a thug in a bar, they'd have used more direct methods. And anyone he'd owed money to wouldn't have wanted him dead, or they'd never have been paid."

"Aye. They'd just have taught him a lesson."

"There's something more twisted going on here, Liam, and the answer is in McCandless' life. You head over to East Belfast now and I'll interview his wife with Annette. Whether Mrs McCandless is aware of it or not, she knows why her husband was killed."

"That works for me. You'll do the grieving widow bit far better."

Craig snorted. "And you can forget the flattery; it won't get you out of doing your expenses. The D.C.S. is looking for them, and you're in trouble if he doesn't have them on his desk tomorrow." His next comment was guaranteed to wind Liam up. "Apparently the word disciplinary was mentioned."

Panic shot across Liam's face so fast that Craig almost relented, but he held his ground, seeing Nicky winking at him from outside the door. She had leverage and he was going to make sure she got to use it. Liam's shoulders slumped as he resigned himself to an evening at the computer, then Craig added an "of course..." and he leaned forward hopefully, detecting a get-out clause.

"What? Tell me. I'll do it, whatever it takes. Anything's better than spending all night on a spreadsheet."

"Well...I think...It's only a possibility now, mind you...But...I think."

"*What?*"

Craig knew Liam was dying to shake it out of him. This was torture for him, but Nicky was enjoying it.

"I think that *perhaps* if you asked Nicky really nicely, and took whatever terms she stated, then she *might*–"

He could see Nicky convulsing outside now, her

31

hand clamped over her mouth to keep her loud laugh in check. Liam leapt in.

"Do them for me! She'd do them for me, would she? Do you think she would?"

His head shot round just in time to see Nicky heading towards the lift. Craig had to admire her timing; she was going to milk this one for everything it was worth.

"It's not her job, but perhaps you two could agree some sort of terms? Anyway, go and speak nicely to her, and then get to Richard Street."

He nodded him out, smiling as Liam molded his best 'suck-up face' before he'd even reached Nicky's desk. If she had any sense at all she would make him suffer. Months of completed expenses should cost him at least two bottles of perfume.

Chapter Three

The C.C.U.

Annette slumped at her desk for a minute, resting her head against its cool vertical partition. Her heart was sore. She'd seen things in nursing that had saddened her, but at least she'd felt that she could help then. With victim I.D.s there was no escape from the relentless sense of waste.

They'd cleaned Ian McCandless up as much as possible before the viewing, and thankfully his face hadn't been badly burnt, the killer's flames spluttering out at his waist. But even his peaceful look hadn't stopped his wife's screams echoing through the desolate room, freezing them all where they stood. The sound had ripped through her, but she was there to support and she wished that she could do more. She wished that she could bring him back; bring them all back for every family.

Craig watched her through his half-glass door, giving her time and knowing exactly what she was feeling. He felt it every time with every murder, and it had turned him into a hunter. Finally, she straightened up and he walked across the squad. He set a cup of sweet, white tea at her elbow and propped himself on the edge of her desk.

"Fancy some lunch before we start? Delaney just called and McCandless' son can't get here until one-thirty, so we can't start until then anyway."

She sipped gratefully, nodding, and some of her usual high colour flashed back to her cheeks.

"Right then. I'll give you ten minutes then we'll head to The James for lunch. Nicky's joining us, and I warn you, she's being Machiavellian."

She raised an eyebrow quizzically, smiling across at the P.A. As she walked over to join them she explained what Craig had meant.

"I'm taking Liam to the cleaners for doing his

expenses. I'll tell you my evil plan over lunch, but all suggestions for his torture will be gratefully received." A few ideas sprang to Annette's mind and she felt better instantly.

****

Richard Street Station. East Belfast.

Liam pushed open the heavily re-enforced steel door, pleased that they hadn't replaced all the old barricades with glass niceties. It made him feel strangely at home. Now all he needed was a Kevlar vest and they'd be back in the eighties, when he didn't have a paunch.

John Ellis was standing behind the desk with his head down, writing; the last man to use a biro in a world of laptops. He was almost as tall as Liam, so his bald patch usually remained a mystery. But the daylight was hitting it now, making his scalp reflect the emergency number from the window, so that he looked like a Satanist.

"Here John, did you know you've got six-six-six written on your head? Hold on and I'll get a priest to exorcise you."

Ellis answered him without looking up, Liam's booming Crossgar accent instantly identifiable.

"Oh aye, that'd be very original, except every probationer's already made that joke. Save your priest, I'd singe his eyebrows with my sins. To what do we owe this honour, Whitey?"

Liam's height and Celtic pallor made him instantly visible, even in a force full of tall men. Years back it had earned him the nickname 'Big Whitey', although Craig said they'd have to change it after the first complaint of racism.

Liam laughed loudly. "How'd you know it was me? I was trying for undercover."

Ellis gave him a sceptical smile and threw open the door to the back office, already knowing what Liam would do first.

"Aye, please *do* help yourself to our food and drink,

Inspector Cullen. We only live to serve."

They both laughed and, after a few minutes banter in the battered staff room over tea and biscuits, Liam ran through the purpose of his visit. Ellis' men had carried out house-to-house enquiries the evening before but returned empty-handed, with only one glimmer of hope.

"There's a wee woman in Harkinson Street who might be helpful. Mrs Ida Foster. The lads said three different neighbours mentioned her."

"Why so useful?"

"Apparently she's the local Agatha Christie. Sees everything. I checked and we've had a few good tips from her over the years. You know the sort of thing; young lads hanging around, casing houses. We'd a spate of burglaries last year and she identified the two lads who'd been casing the houses when people were on holiday. We convicted them on her evidence. Otherwise, there was nothing in the whole area."

"OK, thanks. I'll pay her a visit."

"It'll have to be this evening; she's not there at the moment. Her neighbour says she stays with family every Wednesday night."

Liam slurped his tea and grabbed another chocolate digestive. "Do you have anything on McCandless himself?"

"Aye, we had words with him last year about the cars on the garage forecourt. None of them was taxed and he'd been test-driving them round the streets. He was pleasant enough. On his uppers like most people round there. One of the lads says he was in the chippy on Bonn Street most lunchtimes. It's called the 'Bacon Butty'; great chips."

"Sounds like my kind of restaurant. Maybe I'll take Danni there for our anniversary."

"That'll be your last meal ever then."

****

Craig and Annette left The James bar at one o'clock and strolled back towards the C.C.U. They took the long route along the waterfront, as advance therapy for the interview. It was a bright October day, with the best mixture of sun and cold that Belfast ever saw. Halloween preparations had made it Craig's favourite time of year as a kid, and it still was now.

The cobbles that had once covered Pilot Street were replaced by characterless tarmac now, but he still remembered playing on them outside his granny's four-storied Captain's house; all the street's past occupants had been employed by the sea in some way. Tramlines still traced some local streets, echoing the life led there for generations.

They walked past the boarded-up Rotterdam bar. There since 1797 and only recently closed. It had been many things in its time: a respite for sailors and a lock-up for prisoners awaiting transportation. In the twentieth century it had been a famous music venue, attracting players that included Bob Dylan and audiences that had held Martin Scorsese. Now it lay empty. Sailortown had been a place full of ships and dockers, sailors and travellers, until the planners' pogrom in the eighties had devastated a community built up over three centuries. Five years to destroy three hundred. And they'd called it progress.

Nicky had left ten minutes before them, with her head full of new tortures for Liam. So they talked as they walked, sketching out the details of the coming interview.

"You lead on this one, Annette. Mrs McCandless has already met you, so it will be better for her. I'll just chip in as and when."

She nodded, feeling much better than earlier. The warm comfort of the relatives' room would replace the cold formality of the morgue, and tea and biscuits would add to the relaxed approach. These people weren't suspects; they were victims, although she knew that Craig would be watching for signs that the McCandlesses were involved. That was partly why he would sit back. Always watching. Everyone a suspect, until they weren't.

The relatives' room was on the second floor, just

above the building's main entrance, so Annette ran upstairs quickly for her notes then joined Craig at the doors to the corridor.

As they walked the short, carpeted length towards the room, a thin youth stood up to greet them. He had dark auburn hair and a light tan that threw his blue eyes into sharp relief. He looked about eighteen. His black jeans and sweatshirt stamped his student identity clearly, a doubly pierced right ear and Chinese tattoo adding 'media or drama' to its title. Nothing was ever as unique as teenagers thought it was.

He put his hand out and Annette took it, holding it slightly longer than necessary, in comfort.

"I'm Joey McCandless. You must be Sergeant McElroy. Mum said you were kind to her this morning. Thank you."

She gave a weak smile. "I'm truly sorry about your father, Mr McCandless."

"Joey, please."

"Joey. I promise you we'll do everything we can to catch his killer." She gestured to Craig.

"This is D.C.I. Craig; he's leading the investigation into your father's death."

Craig stepped forward and shook his hand firmly, giving the young boy his new role as man of the house. He spoke quickly in his deep, mixed accent.

"Joey, I'm going to apologise in advance, but we need to ask quite a few questions today, and some of them may be painful. Any help that you can give us in lessening that pain would be welcome. We need to find out why anyone would have done this to your father. So any information you have, no matter how insignificant, will help us, believe me."

The younger man nodded, tears flooding his eyes suddenly, reminding them of his age and hurt. Annette took his arm tightly and led him into the small, furnished room where his mother already sat, curled into herself like a small child. Then they began trying to make the next few hours less painful, something they already knew was impossible.

****

Lough Neagh.

Jessie pulled her long floral skirt down over her knees and lifted Pia onto her lap. The little girl stared up at her mother with soft brown eyes, smiling the gummy smile of a happy child. Two small white teeth poked through her bottom gum and Jessie knew that it must be sore for her, remembering her own wisdom teeth. But her beautiful baby never cried; perhaps she knew how much she was loved.

Tears of injustice pricked Jessie's eyes suddenly. Her children had done nothing wrong yet they had suffered so much. And regardless of who or how many she killed, she couldn't stop that.

But her killings would keep them safe in the years ahead, and no matter what her conscience said she *had* to finish what she had started. And as soon as possible; time was running out.

****

Meg McCandless had unfolded herself from her foetal position when the detectives had entered, and was sitting bolt upright at the edge of her leather chair now, her coffee untouched. She held up her head, her eyes shut tight, and the neon light in the windowless room threw each line on her face into harsh relief. But the fiercest signs of loss were in her hands. They were knotted together on her lap, wringing hard at a white handkerchief; as if all the pain she felt could be erased by her constant twisting of the small square. Joey sat beside her, watching her dry eyes anxiously, his own tears falling freely in compensation. But her eyes remained closed, shutting out the world and the reality that opening them would force on her.

She hadn't moved except to straighten up since they'd entered thirty minutes before, despite her son's touch and Annette's kind words. So they sat, matching her silence, until finally she opened first one eye and then the other, staring at her son vacantly.

Craig reached over and touched her hand. She

stared down at his long tanned fingers, her eyes moving slowly from his hand to his face. Then to Annette's and finally to her son's again, expressionless and uncomprehending. Annette had seen the reaction before and she motioned Craig outside the room.

"She needs a doctor, sir. She hasn't said a word since the I.D. this morning, and if anything she's blanker now than she was then."

Craig nodded. Any hope of getting information from Meg McCandless had left him five minutes after they'd entered the room. He raked his hand down his face tiredly.

"OK, Annette. Call the medical examiner to see her. Then see what you can get from Joey. Anything he can give us at all."

She nodded and re-entered the room, leaving him to drive to the lab, angrier by the minute at the destruction of a family, probably for the rest of their lives.

****

The Saintfield Road, Belfast.

The newly built pathology labs were set in a secure science park on Belfast's Saintfield Road, two miles from the city centre. They shared the park with valuable research facilities, whose high security and alarms were a condition of the huge grants they received. Craig abandoned his black Audi in the nearest free space and pushed through the PVC doors headed Pathology, aiming straight for John Winter's corner office. The door was lying open, the office unexpectedly empty, so he helped himself to a coffee with the rude familiarity of a long-time friend. John's machine produced seven types of coffee with bastardised Italian names, but only espresso had the hit he needed after that interview.

He was sitting at the desk flicking through an old newspaper when John clattered in, dropping an armful of papers onto the desk and knocking Craig's drink onto the floor. They watched as the dark brown liquid spread, laughing as John frantically grabbed towels to curtail the damp patch. He'd dropped, spilled and ripped everything he'd touched since they'd been at school and it had cost his parents a small fortune.

"At least I missed the notes this time. I didn't yesterday. Fancy another one?"

Craig jumped up with a parental look. "I'll get it."

They settled into an amiable silence, John knowing from the darkness of his friend's expression not to speak until Craig broke it. Eventually he did.

"Sorry to pressure you, John, but what do you have? Des asked me to drop into the forensic lab and he's got to leave by five."

"Part-timer." They both laughed, before John added.

"Still, I suppose your wife going into labour is a valid excuse. She was admitted to St Mary's about an hour ago. I tell you what, we'll head up there now and let him leave, then I can update you afterwards. Bring your coffee and I promise not to spill it."

They took the stairs two floors up to Des Marsham's world, where things went bleep in the night. As they entered he was leaning over a souped-up microwave, his thin tie stained with some nameless chemical.

"Making dinner, Des? That's decent of you."

"I'm cooking something, but it's not your dinner."

"I hear Annie's in labour. Congrats."

"Don't congratulate me too early, I've hours of swearing to go through first. I was called names I never knew existed when she had Martin, and she's learned some new ones since then. You two won't know this yet, but labour is all men's fault."

John nodded sagely, "Every woman swears and every man gets sworn at, it happened with every baby I delivered. Think of it as a rite of passage." He waved at a fuming cabinet where a fingerprint was appearing through the mist. "OK, what do you have for us?"

Des pulled up a stool and sat down.

"Well, there are a few interesting bits and pieces.

We have a clear fingerprint on the doorjamb and another on the victim's phone; that's what's cooking now. We also have a distinctive white cream on the petrol pump, the wire and the victim, with a smaller amount beside the door print. And we have two very unusual weapons; the wire and the weapon that fractured his skull."

Finding the prints made Craig immediately suspicious, but he wasn't sure why. He knew that he should welcome any print, but somehow he thought the fact they'd been left was bad news not good.

"First of all, the print by the door. It's a clear index finger, small enough to belong to a woman or boy. If we had the technology we could try for a sex."

"I didn't know you could sex a print."

"In theory, yes. The technology uses urea levels; men's are higher than women's. But we'll have to make do with size today. It's not in our system so can Davy do a wider search for us, Marc?"

"Sure. Send it over."

"Thanks. Number two, the cream. It's white, and there were two sizable smears on the pump and the victim's face. Also patches on the wire and beside the print. Its main constituents are zinc oxide and benzyl derivates, with a few other substances like lanolin in small quantities."

"Some sort of diesel or lubricant? Maybe car wax? There were used cars for sale at the garage."

Des took out a notebook and smiled as he turned to the relevant page, shaking his head knowingly.

"I know exactly what it is but I'm in the mood to make you guess. Here's a clue. It's a cream that I'll be using in huge quantities for the next year, and that I've had to use before."

Craig stared at the scientist's beard. "Well, it's definitely not shaving cream."

Des laughed and Craig looked at John, puzzled. Every cream that sprang to mind was either too strange or too deviant to name. Finally the detective gave up.

"I've absolutely no idea. Put us out of our misery."

"It's Purecrem. Not exclusively but most commonly used for...nappy rash!"

"Nappy rash?" John looked at him incredulously. "Was it definitely linked to the body? Couldn't it be an old patch? Maybe McCandless was a grandfather?"

Craig shook his head. Ian McCandless had had no grandchildren.

"Yes, yes and no. The cream was fresh; it hadn't dried or congealed to any extent. I've spoken to the manufacturer and carried out some tests, and it would have taken eight hours to congeal at yesterday's temperatures anyway. It was found within ten millimetres of the clear fingerprint, so, if you ask me, I think our killer was either changing a nappy, or perhaps working in a nursing home or hospital ward, less than eight hours before they killed McCandless. So that's interesting, isn't it?"

"Why nursing home or hospital?"

John answered before Des could. "Because it's often used to prevent pressure sores in immobile patients of all ages."

They shared a puzzled look but moved on. "OK, what about the wire?"

Des shot them an excited look. "The wire's even more interesting. It's razor-barbed wire in a flat-wrap type. Our wire's made of stainless steel, although it comes in electro-galvanized and hot-dipped galvanized as well."

He began digging into the detail with excitement, expecting Craig to be equally 'turned-on'; the delusion of the true scientist.

"There are lots of types: straight, crossed, spiral and flat-wrap, which is ours. It's one of the newest types, so it's quite unusual, and very unlikely to have been in domestic use. It's mainly used in prisons, farms, national defence locations and so on. The C.S.I.s didn't find anything similar at the garage, and there's Purecrem all over it." He frowned suddenly. "The more interesting question is how it was cut? It has a carbon core that makes it impossible to break through with normal tools."

He stared into space distractedly for a moment then continued, talking to himself.

"And then of course, there's handling it. How the heck would that work?"

He caught himself rambling and turned back to the others eagerly, expecting his enthusiasm to be reciprocated. Craig's blank expression indicated that he'd lost the will to live, so the scientist sighed and continued with heavier emphasis.

"Basically, it means that whoever did this either wore very strong gloves and then left the print deliberately, or...they were completely immune to pain. In which case they tied the wire bare-handed and you're looking for someone whose hands are torn to shreds. See why it's interesting?"

John couldn't feign disinterest any longer and Craig saw the excited gleam in his eye. He interjected quickly, before the other men went to 'nerd' heaven.

"What about the hammer?"

"Ah now, that was even more interesting. Come over here."

Des led them to a small table at the back of the lab, where there sat a plaster reconstruction of Ian McCandless' skull. Copies of its shattered fragments were laid out to reveal a small gap in the bone, the size of a large coin.

"That's where he was hit. I can see why you thought it was a hammer. Size-wise it's not far off. But it definitely wasn't a hammer."

"What was it then?"

John spoke eagerly before Des could. "I think I can answer that. There was a tear in the brain's covering, the Mater. And that, plus the shape of the brain contusion, makes it much more likely that this was done with a sharp penetrating weapon, not the rounded head you'd see on a hammer."

Craig repeated his question. "What then?"

Des reached into a drawer and brought out a book, filled with page after page of implements nasty enough to cause similar damage to the human skull. He flicked quickly through the pages and then stopped at a section marked 'trauma: sharp' containing hundreds of pictures, ranging from household implements to unrecognisable objects. They made unpleasant viewing.

"All of these?"

"Sorry, but yes. These could all leave similar marks and it's as close as we'll get without the weapon to compare. When you find it we can match it, but any of these could have caused that injury. I'll send this over to Davy."

Suddenly the scientist looked at his watch. "God, I'd better shift myself to the hospital otherwise it won't just be today I'll get sworn at. I'll leave you two to solve the case, but call me back if you need me. Anytime, day or night. I *really* mean it."

The pleading look in his eye showed them just how much he meant it, and they laughed, waving him out. Then they sat beside the skull in silence, Craig sipping thoughtfully at his cold espresso as John fingered a sample of the razor-wire gingerly. A red streak sprang suddenly from his fingertip and he dropped the wire urgently, swearing.

"Bugger! I didn't even feel that cut me. This stuff's vicious; I wouldn't like to handle it even *with* gloves. If Des is right then our killer has no hands left. Although it would certainly explain the findings on McCandless' shins. Come downstairs and I'll show you."

They walked down three flights of stairs into the ice-cold mortuary, where Ian McCandless was taking his final nap. John lifted a clipboard to check something and then walked quickly down the room, past rows of wall fixtures with numbered segments, until he'd reached number one hundred and nine. He opened the door, and pulled the drawer containing their victim out into the freezing air.

The sheet covering the body was plain and white, like any bed-sheet. If they hadn't been where they were it could have revealed a sleeping man instead of a dead one.

The pathologist pulled back the sheet and their victim's face came into view. Craig gazed down at Ian

McCandless sadly. Death was a waste, but it formed the baseline to both their days, and the 'puzzle', the bit that they both loved, started here.

McCandless had been a handsome man in life, stocky and strong, with a weathered face and arms that showed a manual, outdoor existence. He looked anywhere between sixty to seventy years old but Craig knew that he'd only been fifty-six. Perhaps financial worry had aged the man, or maybe it had just been life wearing him down. He knew how that felt.

John began reporting, breaking through his thoughts.

"Starting from the top. He has marks of forced trauma around his mouth where the petrol pump was pushed in very hard. The rubber handle hit the area surrounding his mouth on entry. The back of his throat also bears testament to the level of force used, they nearly pushed the metal spout through the back wall of his pharynx, implying?"

"Revenge, personal motive, unaware of their own strength perhaps? Maybe all of those things. Although I still feel this killer is physically small, hence having to trip McCandless up to disable him."

"Maybe they're small but very strong. Or if Des is right, they may simply have no sensation in their hands to moderate the force. Sensory feedback is part of what tells us how hard we're pushing."

Craig looked puzzled. "What would cause a loss of sensation without a loss of power?"

"If that's what it is, then we're talking about a sensory neuropathy and there are lots of medical conditions that could do it. Anything that causes sensory nerve damage: diabetes, some tumours, it's quite a long list; although most would cause a loss of strength as well. I'll narrow it down for you."

He gestured at their victim.

"I won't lift his head, but you saw the skull model so take my word for it; he has a depressed fracture and severe contusion of the brain surface about the size of a two-pound coin. It doesn't fit a domestic hammer, so we're looking for the weapon that Des described."

He covered McCandless' face.

"OK, moving down. The lower part of his body was charred even though the top half wasn't. The worst burning is at his feet so they definitely didn't set light to the petrol around his mouth, they set light to the pool at his feet. And they poured some on him. The C.S.I.s found some random splashes on his shirt, so it was probably tossed over the body as well."

Craig interrupted him.

"The fact that they didn't set fire to his face makes it less likely that there was a personal relationship, and they definitely weren't trying to hide his identity. But the hands-on method still means that this could be vengeance for something."

John thought for a minute and then nodded. It made sense.

"Right. His hands are newly abraded by gravel and stones, and they match the ones just outside the shop door, so it makes complete sense that he fell when he was tripped. He cut his hands on the gravel when he extended his arms to save himself. But apart from nicotine stains from smoking, there's nothing else on his hands to note. His legs tell the main story. His thighs, knees and shins have abrasions consistent with a fall and then being dragged face-down across the forecourt to the pumps. The wire matches perfectly with the narrowness and depth of the straight horizontal cuts on both shins, and the depth backs up Des' razor-wire theory. I pity any animal caught in that stuff. I agree they weren't trying to hide his identity but I do think they were trying to hide the wire cuts. That's why they set fire to him feet first. They didn't want us to know about that wire for some reason, so I think it's a clue to your killer."

"That and the print."

"Yes, the print's interesting. I'd like to see who it goes back to. Anyway, McCandless' lower limbs were still smoking when he was found and they were flexed in what's called a partial pugilistic or boxer's pose, where the tissues had contracted from the heat. But they weren't fully flexed and the fire had gone out. So that, the body temperature, and the lack of rigour, gives me a time of death less than an hour before he was found. Anytime between one-thirty and two-thirty pm."

Craig nodded. "His last outgoing call was at two-fifteen and he was found at two-thirty, so that fits. OK. He was killed soon after two-fifteen, in broad day light."

John nodded. "Quite the daring little killer this one."

"Someone must have seen them."

"How's the door to door going?"

Craig shook his head. "Nothing so far, but Liam's on it."

John smiled. Liam Cullen was like a bloodhound and he'd never come back empty handed yet. He covered the dead man's legs with the sheet and continued.

"The other thing worth mentioning is his last meal. Chips, less than two hours before death. The wide-cut chippie type, not the narrow burger-joint ones. His arteries were in a shocking state for a fifty-six-year-old, so I imagine they weren't his first chips. He drank a fair bit as well, although not yesterday, but I wouldn't want his liver."

"Maybe one of the local chippies served him."

"Maybe. Finally, his lungs." John looked solemn. "He was nearly killed by the blow to his head, but the lungs show that his final cause of death was drowning. Whether by accident or intention who knows, but he definitely drowned in petrol."

"God."

They gazed down silently at the body, imagining what Ian McCandless' last minutes must have been like. Tripped with razor-wire, legs cut, skull fractured, dragged, drowned and then set alight. The killer had to be a sadist, or mentally ill. But either way, they had hated this man for something.

They put McCandless back to sleep and headed back to John's office, drinking coffee and outlining theories until nearly six pm. Eventually Craig straightened-up, preparing to go, but something about John's manner made him hesitate. There was definitely something more that he wanted to say.

"Something else bothering you?"

The way John was kicking the desk said 'yes' and he started speaking quickly, without meeting Craig's eyes.

"Marco, there's something you need to know."

Craig became immediately uneasy at John's use of his Italian name. It always preceded trouble.

"Camille's coming to Belfast."

Craig strained for breath as if he'd been kicked in the stomach and fought the reflex to throw-up. He couldn't think for a second and then he thought too much. His questions formed rapidly and the main one was 'Why?'

He'd thought he'd never have to see Camille again. She'd been his girlfriend, partner, whatever the modern euphemism was, for nine of the fifteen years that he'd lived in London. They'd been in love. Heart-flipping, euphoric love. But she was an actor and an ambitious one, whose desire to perform eventually passed her desire for him. And that was the truth, no matter how she'd tried to dress it up.

In the excruciatingly drawn-out death throes of their relationship, she had gone to New York. Where, although she'd always denied it, he knew that he'd overlapped with a studio director called something suitably cool, like Zack or Kirk...or Prick. She'd ripped out his heart, leaving him a far more distant man than the one who'd grown up with John Winter.

It was five years since she'd left him and four since he'd come home, but every birthday he got her card with one kiss on it. He'd always wondered whether Prick knew. Now she was coming to Belfast and Craig knew with absolute certainty that he couldn't deal with it. He turned to walk out but John stood bravely in front of him.

"Hear me out, Marc. You need to know the details, if only to avoid her. Belfast's a small place."

Craig stared at him coldly, hating him; as if he'd somehow colluded with Camille by even mentioning her name. His rational mind knew that John had never even met her, but the animal in him wanted to rip his head off. He stood completely rigid, his fists clenched.

John fell over his next words, defending himself. "She's coming as part of the Festival – they're on tour with 'A Midsummer Night's Dream'. I only found out because she e-mailed me."

When Craig spoke the sound of his own voice shocked him - it was a guttural snarl, like an animal. "How did she know your bloody e-mail address? Have you been in contact with her all along?"

His suspicion cut John deep and he hit back angrily.

"Why the hell would I be in contact with her? *You* may have loved her, but to me she was nothing but the heartless bitch that wrecked you. For God's sake, think clearly. The contact came through on my hospital e-mail, so you must have mentioned my name to her. After that it wouldn't have been hard to find out where I worked. Winter's not that common a name, especially in Northern Ireland."

He stepped back and raised his hands in peace, knowing that Craig was hurting and didn't need another fight from him. His voice softened as he delivered his next few words.

"She just e-mailed me to tell me she was coming over. She'll be here for five days from the twenty-fourth and... she'd like to see you. But she won't force it. She knows it has to be your choice."

He hesitated for a second before continuing. "No-one would blame you if you didn't see her Marc, but you have to consider whether you'll regret it if you don't."

They stood in silence for a long moment, as Craig's anger seeped away, echoed by a dull retreat in his eyes. Then he reached a hand out to his friend, his lips moving to form some words, but he gave up defeated and turned away, leaving the words for him to say.

John knew exactly what they were. "I'll regret it either way."

Chapter Four

Northern Ireland was many things. Verdant; green and plush. And Orange and Green. Young and arty: MTV and the City of Culture. And sedate and elegant, like an elderly lady wearing white gloves on her way to church.

It was cosy and welcoming, or parochial and interfering like 'small town anywhere'. It was small or it was compact. Everything plus or minus, depending on your point of view.

Jessie knew exactly what her view of Northern Ireland was. It was perfectly sized, especially for prisons.

****

Near Holywood, County Down.

Craig shoved his hands deep into the pockets of his leather reefer, and stared out across Helen's Bay. The grey waves were rolling forward and then pulling back flirtatiously, inviting him to enter and take part in the ritual dance. He was tempted. It wasn't the first time he'd thought how much easier life would be if you were dead.

John had meant his words kindly, but hearing that next week he and Camille weren't going to be separated by the water stretching in front of him. Or even better, by the larger pond on the other side of Ireland, left him with the dilemma that choice always brought. And this at a time when he thought he'd finally found some dull peace.

While she'd been out of touch and out of reach, he could pretend that she was just a memory. Someone he'd known when he'd lived some other life. It was only when her card arrived with its fatal constancy that he was reminded of the life he'd once led with her; one where he'd allowed himself to love. Not the safe love of family or friends, always returned and never costing, but the fierce, dangerous love where someone bought your heart with promises, promises that Camille had broken long ago.

And now, choice again. Not even the certain choice of her love, only the choice of whether to see her. See her and let her face and voice and touch rip through the wall that he'd built between himself and the world. He hated her for coming and he hated John for telling him, and he hated himself more than either of them for being such a bloody coward.

The water still stretched ahead of him, grey and frothing white, unfeeling and careless. He envied it for that. But thirty minutes of staring hadn't answered his questions, and thirty more minutes shivering wouldn't answer them either. So he pulled up his collar and turned on his phone, reconnecting with the world. The instant beeping reminded him that life went on without him and he still had the job, something that he could always control. And somewhere else, Camille was getting ready to do something to someone, with whatever awareness of the turmoil she created her selfish heart would allow.

He hit the symbol and picked up his messages. Three: John sounding anxious, Liam sounding cheerful and John again with just one word. 'Sorry'. He had nothing to be sorry about.

It was his mess and his life and his fault. Craig dialled his friend's number and it cut immediately to answerphone. He was grateful for that, not leaving a message, the call itself indication of the apology that meant they could pretend their earlier conversation had never happened. He'd make unspoken amends over beer and football another day.

He dialled Liam.

"What were you sounding so happy about?" He was aware that he sounded like a grumpy shit, but he still acted like one.

Liam missed his mood completely.

"Two things, boss. One, McCandless was in the local chippy about one o'clock." Craig nodded to himself, it fitted John's findings.

"And two, we might have a witness. An old lady across the road, Ida Foster. She's away until tonight so I'll nip down there later. Apparently she's the local Poirot, so well worth a chat. One neighbour said she thought she saw a young man entering the garage about two-ish but couldn't be sure, but she says Mrs Foster's our woman for the details."

Craig knew he wanted a 'well done' so he grunted. "Good" adding "OK, it's seven now so I'll see you in the morning. Annette has some leads she's chasing and we'll follow up on Mrs Foster's info when you get it. And let's see if we can make an arrest before the press realise that a two hundred pound man was probably killed by someone half his size, or most of the wives in Northern Ireland will be following suit."

He cut the call quickly, realising that it was too abrupt and feeling bad about his people skills. Must try harder tomorrow.

The light on his phone suddenly flashed with a text – John. 'Beer in town. 8?'

Forgiven already; brilliant. Apology-free friendship, available only with a man.

****

The Lower Bann River. 7 p.m.

The team of C.S.I.s stood respectfully beside the river, as Detective Inspector Julia McNulty knelt by the bloated, still body, oblivious to the sharp stones cutting her knees.

The dead girl wasn't much more than a teenager, her thin wrist and fine chain bracelet echoing her youthful fragility. Her soft, long hair was spread across a swollen face that told of her time in the water. The brown strands were smeared bloodily, as if their ends had been dipped in dark red paint and then stroked deliberately across her pale, freckled cheeks.

The girl's arctic white T-shirt with its logo of Kasabian was caked with mud, and half-pulled from the waistband of her dark mini-skirt. The T-shirt's thin fabric was so incongruous in the cool October air, that Julia knew a jacket wouldn't be far away. The C.S.I.s would find it.

She looked up from the sadness of the body towards the vibrant, early-evening sky, and then dragged her gaze haltingly down again. Past the famous beauty of Portglenone's Lower Bann River, through the streaks of sun lighting the green bushes and then back to the death that was her job. Then, even more slowly, she forced her eyes further down. Towards the girl's torn knees, where a rope of tights and once-white pants was hooked awkwardly between her tangled limbs.

An elderly sergeant had recognised the girl as Maria Burton, a young constable from his station. He stood solemnly now, his eyes straight-ahead, as were everyone's but Julia's. As if to look at the girl's last damaged tableau would be the final act of disrespect.

Julia reached behind her, lifting the approved cover, and laid it gently over the girl as if tucking her into bed, careful to disturb nothing. The signs of death and damage by her killer would be the only things to give her family justice, and they had to find Maria Burton's killer. For her, and for every woman on the force.

****

Jessie fed the children, leaving Fiona to tuck them in, then she ironed her outfit before disappearing into the bathroom with the cardboard box and scissors. It wouldn't serve any of them to have her recognised before she'd finished what she had to do, so she had to look very different this time. It had all gone well so far; she couldn't fall at the last two hurdles.

Life in Northern Ireland hadn't always been easy for her, but as a country it was perfect in some ways. Yes, it had its share of criminals, like anywhere else, but thankfully, also like anywhere else there were more males than females committing crime. So it was no great surprise that the country had only one women's prison; Wharf House. It would make her next step very easy.

She knew that she could get there right now, just by confessing to the police what she'd done. But that would leave her last target completely untouched, and there was far too much danger in it. Danger that they'd take her to hospital instead of prison, danger that they'd identify her and find her girls before she'd tied everything up. And danger that they'd link Fiona to her. No, tonight's plan was the best way and their only guarantee.

She changed into her outfit, smoothing the short skirt down over her too thin thighs. Then she smiled at the low-cut top she'd chosen – it was perfect for what she had in mind. Her make-up was heavier than she'd ever worn but it suited her newly blonde crop. And she needed it nowadays, to cover the dark hollows and lines brought on by pain. Suddenly her head swam, and she half-fell backwards onto the bed. Her balance was a growing problem but even that could serve a purpose; it made her look drunk when she wasn't and that would be doubly useful tonight.

She pushed gently at the swinging cot beside her bed, setting up a soothing rhythm, and watching two small white hands curling in happy answer. Pia's bright, wide eyes stared up at her and their smiles matched - her children's world was safe and Jessie was going to keep it that way.

Opening the bedside drawer, she pulled out the small bottle of tablets. Three now and three in six hours' time, and many more for the small bag she'd packed, for Fiona to bring to her the next day. She drew herself up and looked down at her baby one last time, then, fixing her smile and lifting the bag, she walked unsteadily into the bright living-room where three smiling faces greeted her: two small and one long grown-up.

"Mammy, Mammy, you look beautiful."

The chorus of praise reminded Jessie that she'd once been thought a pretty girl. Two warm, soft bodies hurled themselves at her, their just-bathed perfume better than any scent she'd ever owned. Small fingers ran wonderingly through her newly shorn blonde fringe.

"Mammy, are you going dancing?"

Jessie turned to her sophisticated four-year-old and laughed. "Yes, Ruby, funny dancing. Like you saw me do last week in the supermarket."

She deliberately wobbled. It didn't take any effort nowadays and it always made them laugh. They didn't understand, and that was how it would stay for years to come, thanks to Fiona.

Fiona smiled at her "You look really lovely, Jessie. When will you be back?"

It was said anxiously and the two women stared at each other above the small heads, having a second, silent conversation.

"I've packed enough for three days. That should do it."

She looked down at their shiny faces again. "You be good girls for Fiona and do everything she tells you. Now, wish me good luck."

A high-pitched chorus of "Good luck, Mammy" filled the air, although neither child understood what it meant. Fiona reached over and hugged hard at the younger woman's thin frame, tears springing to her eyes.

"Good luck, Jessie." Then she whispered. "For both of us."

****

Danni wasn't happy about him doing overtime but Liam's gut told him that this witness would be important, so evening or no evening he wanted to take Ida Foster's statement himself. He scanned the terraced street as his young driver grabbed his cap, then they entered the garage forecourt in Harkinson Street and stood for a minute, gazing around the derelict lot. The cars had been towed and metal shutters were locked to the shop's windows now, guarding its precious chocolate bars. Yellow crime tape made it clear that entry was definitely 'verboten'.

"What are we looking for, sir? Wouldn't the C.S.I.s have got everything already?"

Liam stayed silent, sniffing the air, but there was only a vague vapour of petrol. Nothing else hinted at yesterday's gruesome scene. He was searching for the unidentified but he'd know it when he saw it. There was usually something if you looked hard enough.

He beckoned the constable over to the guilty pump. "Have a look around and see if there's anything they might have missed, son. Give me a yell if you spot anything. It doesn't matter how stupid it sounds."

He walked quickly out of the forecourt, past the marked police car and pushed open the low garden gate of an elderly terraced house opposite. The house that three neighbours had said held his eyewitness.

Although the gate was warped and split, the house itself was made of clean, red brick and boasted a new wood and glass front door. Four small windows overhead were dressed in crisp, white netting and the front bay held a green plant that reached out hopefully for the sun. There was no movement and no sound, but the house was definitely alive; Liam could feel someone at home.

He hunkered down and lifted the low brass letterbox, peering into a narrow hallway. A sudden flash of movement at floor level was followed by something cutting his face, and he jerked back quickly. Too late to stop a sharp claw gouging the skin from his nose.

He lost his balance and felt backwards onto the gravelled path, ripping his trousers in the process, his bellowed, "ah shit" bringing the young P.C. rushing from the forecourt. Liam waved him back quickly, more embarrassed than hurt.

He knelt up to have another look, at a safer distance this time, and a large ginger cat stared defiantly at him from the far end of the hall. It looked clean and well fed which was something at least. It wouldn't save him from a tetanus jab, but it did imply a caring owner, so he'd learned something already.

With Danni's regulation-issue white hankie held firmly across his nose, he rose to his feet and knocked the front door hard. "Police. Open up please, Mrs Foster."

A small shadow appeared slowly behind the glass and remained stock still, halfway down the hall. It looked like a small woman or a child and Liam could sense that he was scaring them, so he softened his voice and hunkered down again, peering in.

Standing half-out of the first doorway was a small elderly woman. She was eighty at least, and not a modern eighty. Her thick brown tights and laced shoes reminded him of his granny in the country. A proper sensible granny, not one of these modern ones filling themselves with Botox.

Her hair was white and curled and she looked at him apprehensively through large glasses. She looked frightened, as if she rarely answered the door. Liam decided on a kinder approach.

"Hello Mrs Foster. My name's Detective Inspector Liam Cullen."

He had a second's thought that in this staunchly Loyalist street 'Liam Cullen' might sound like a Republican Dissident and scare her even more, but he carried on regardless.

"Could we have a quick chat about what happened across the road yesterday?" He lifted his warrant card and pushed it through for her to see, hoping that the cat wouldn't see it as a new invitation to assault.

As she edged her way slowly down the hall, he could see that her left leg dragged slightly, and her frailty touched him, reminding him why he did the job. She reached out hesitantly, steadying herself, and took the proffered card, holding it close to her glasses for what seemed like minutes before she looked satisfied. Then she leaned over and opened the front door inwards, allowing him to enter.

Liam's heart sank at her eyesight. How could she possibly have seen enough to be a good witness, no matter what her neighbours said? But he always lived in hope.

He stood in the tiled hallway looking down at her. His six-feet-six height made him stand above most people but this tiny woman barely reached his hip. Yet her large eyes danced, hinting at a lively girl inside. She looked up at him trustingly and smiled, handing the card back. "My name's Ida Foster, officer. Please come in."

Her voice was much stronger than Liam had expected, with a lilt from somewhere that he couldn't quite place. As she turned slowly into the small front room, decorated, not as he'd expected with chintz and china but with Australian arts and crafts, her accent slotted into place. Despite his protests, she insisted on making him tea. Remembering the constable waiting by the car, Liam called him in, and together they kept the old woman company over tea and biscuits for an hour. An hour that would help their investigation more than he could ever have hoped.

****

Limavady Police Station.

Julia McNulty sat at her desk in Limavady, sucking at an un-lit cigarette and working out the order of play. Was their drowning victim a girl who'd been beaten, raped and dumped, who just happened to be a police officer? After all, being in 'the job' didn't provide you with a force field, although she sometimes wondered if everyone realised that. Some of her colleagues acted as if they wore superhero suits under their uniforms.

Or, had Maria Burton been raped and murdered *because* she was a police officer? The answers to the two questions would mean something very different. The first, a sad fate for anyone, the second carrying implications for the whole force. Especially its women.

She already knew that her answer didn't matter, because she had to treat it as both. Work it as a rape murder, but use wider intelligence to find out if the whole force or its women were under attack. She lifted her desk phone with a heavy heart, dialling and waiting to hear the deep voice of the man she studiously avoided. She dreaded contact with him, but accepted that it was part of her job, and she'd been prepared for it by her years in the army.

She was surprised then when a quietly spoken woman answered. Julia paused, deciding between the man's wife and daughter, and then hid her pity for the woman as she spoke.

"Mrs Harrison, could I speak to the Detective Chief Superintendent please?"

Chapter Five

The room was small and still, with furniture well past its sell-by-date and that air of peace that the elderly seemed to carry with them. The only nods to two thousand and twelve were a huge flat-screen television and a pile of lottery tickets that poked out from behind the clock. It reminded Liam of his granny's farmhouse – she'd had a huge TV as well, and when he'd asked her why, she'd just laughed and imitated a jockey. Her lottery tickets had been betting slips.

The two men perched on the edge of the too-small chairs, drinking their tea from the china cups brought out only for visitors. Liam's huge fingers couldn't fit through the handle, so he held the cup like a pen and tried not to drip tea on the rug, draining the cup in one swallow. Ida topped him up again, smiling and handing him ginger cake that was the best he'd had in ages, and he said so. She beamed at him proudly.

"We used to run a tea-shop in Dundonald, but now I just bake for myself and visitors. I'll give you a few cakes to take away."

She smiled at the young constable. "So nice to see a man in uniform" casting a slightly disapproving eye over Liam's grey suit.

"In my day, any man who wasn't in uniform wasn't a man at all. They were so handsome. We used to go dancing at the Floral Hall near Bellevue and have such lovely times." She looked wistful for a moment. "So much more romantic than those disco things."

Liam watched her as she spoke. She was one of those elfin creatures typical of the war years. Enforced rationing and healthy walking had left them with a legacy of slimness in maturity and frailty in old age. She still wore the strange fashion mix of a generation where clothes had been in short supply, as if she'd never quite caught up. Her thin hands bore rings that hinted at marriage and children.

"Do you have family nearby, Mrs Foster?" The

constable's loud voice broke through the musty air like a siren and she smiled at him again, as if he was her own child.

"Yes, thank the lord. My daughter lives two streets over and I have seven grandchildren and a great granddaughter – she's getting married in June."

She moved suddenly, far quicker than earlier, over to a dark sideboard, pulling a sheaf of photographs from its top drawer. Liam silently cursed the P.C. for his question, but part of him smiled at the certainty of viewing baby photos, accepting that the small kindness might mean a lot to Ida Foster. Annette's people skills were rubbing off on him.

They admired her photos, and drank and ate for about thirty minutes, until finally Liam shifted the conversation to the reason they'd knocked at her door.

He outlined the murder without revealing its gruesome detail but as always, he was surprised by the pragmatism of the war generation. Nothing seemed to shock them, but then they'd seen so many die. Or maybe age brought calmness. He thought wryly that Craig could do with some of that nowadays.

"So, did you see anything across the road on Wednesday? Anything that stood out at all, Mrs Foster?"

"Ida."

"Of course. Ida."

"What time do you mean, Mr Cullen? I'm in the neighbourhood watch so I see a lot through my windows. I sit there and watch the world. See ..."

She pointed towards the net curtains and Liam peered through the room's dim light, spotting a window-seat that he hadn't noticed before. It was the perfect vantage point. He walked over and lifted the curtain. Yes! Ida had had a clear view of the garage.

"Any time at all yesterday – were you looking out?"

"Oh yes. Now let me think.... yesterday... Well, Lizzie came in after eight on her way to work. Did I tell you she has a very important job? Up at Stormont; she's one of those civil servants."

He half-smiled and nodded her on, encouraging

her to stick to the story.

"And when she left?"

"Oh yes. Well, I had breakfast, then I took a cup of tea and my crossword to the window and I sat there. I was probably there until five-ish when Lizzie came back to take me to stay with her. I always stay over with Lizzie on a Wednesday night – until Thursday evening."

Suddenly Liam felt excited; she'd been sitting by the window all day! He'd expected an hour if they were lucky, but this was brilliant. He was even more impressed by her ability to exist without food for eight hours.

"Didn't you leave the window at all in that time? For more tea or whatever?" He hesitated to mention the word 'toilet' to a lady of that generation; he'd said it to his granny once and could still remember the resulting sore ear.

"Oh no, I had my flask with me."

She looked at him as if she'd suddenly realised something.

"Now I remember. I stayed there until Countdown started on Channel Four plus one, at four-twenty-five. I always watch it with some tea and toast. That's when I sat back down there." She indicated the P.C.'s chair, smiling, satisfied that she'd been accurate. Both men stared, impressed that she knew about the Plus One channels; Liam had only found out they existed a few months before!

"Then Lizzie came round at five with Gina and Roy, her youngest. She brought in fish and chips. A lovely piece of cod from the corner of the Belmont Road. Then the children did their homework while we chatted and we left at about six-thirty. I watched 'Midsomer Murders' over at hers."

Liam was almost afraid to ask the next question, the possibility that she might have seen something useful almost too good to be true. But he needn't have worried about framing his questions to tease information out of her, because Ida suddenly reached up to the mantelpiece and grabbed at a worn red notebook, opening it at the second last page. She peered at it for a moment and then started to read.

"At ten-past-ten in the morning the postman walked into the garage and put some letters through the shop door. He's my postman - Mr McGimpsey - such a nice man; I always give him something at Christmas. Then at eleven-forty a boy on a bicycle rode around the forecourt a few times, doing those dangerous one-wheel things." She pursed her lips disapprovingly.

"Wheelies?"

She nodded and pushed her large glasses further up the bridge of her nose, without taking her eyes of the page. "Yes, I think they're called something like that. Roy does them in the park and his mother shouts. I recognised the boy; his father owns the grocery shop."

She squinted hard at the page and Liam's heart sank again at her eyesight, but what she said next removed all his doubts.

"At twelve-thirty-seven a young man walked onto the forecourt and over to the cars that were parked at the back." She glanced up accusingly. "They've all gone today. Have they been stolen?"

"No, don't worry, we've just taken them to our compound to stop them being vandalised." Satisfied with Liam's explanation she moved on.

"He walked around a few times and looked at a couple of them very closely. He didn't look like a criminal, but I've written a description of him anyway."

She tapped the page emphatically, "Six feet, about thirty, wearing a suit. Balding dark hair and overweight. He looked like a spiv – we had lots of those during the war."

The two men laughed and she smiled, pleased that they appreciated her work.

Ida continued.

"At one-forty-five in the afternoon a young woman walked up and down the street a few times. She looked very shifty so I paid special attention to her. She was in her twenties somewhere, very thin and pale looking. You know that pale that says you're not healthy? And she had on those jeans things – I hate those. Doesn't anyone dress like a lady nowadays? My Lizzie does. She's always nicely turned out."

Liam leaned forward encouragingly, desperate not to be drawn into a fashion diatribe, and he noticed her eyes again. They were huge and the palest blue that he'd even seen; almost translucent, as if you could see behind them. Ida looked thrilled by his keen interest and continued eagerly.

"She was small and she had her hood up, but you could still see she had dark hair. Not black but dark brown, down to about here." She indicated her shoulders.

"The ends were sticking out; it looked like she hadn't put a comb through it for weeks." She pursed her lips again, sniffing disapprovingly. "Her jacket was very rough looking; dark green like the ones the trainers wear at racecourses, but the hood was grey."

She was describing a green Barbour jacket and a grey hoody, Liam was sure of it. The constable leaned forward, desperate to assist, but Liam shook his head slightly, motioning him not to lead her. Ida Foster was going to be a valuable witness.

"Then she walked onto the forecourt, and cheeky as you like just walked on into the shop! And the owner definitely wasn't in there."

"Was the door open?"

She paused for a moment, thinking, "It must have been. She didn't use a key, she just pushed it open. She was in there for about ten minutes."

She consulted her notebook. "Yes here it is. She went in at one-fifty and came back out at two pm on the dot." Liam could have hugged her for her accuracy.

"Which way did she go then, Mrs Foster?"

"Ida."

"Sorry. Ida."

She smiled at him forgivingly. "She walked out the door and turned to her right towards the cars, and then she stopped and looked at one of them. I thought she was going to steal it, so I kept a very close eye on her."

The hairs on the back of Liam's neck stood up. "Which car?" Knowing the answer even before she spoke.

"A red one. A small, fat car. That's what I call them anyway."

She smiled and looked up at him, hopeful that he'd laugh at her joke. And he did, so loudly and for so long that it verged on hysteria. He'd spoken to the killer! He'd actually spoken to the killer - the red car confirmed it. It was the woman who'd called Ian McCandless' mobile; Monica Gibson. That wouldn't be her real name of course, but at least they had a number; and even if it was false, it might give them something.

Ida was still talking and Liam was pulled out of his self-congratulation by her next few words.

"Then she walked around the corner and disappeared."

"Did you see her later?"

"I can't be sure. I saw the man who owned the garage driving up in his navy car at eleven minutes past two. He walked right into the shop. But then my phone went. It was my sister Jane in Sydney and we were chatting for ages, so I stopped watching. When I looked again, it was three-fifteen and all your cars were there. Did I miss anything important?"

Only a murder, Ida.

Liam bit back his disappointment. It had been too much to hope that she'd actually witnessed the killing. They'd already been spoiled, and now she'd confirmed McCandless' time of death as well.

"No, you've been brilliant, Ida, really brilliant." She beamed at him, and he felt sure that his next words would bring an even bigger smile to her face.

"You've given us very valuable information, so could you work with our sketch artist to produce likenesses of the people you saw yesterday? Especially yesterday afternoon."

"Are they all murderers?"

"No, I'm sure they're not all." He fervently hoped that one of them was. "But one of them might be." Ida looked as if she might burst. "And the rest we'd like to rule out of our enquiries, with your help."

He paused for effect. "Would you be free if I sent a patrol car to collect you, in the morning? Say about ten o'clock?"

She nodded vigorously, immediately lifting the phone to tell her daughter, and they said their farewells, leaving her chatting happily. Then Liam called Craig to give him the biggest break they'd caught yet.

****

Shaftesbury Square, Belfast.

The taxi driver dropped Jessie at the strip of bars and clubs that made up the rough end of Belfast's 'Golden mile'. What started with drinking and fighting at the Shaftesbury Square end, finished one mile further up in Malone, with multi-million pound houses and shops selling Armani and Chanel. Belfast's small size prevented the light and dark shades of life being very far apart.

Jessie paid the driver and got out onto the pavement, gazing up at the Square's neon lights. She caught the admiring glances of the burly, T-shirted men queuing outside The Ark, a popular nightspot for the under forties, their attention guaranteed by her blonde, mini-skirted stereotype.

They ran their eyes across her breasts and thighs, mentally salivating, and she had a sudden image of wolves licking their lips, like something in a Roadrunner cartoon. Men were so predictable; Pavlov should have just forgotten the dogs and taken a blonde to inner city Britain.

But their predictability would be very useful soon and she had nothing to lose nowadays. Protecting her virtue was redundant; her body was her weapon tonight, no matter how defective it was.

Jessie glanced up at the red lights and suddenly a

searing pain cut through the bone behind her eyes, sucking out her breath. She staggered backwards, a fortuitous lamppost halting her fall, her hearing suddenly dulled by chords of high-pitched bells. Droplets of cold sweat trickled down between her small, high breasts and she fought the urge to vomit, shutting her eyes quickly. She was half-deaf to the calls of "Hey Blondie!" that passed for foreplay to the men walking past.

For seconds that dragged like minutes she leaned against the post, eyes closed, until the ringing passed and her sweat had dried. Then she opened her eyes to see the traffic still running, and her taxi driver still sitting at the kerb, counting his fares. It was over for another while, but she knew that she needed to hurry now, if she hoped to complete her task.

Moving as quickly as her high-heels allowed, Jessie joined the short queue into one of Belfast's roughest nightclubs. Her hand was stamped with dye then she was waved into the darkness where rhythmic strobes crossed the faces of the young and not so young. She prayed that her extra medication would prevent the seizure that such lights would normally provoke.

It was like walking into a safari; the females huddled to one side, the males prowling and watching. She knew she had to act quickly so she scanned the room desperately, searching for only one thing. Couples. Especially couples where the man faced the door deliberately, so that his eyes could wander over each new female entrant without his clinging girlfriend spotting his crime. It didn't take her long to find the man she was looking for.

He was tall with short dark hair and a strong jaw, handsome in a half-pretty way, but overly groomed and self-aware. He admired his reflection frequently in the glass beside him, and cast around constantly for an upgrade from the slim brunette hanging from his neck. Perfect! An arrogant prick with a possessive girlfriend – just what she'd been looking for.

The girl around his neck sensed something and gazed around hostilely, searching for someone but unsure exactly who. Just any woman who would steal her prize.

Jessie walked quickly to the D.J. and whispered seductively in his ear, gifting him a long enough look at her breasts to ensure that he finally nodded and moved to the pile of unplayed discs at his side. He selected one in particular and she moved back onto the floor, readying for her performance.

She caught the eye of the half-pretty man with a silent promise and began to dance, slowly and sensuously. Ignoring any looks but his, she felt the music with its soft French words running through her, promising sex and creating heat. Her hands wandered down her body, touching her breasts and thighs, her eyes half-closed.

When she could feel the room watching her, Jessie half-opened her mouth and widened her eyes, ignoring the crowd of staring men and fixing only on her target. She beckoned gently towards him, seeing him and only him; ignoring his companion, dismissing her as totally unimportant, and prepared to do whatever damage it took to get her where she needed to be that night.

The man's eyes wandered over her body, a smile touching his full lips. His pupils dilated in the darkness as he moved towards her, pushing the obstacle in front of him to one side. He crossed to the centre of the floor and began touching her hair, kissing her lips, stroking her thighs. The two of them moving in time to the music, pulsing and soaring, his arousal forcing her to see him. He was strong and hard, and involuntary responses came from Jessie's body. This wasn't the plan but could add to the plan. She returned his pressure firmly with the full length of her body, oblivious to the other couples beginning to dance.

She shifted her gaze and was rewarded by the sight of the man's old companion standing beside them. There was fury in the brunette's eyes as she grabbed her errant lover's arm, only to be pushed away in response. Now it was time for Jessie to perform.

She turned to the spurned girlfriend in mock anger. "Can't you take a hint? He's with me now." Then, for added effect. "Piss off!"

She dismissed the girl sneeringly and seized her new lover's face in her hands, kissing him with a sensuality that she thought she'd forgotten. Then, just as she'd hoped, the other woman grabbed her arm and Jessie spun round viciously, pushing her hard across the floor. It was working.

The floor emptied and the bouncers stood watching with folded arms, while calls of "Cat-fight, Cat-fight," echoed around the room.

Jessie saw the girl coming at her again, so she shrugged off her partner and threw herself at her assailant. She'd seen women fighting on television so she knew exactly how much to do to get arrested, and that was her only aim.

She moved slowly to the edge of the floor, with the brunette following just as she'd planned. She reached for Jessie's hair and Jessie stepped forward to let her, falling deliberately to her knees beside a small table. Gripping its edge as if to help herself up, she seized a half-full beer glass, tossing the beer on the floor and breaking its edge against the table. Then, with an almighty effort, she got to her feet and ran towards her adversary, skewering and twisting the broken glass firmly into the girl's bare upper arm. She knew exactly where to cut without hitting a major vessel – this girl wasn't her enemy, she was just the means to an end.

Blood spurted onto the floor and the dark-haired girl fell to her knees startled, her eyes locked onto her own blood in fascinated horror. Jessie went for broke and stalked the floor with the bloody glass, holding the bouncers at bay. She swore and threatened them with its broken edge for what seemed like an endless time, giving her audience a free show, until eventually she was grabbed from behind in an arm-lock and she dropped the glass, feeling the tight restriction of a police cuff around her thin wrists.

She smiled inwardly, while outwardly her spitting wildcat entertained the crowd as they watched her exit. None of them were aware that her real game was just about to start.

****

Limavady Station.

"Maria Burton was only twenty-four. Joined up last year."

"And now this happens."

Detective Sergeant Gerry Shaw shook his head. "It mightn't be anything to do with the job, ma'am. I know I shouldn't say this, but I really hope it *was* personal. The last thing we need is some nutter out there randomly targeting female officers. I've got the intelligence boys checking the usual suspects just in case."

He paused for a second. "Was she married?"

Julia nodded and took a deep, comforting drag of her cigarette, blowing the smoke into a long white funnel in the night air. They were standing in the brick alcove outside the station's back door, full of hardened smokers whatever the weather. The fresh-faced sergeant tutted deliberately slowly.

"That'll kill you, ma'am."

"For God's sake, spare me the lecture, Gerry. Everyone dies sometime."

"Aye, that's so."

His soft Derry drawl dragged the last word into a song and Julia smiled. She loved any accent but her own, especially the soft ones.

"But not at thirty-five, ma'am."

He shook his head disapprovingly and she dropped her spent cigarette, deftly crushing it with her foot. Gerry had 'Ma'am-ed' it to death.

She sighed heavily. "All right, you win. God, but there's nothing as boring as a reformed smoker."

He smiled in victory, careful that she didn't see. You could only take the piss so far with the D.I.

"What else do we know about Maria?"

"Separated six months ago and just got her decree nisi. She told her sergeant that she'd married too young."

"Never a right time, is there? Have uniform

brought the husband in yet?"

"For identification?"

"For a suspect. You know fine well most of these turn killings out to be someone they know. The bogey man in the bushes is an urban myth, Gerry, no matter what the press say."

She groaned, reminded of the media briefing she had coming. If Maggie Clarke was there, she'd focus on her. There were good journalists and then there were hacks. Maggie was one of the good guys, giving unbiased reporting in her column for the Derry Telegraph. The others could go to hell.

"Anything back from forensics yet?"

Gerry nodded. "They found semen, so that's good news. The bad news is that all the sperm were dead."

"Isn't that to be expected in the water?"

"Not the intrauterine ones apparently, and they're dead too. Still, they're running it for matches; known offenders."

"And the husband?"

"And the husband, ma'am."

He was about to say something more but then thought again and shrugged. Julia saw the gesture and knew what was coming, so she thought she might as well bring it on.

"Go on then, say what you're thinking."

"Aye, well, it's just...aren't we being a teeny bit cynical, ma'am? Not all ex-husbands are axe murderers."

She turned to look directly at him, ready to whip out a sarcastic remark, but the genuine naivety in his eyes reminded her that there were still some nice guys. She bit back the comment and turned to go, then, unable to resist the last word, she threw "you haven't met my ex then" over her shoulder.

It wasn't the whole truth, but it made her feel better, and the boss always made the closing speech. Rule number one.

****

High Street Station. Belfast.

"Name?"
"Kate Rogers."
"Age?"
"Twenty-seven."

Jessie really couldn't believe it. It had worked; she was actually being booked! Tonight she'd be in a cell, and she'd act up so much that tomorrow a judge would have to remand her. And there was only one place to remand women in Northern Ireland. Wharf House. Exactly where she wanted to be.

Chapter Six

Limavady. Friday, 8 a.m.

Julia couldn't sleep, so at six am she'd decided that she might as well be paid for her insomnia, instead of lying in bed alone. So there she was, knackered and standing in the hallway of headquarters dying for a cig. She reached into her bag for the comforting shape of the small box, wondering again why no-one had started a religion where the deity was a giant cigarette, the answer to all troubles. She'd definitely join it. Hell, she'd be a Priestess!

Her mobile would have to substitute until she got outside, so she flicked it open and pressed 'Gerry', feeling, and not for the first time, like a complete loser for having her three quick-dial numbers as Gerry, the Chinese takeaway and her mum. She really needed to get out more.

It was answered within four rings.

"Hi chief, what can I do you for so early?"

"Is Paul Burton ready for interview yet?"

"Give me a break, it's eight o clock! I'm still at home and no-one human is even awake yet, except you ex-army types. But I've got some good news for you."

"What's that?"

"Burton's denying everything, so that'll give you something to sink your teeth into."

Julia perked up instantly – she loved a challenge.

There was no-one around to tut at her, so she lit a cigarette just before she left the building, defiantly blowing the smoke through her nostrils like a dragon, just as she opened the door. The tut came anyway, by telephone.

"You've just lit a cig, haven't you? I can hear you."

"Yep, and you're not here to tell me off." She blew more smoke into the receiver in a 'fuck-you' exhalation. Pity it was soundless. "And I'm going to have another one after this, so that'll give you about ten minutes to meet me upstairs with the reports. The D.C.S. wants me at ten; to get the press off his back, so let's get Paul Burton down for eleven. We need something definite on this today, Gerry. And you do want to see your wife and kids tonight, don't you?"

****

The C.C.U.

"Joey McCandless said the debt collectors were always calling them. Poor woman – at least that'll stop now."

Liam raised an eyebrow. "Will it? Won't she inherit his debts?"

"No, not on the garage, he'd sewn it up tightly in his name. And the house insurance will leave her pretty well off." Annette caught his quick look. "No! Not enough to justify bumping him off. God, but you're cynical, Cullen."

Liam winked at her and grinned.

"I keep telling Danni *I'm* worth killing, but she says not to tempt her. By the way, my witness is a complete star and she's coming in this morning to give us a sketch. She described four people at the garage that day, plus McCandless. Three men and a woman."

"A woman! Are you sure?"

"Yep, I'm sure. She saw a small woman. She even described her hair and face, despite her wearing a hoody. She caught a good look from the front."

So Craig had been right; their likeliest killer was a small woman. It certainly fitted with the tripwire. And the fact she'd killed in clear daylight meant that either she thought she was flameproof and would never be caught, or she didn't much care if she was which was much worse. People who thought they had nothing to lose were always far more dangerous.

Craig heard them talking and wandered out of his office, pulling up a chair.

"The description certainly fits, Liam, but how reliable is your little lady?"

"Sharp as they come, boss. I tried to test her

memory about general things and she told me to stop being cheeky, and then calculated the seven-times-table in her head while she was pouring out the tea. And you want to see the notebook she keeps! It's full of details about people coming and going. She watches the whole street from her bay window."

Craig nodded, thinking of his own mum. She was only sixty-nine but he could imagine her still running rings round some cheeky young copper in ten years' time. She'd eat them alive if they underestimated her. Annette smiled at the thought of Liam perched like the Jolly Green Giant in a world of doilies and chintz. She'd pay money to see that photograph.

At least he'd spent his afternoon more pleasantly than they had. Mrs McCandless' silence would live with her for a long time, that and the way Joey had wiped the tears from his cheeks as he'd talked about his dad.

"She's coming in at ten."

"That's great. Hopefully we'll have a likeness by later today. Meanwhile here's another little gem to get your grey cells working." He told them about the Purecrem and Annette's mouth dropped. It hung open until Liam leaned across, tipping it shut.

"Aye, I was going to mention that, boss. My P.C. spotted a smear of cream at the garage yesterday."

Annette found her voice. "What do you make of it, sir? A baby? Maybe McCandless had a mistress and a love child. Maybe he'd promised her things and then reneged on it? She wouldn't be the first woman to do a man damage in that situation."

Liam crossed his legs pointedly, "Danni would put my nuts in a vice."

"She'd have to join the queue."

Craig furrowed his dark brows. "That's not a bad suggestion about McCandless, Annette."

She made a face. "Except there was no word of infidelity when we interviewed his wife, sir. But then, I don't suppose there would be, especially not in front of her son." She went quiet suddenly then offered up something reluctantly. "A lot of those creams are used for adults as well."

"That's what John and Des said. What made you think of that?"

She hesitated over her next words.

"Come on, Annette. What is it?"

"Well, it's Joey, sir... He works in an old people's home to supplement his student loan." She added hurriedly. "But I'm sure it's not him, he's really cut up about his dad."

Liam snorted at her naivety. She was always giving people the benefit of the doubt, but it probably balanced out his own cynicism.

"Right, Annette. Go and talk to the wife alone. Softly, softly please. If there was a mistress and she didn't know then we could damage her badly, so just tease out whatever you can. And I want Joey looked into as well - he's small and slight enough to pass for a girl in some lights, and he wouldn't be the first to kill a parent."

"But he was genuinely upset, sir."

"He could be upset even if he had killed him. Crimes of passion aren't rational, you know that. Liam, I want you to chase down this razor-wire, Des says it's a very unusual type. He can give you all the information you need on it, although John said he was still in St Mary's maternity being shouted at an hour ago."

"What?"

"Annie's in labour."

Annette and Liam nodded at each other knowingly.

"Aye, Danni found a few new names for me when Erin was born last year. I hadn't heard them much outside the barracks before then. I must say I was quite shocked to hear my delicate flower of a wife say such words." He pursed his lips primly and then burst out laughing. "Actually I'm quite looking forward to a repeat with this next baby, it's been great ammunition against her ever since. All I have to do is threaten to tell the priest what she called me and she makes my favourite dinner for a week."

Suddenly Nicky approached, and they watched

Liam's colour heighten, underlining his schoolboy crush.

"Good morning all. Sorry to interrupt you, sir, but the D.C.S. wants to see you this afternoon. He'll be back from Limavady at one o'clock."

Craig rolled his eyes. "Deep joy. Any idea what he wants, Nick?"

"He said an update on the new case." She looked around as if she'd just noticed Annette and Liam sitting there and shot them both a kilowatt smile, throwing Liam's cool even further into the bin. Annette noticed that she was particularly perky this morning.

"You look happy, Nicky. Anything exciting happening?"

The P.A. glanced at Craig hesitantly, and then used her best wheedling voice. Combined with her usual growl it made her sound like Mariella Frostrup with a head cold.

"Well...there could be. That's if the D.C.I. will very kindly let me have a week's holiday at short notice?"

"How short?"

"Monday week. The twenty-ninth."

Craig raised his eyes to heaven at the thought of breaking in a new temp. "Tell me..."

Nicky grinned. "I won a holiday in our Jonny's school raffle. A week in Venice for me and someone else."

Liam couldn't resist it. "Are you taking me then?"

She tossed her hair and ignored him, continuing.

"I'm taking our Denise. Gary can't get away from work and she's just getting over her appendix op, so I thought it'd be brilliant for her. And if Gary's not there we can just shop twenty-four-seven." She looked at Annette for an understanding retail audience.

"Just think of all those shoes and bags. Brilliant."

Nicky glanced hopefully at Craig from under her lashes and he glanced at Liam. Both had complete sympathy for Gary. Seven days of shopping was man hell. He smiled at his P.A. and nodded.

"On you go then, but you'd better get me a good

temp or you'll be coming back to a very grumpy boss. I'll get my mum to call you; she has cousins in Venice so she'll find the best shopping and eating places for you. In fact she could probably get you a tour-guide if you'd like."

Craig's mother Mirella was a Roman Italian who'd been a professional concert pianist for many years. She'd brought up her two children to be musical and bi-lingual and named them Marco and Lucia, but the teasing had been too much in a Belfast primary school, so in the first week their Belfast father Tom had shortened the names to Marc and Lucy outside the house, much to Mirella's annoyance. She still ranted at him about it.

Nicky teetered over and gave Craig a peck on the cheek and was rewarded by a blush that matched Liam's. She smiled and left, throwing Annette a secret wink on the way out. Fifteen – Love.

Craig picked up where he'd left off. "OK. Liam, the wire. Annette, the wife and Joey, and I'll meet you both at the lab at eleven. We need more details on that weapon."

He lifted a file and headed back to his office. There was nothing urgent in it but he needed some space. He and John belonged to the 'you can sleep when you're dead' school of partying and last night had been a heavy one spent ricocheting between the Cathedral Quarter and the bar at Ten Square, with the added dimension of John desperately trying to avoid mentioning Camille's name. Craig knew that he needed to decide what to do about her: see her, not see her, walk into the sea, emigrate.

He sat staring at the file reading the same passage four times, until the steel desk clock that had been a present from Lucia said ten o'clock. His parents were always awake from seven, even though they were both retired, his mother from touring and his father from his university physics post, so he decided to call them.

He didn't need an excuse but Nicky's trip would give him one, and he wanted to hear a friendly voice. He dialled their number slowly, feeling pathetic for calling at all.

It was lifted within three rings and his father's deep voice answered. Craig could picture him, still in his shirt and tie. He'd never quite got the hang of retirement.

"Hi, Dad."

"Ah, hello, son. How's work? Did you catch that garage case?"

"Yes."

Tom Craig knew better than to ask the detail so he went on. "Are you calling for anything particular?" Craig's hesitance answered him immediately and he knew that he wanted Mirella's input.

"Right, I'll just get your mother and we'll see you tonight I hope? Lucia's bringing some new young man round to meet us." The words 'young man' always made Craig smile. Lucia was thirty-two and most of them were at least that age.

"I can't miss that. Let me guess; is this one a struggling musician or a struggling poet?"

Lucia's taste in men ran to talented waifs and strays. She was the arty, 'friends of the whale' one, which was probably why she was the fundraiser for a charity and he was playing cops and robbers with John. His father laughed; a warm, low growl that came from deep inside his chest. Craig remembered making him laugh as a kid just to hear it.

"You guessed it, although this one isn't starving or struggling apparently. He's a pianist with the London City Orchestra."

Craig was impressed. A pianist! His mum would be ecstatic. Lucia had better marry him or they'd never hear the end of it.

"Here's your mother."

"Marco, what is problem? What you need?"

The time of his call had made her maternal antennae twitch and she knew that there was something wrong. But Craig just let her lilting Italian cadences wash over him for five minutes, chiding himself for being pathetic enough to still get comfort from his parents at forty-two. Then he told himself the lie that he could live with, that he'd given her Nicky's number and that was the only real reason for his call.

****

Limavady Headquarters: D.C.S. Harrison's office.

"I know it's making everyone anxious and it's bad for morale, sir, but we can't rule out that it was an anti-police attack until we're sure. That wouldn't do anyone any good. Let's hope it *was* the husband; I'm interviewing him at eleven and we should have preliminary reports from forensics and pathology later, so I'll know a lot more by close of business."

Julia was standing, hands clasped behind her back, looking straight ahead; just as she used to do as a young army captain. She'd never managed to shake the habit, although she had left the army ten years before; even she wasn't macho enough for that life. Plus the cigs were making the assault course harder by the year, and in a choice between smoking and the Regiment, the Regiment would lose every time.

She preferred being in the police anyway. At least she got to dress like a woman at work. Although not today; today she'd deliberately chosen to wear her baggiest trouser suit and frumpiest heels. It didn't do to look too attractive anywhere near the D.C.S. His reputation for leching preceded him.

She pushed back a strand of her dark red hair, a legacy of her Scottish grandfather, and waited for him to speak. Terry Harrison looked up at her, smiling inwardly. She was a pretty woman but not really his type. Her insistence on being 'one of the boys' did her no favours; she would look far better in a dress.

"You can sit down you know, Julia. You're not on parade."

He motioned her to the chair opposite and she took it, blushing. He noticed her heightened colour and the vulnerability behind it and his 'victim radar' pinged. Vulnerable. Maybe she was his type after all.

"I appreciate what you're saying, Inspector. The investigation has to be robust. It would be worse to charge the wrong person, for everyone's sake. But you have to appreciate *my* position."

Your position's sitting on your backside usually, sir.

Julia thought to herself, and not for the first time, that it was just as well telepathy wasn't a D.C.S. job requirement.

Harrison droned on without inhaling.

"I have the media to deal with and they're baying for blood at the moment. So I'm going to draft a holding statement, saying that we don't feel this was an assault on the police generally, but rather the very sad loss of a colleague who has been the victim of a heinous crime. I won't release it until six pm, so that should give you plenty of time to get back to me with your *confirmatory* findings from the husband."

She cast him a sullen look but said nothing. His tone hardened.

"Are we clear, Inspector McNulty?" She was sorry she'd sat down now.

"Yes, sir. Crystal clear."

Harrison perused her face slowly. Her words had verged on the sarcastic but her tone was all sweetness. Hmm...

"Good, then I'll send you the draft for comments at five-thirty. That'll be all."

He reached out his hand for the phone, the action dismissing her if his words hadn't already done so. She rose quickly and left the room, the blush burning her cheeks, completely missing Harrison's quick scan of her body as she turned.

Bastard. When was the last time he'd worked a scene? Bastard, bastard, bastard.

****

It was late morning when the Craigs' phone rang in Holywood, 'Best kept medium town of 2009', and Tom Craig had just eased himself out of his chair to answer it when it cut off. He tutted quietly, returning to his computer screen. He had just taken a sip of sweet tea when it rang again.

"Mirella, that's the phone. I'm working. Can you get it, pet?"

He wasn't really working. Well, not what he'd called work for thirty years. Writing papers and preparing lectures, marking illegible scripts from bored students, whilst all the time searching desperately for one vague glimmer of understanding amidst the plagiarised reams.

No, this wasn't 'real' work; this was fun. Plus it got him out of dishwashing duties, although why Mirella wouldn't let him buy a dishwasher he would never understand. Some sort of Italian 'love thing' probably, like most things were with her.

He was drafting an article for the local newspaper. They'd taken him on the year before as a freelance science writer. It used his physics background, it was light-hearted reporting on the latest weird and wonderful advances across the world and, best of all, they actually paid him. Not much, but enough for their twice-yearly trips to Rome, and wine and pasta money when they were there. And it meant that he could legitimately ignore the phone and leave the dishes dirty.

Mirella bustled past him, muttering in Italian. She knew exactly what her husband was up to, but pretended that she didn't because she loved him anyway. She grabbed at the mock nineteen-forties receiver, playfully flicking a dishcloth at his back.

"Si. Yes, Mirella Craig. Can I 'elp you?"

The female voice was so soft and hesitant that Mirella didn't recognise it at first, straining to hear what it said.

"I am ve-ry so-rry, I cannot 'ear you, please."

"Hello, Mrs Craig." Silence. Then, even more hesitantly. "It's Camille...Camille Kennedy. Is Marc there?"

Tom Craig knew something was up by the icy silence that suddenly descended on the room, and he glanced over at his wife questioningly. She was gripping the receiver so hard that the blood had left her hand, and staring at it as if it was a snake. He left his laptop and moved quickly to her, convinced that she'd had bad news, until her angry look took him by surprise.

He realised in an instant who was on the other end of the phone and reached over quickly to remove it from Mirella's grip. Too late. The stream of Italian/English invective that shot down the receiver was pure maternal instinct and contained words he'd only heard her use once before, when someone had beaten up Lucia at school.

"You dare call my house. Heartless trollop! You stay away from Marco, you..."

He turned her towards him and stared straight into her eyes, his finger firmly on her lips. Slowly, he loosened her grip on the handset, finger by finger, finally lifting it above her head out of harm's way. Marc wouldn't thank her for her anger. This was his business.

He turned away from his wife, speaking into the receiver as if it had just been answered, feeling her eyes boring into his back.

"Just one moment, please."

He walked out through the French doors into the garden, with a look that warned Mirella to stay behind. Then he spoke again, already knowing who was on the other end, but pretending that he didn't.

"May I help you?"

The voice was tearful now and ready to run, and he almost felt sorry for her. Almost, but not quite. He'd seen the damage Camille had done to his son, and it wasn't over yet by the sounds of it. But he knew that adults couldn't be shielded by their over-protective parents. Life wasn't like the playground.

"It's Camille Kennedy, Mr Craig. I'm sorry to bother you, but ..."

"Yes, Ms Kennedy."

Not "Camille" or "It's lovely to hear from you", even though they'd known her for many years and stayed with her and Marc many times in London.

"I take it you're looking for Marc?"

"Yes...I wondered..."

He could see Mirella prowling just inside the French doors, eavesdropping, and he turned his back firmly to her, knowing that he'd pay for it later. Her protective Mama side would give him a special kind of hell, but it wouldn't last, and by bedtime they'd be friends again. She never held a grudge, unless someone hurt one of her children, and then she would hold it forever.

"He doesn't live here, Ms Kennedy, and I'm sorry but I won't give you his number or address, so please don't ask."

A quiet sob at the other end made him soften slightly and he relented, adding.

"But I will take your number and tell him that you called. That's all I can or will do. Please give me your number."

He walked into the living room and lifted a pen, shooting another warning glance at Mirella, which she returned with venom. He took a note of the number and with a short "Goodbye" cut the line, walking quickly past his wife to return the phone to its cradle. Then he waited for the explosion.

****

Limavady.

Paul Burton sat in the small neon-lit interview room fidgeting nervously, folding and unfolding a gum wrapper in the way Gerry remembered doing, when he'd been in nicotine withdrawal. The detectives stood on the other side of the two-way glass watching him, while Julia's brain turned over, slowly configuring her plan of attack.

Burton had been lifted from his house outside Templepatrick six hours before, told only that he was needed to help them with their enquiries. All of his questions were met with silence or "the inspector will explain" and there was no sign that he even knew his wife Maria was dead. Although that told them nothing; self-denial was almost as good as the truth for portraying signs of innocence.

He'd even told them his wife was in 'the job' and suggested calling her. Again, silence. They already had Maria Burton's positive identification, and a weeping set of parents who had confirmed her difficult marriage and unhelpful estranged husband. Now here he was, professing not to even know that she was dead.

Burton had declined legal support, but that could mean innocence or bluff. So for the past hour he'd been left with tea and quiet in a starkly-lit interview room, working up a sweat. He'd been cooking nicely and now he was ready to eat.

"Have you got the forensics, Gerry? I need them before I go in." He pushed a small folder into her hand.

"I hope there's some good news in here?"

"Well, it's interesting anyway – especially the swab results. We know she was seen alive at eight o'clock Wednesday morning and found at five pm Thursday, so she could have been in the water between twenty-four and thirty-three hours. The pathologist says nearer twenty-four. She had abrasions on her hands and knees, thin linear cuts across her shins and a basal skull fracture."

Julia was puzzled but she waved him on.

"They found semen inside the uterus and her clothes were disarranged, so she was raped and killed somewhere on Wednesday, and then dumped in the river. The C.S.I.s took the vaginal swabs at five-thirty yesterday and rushed them to the lab. OK?"

"OK, yes, what's your point?"

"The lab report is timed six pm."

"Yes, and? Oh, for God's sake Gerry, do you want a fanfare?"

He sighed. "Well, it doesn't add up. The lab report says the intra-uterine sperm were all dead…by six pm?"

"Maybe it was her contraception. Spermicide?"

"Well, one, she probably wouldn't have used

anything like spermicide if she was being raped. And two, I don't think hormone-based contraceptives like the pill are meant to do that. I think they stop women producing eggs not kill the sperm. I'll check, but I'm pretty sure."

She looked at him as if he was an anomaly; a copper in touch with his feminine side. Lucky wife.

"I still don't get it."

He resisted sighing again and adopted a brisk tone. "OK. According to the pathologist, she was in the water for at least a day, so raped somewhere between eight am and five pm Wednesday. Sperm usually live for about six hours in the vagina and six days inside the uterus. Spermicide kills sperm so they likely wouldn't have reached the uterus at all, and the pill doesn't kill sperm so they could have reached the uterus, but if they had they'd still be alive."

"Summarise, Gerry, and quickly."

"It means that any sperm that *had* reached the uterus should still have been alive by the time the lab examined the semen at five-thirty pm on Thursday. Maria was healthy and her husband looks healthy-ish, and there are no signs of infertility on the report."

Julia still looked blank so he pointed to the pink sheet inside the file, his voice rising in exasperation. She squinted at him in warning.

"There were millions of sperm inside the uterus and most were a normal shape so, in other words, it's an otherwise perfectly normal sperm sample. So how come they were all dead in less than six days?"

She stared into space, longing for a cigarette, and then snapped her fingers.

"I've got it – the water?"

"Nope, the lab says that shouldn't have killed the ones inside the uterus, just the sperm outside. And *they'd* have died anyway at six hours, long before we found her."

"OK, in which case the sperm had to have been dead before they ever went into her uterus. Which....which means they were produced days ago!"

Gerry nodded, looking embarrassed, and she swore

she saw a blush starting. He was a good church-going man, not a heathen like herself, and she knew this sort of case made him uncomfortable. He urged her on.

"So why would Burton have been carrying old sperm with him when he attacked her, ma'am? When...when..."

He blushed even deeper and Julia had a random thought that she'd never seen that shade of purple before.

"When, when...what, for goodness sake?"

"When men can always make new stuff!"

He spat the last few words out as if he didn't belong to his own sex and she had to stifle a smile. Suddenly the answer hit her. Of course. It was so obvious.

"I'll tell you why Gerry, because Burton didn't do it, and now I'm going to prove it."

****

Laganside Courts, Belfast.

"Please stand, Ms Rogers."

Jessie gazed curiously around the small courtroom; like a spectator, rather than someone on trial. She hadn't been inside a court for five years, and it still held novelty value for her.

She screwed up her eyes and blinked a few times, trying to clear her vision. She was exhausted from last night's clubbing and a night in the cells, spent yelling and screaming enough to warrant her bail being refused. But it had all been worth it to stand here now.

The judge looked through her as if she was invisible, and she understood why. He must have spent years listening to people with behaviour worse than her farm animals. She hadn't really seen them either.

"Kate Rogers, you are accused of committing a criminal act, the crime of Actual Bodily Harm. This led to your victim requiring medical attention, and has left her with the likelihood of significant future scarring. Furthermore, it appears that you committed this act with little provocation and with no reason other than your own aggression. It was not in self-defence, nor was it in the defence of others."

He paused to adjust his glasses, before restarting with a loud tut.

"Your blood tests show that you were not drunk nor under the influence of illegal substances, and you have no known past criminal history. Therefore, I am at a loss to find any explanation or mitigation for this offence. In addition, you have no apparent fixed abode or means of support. And the officers have told me that you were violent; biting and kicking them when you were arrested and cautioned, and abusive throughout the night to the personnel at High Street police station.

Therefore, I can find no reason to allow bail and I am hereby remanding you to Wharf House Detention Centre, until your case can be heard for trial."

He turned tiredly to the officer beside her. "Please remove the prisoner."

Jessie dropped her head as if in shame, and no-one saw the smile that she was hiding. This was exactly what she had wanted.

As they said on television; 'result'.

Chapter Seven

The C.C.U.

Ida Foster sat forward excitedly in the chair that Liam had found for her. It was the most comfortable chair in Docklands, which wasn't saying much, but Nicky had provided a tray of tea and biscuits to soften the experience even more. Not the usual fare for a police sketch session but they were all going to get old someday, or die, and somehow Liam doubted that anything could kill Ida.

She was wearing her best coat and gloves just for the occasion. Only good manners had made her remove her hat, a cake of velvet and voile that looked so new that Liam would have said she'd bought it especially for today, if time hadn't prevented it.

The constable who'd collected her said that she'd posed for at least five minutes beside the marked police car, before allowing him to help her in. It was long enough to attract curious looks from the neighbours, and she was finally rewarded by old Mrs Wolsey from three doors down ambling up to them, unable to control her curiosity any longer.

"What're you doing in your Sunday best, Ida?"

In a pensioner's show of 'cool', Ida had rested her hand on the car's newly washed bonnet, as if she did it every day. Then, drawing herself up to her full four-feet-eleven and looking around exaggeratedly, she had uttered, in a voice that movie trailers would be proud of "Helping the police catch a murderer."

Then she'd entered the car like a secret agent, the constable entering into the spirit of events with a small salute before driving off, certain that Ida would enjoy afternoon teas on the back of her adventure for years to come.

Now, here she was, crunching a Hobnob with her best dentures and describing the four people that she'd seen in Ian McCandless' garage to the sketch artist, with all the creative panache of Da Vinci.

****

Limavady.

Julia tapped her silver lighter rhythmically on the hard Formica table, falling into some internal groove that Gerry thought was a recent chart number. Whatever it was, it was irritating the hell out of him, but the effect on Paul Burton was far more interesting. His distress was increasing visibly with each tap.

He was a round faced man with strangely recessed eyes, buried so deep in fat that their colour was impossible to see. He looked like a giant Shar-pei.

His hands matched his face, with short, stumpy fingers like sausages, clenched together in a shiny fumble, the hairs on each finger dripping with sweat. He looked pleadingly at Gerry, somehow sensing that Julia was a less sympathetic audience.

Burton didn't know what they had on him, but, although they'd only told him five minutes before that his wife was dead, his concern for his own predicament seemed much stronger than any regret at the news. They'd watched his face carefully as he was told, and although it wasn't uncommon in an acrimonious divorce that the spouse was less than devastated, he hadn't even asked them how she'd died, and that was interesting.

Instead he'd rushed to answer their "when did you last see her?" with an urgent, "six weeks ago" in an irritating high-toned whine.

Not for the first time Julia marvelled at how an attractive woman had married such a slug of a man. Maybe he hadn't been such a mollusc when they'd said, "I do" but she was sceptical.

She nodded at Gerry and he reached over and pressed the tape machine into action, while she placed her lighter purposefully to one side, lining up the thick sheaf of paper in front of her. Every sheet but the top one was blank, but Paul Burton would never know that, and the pile's volume added to its import, which added to his fear.

"For the benefit of the tape, could you please confirm that you are Mr Paul Burton of 35, Minsk Drive, Templepatrick?"

He nodded.

"Please say it for the tape, Mr Burton."

A high-pitched "Yes" squeaked from his fleshy mouth.

"Thank you. Now, do you know why you're here, Mr Burton?"

"Because Maria's dead?" The rise in his tone far higher than a question required.

"Yes. But do you know why we wish to speak to you?"

Julia's 'exasperated mother' tone said Burton was being a very irritating child, and he immediately glanced down in response, probably from years of being one.

He answered her quickly. "To help with your enquiries. That's what the man said when he came to the house." He looked up at her again, slightly more defiant. "I'd like to help, even though I really hated her."

The last words were said matter-of-factly, with no hint that he realised how incriminating they were.

"Why did you hate her, Mr Burton?"

Julia's voice had become calm and almost confiding. You can tell me. You can trust me. I'm your friend.

Gerry had always marvelled at her ability to control her pissed-off, cynical and angry moods when she needed something from a suspect. And to know exactly when to use them to best effect. She would be their new best friend or their angry mother until the case was cracked, if that was what it took. But then she *had* worked in the oxymoronic Military Intelligence. He worried about what else she had learned there.

"'Cos you lot have no idea what a bitch she is...was. She was a cow and I couldn't wait to be rid of her."

It was said without any hint of irony and Julia

leaned forward, narrowing the distance between them amicably. Paul Burton echoed her encouraging movement, warming to his theme.

"She said I watched too much TV."

His tone was offended, as if she'd accused him of something criminal or untrue. But his swollen torso said it was a fact and conjured up a clear image of crisps and beer stored beside a TV chair.

"And she always wanted to go clubbing. For fuck's sake, that's what you do before yer married! To catch them, like. You don't keep going when you've got a woman."

Julia could see exactly why Maria Burton had left him; it had been a match made in the darkness. But she nodded understandingly anyway, her true sympathy with Maria not him.

"So would you say that you argued a lot?"

He shrugged. "Nah, I just told her to catch herself on and she went out with her mates. Suited me, until she started to hide my remote." The sudden indignation in his voice almost made her laugh.

"Well, that was it, I threw her out, didn't I. No amount of shagging is worth putting up with that."

What a prince.

But her technique was working. Playing it hard and then soft was making Burton comfortable and he spoke unprompted now, encouraged by her occasional reassuring nods.

"Anyway, she moved out in April, then I saw her six weeks ago, at the solicitor. For the Nisi. She looked like shit – got fat. I'd a near miss there; she was going to end up like her ma."

He looked at Gerry in male solidarity against the swelling sea of female obesity. Gerry nearly choked at the idea that this fat layabout would think that the nine stone Maria Burton was overweight, but he nodded in sympathetic agreement instead. He was learning from his boss.

Burton half-lay back in his chair, elbows on the table, indicating just how comfortable he was with his new best friends. Julia mirrored his postures perfectly, leaning backwards and forwards in echo. It was called neuro-linguistic programming, and it worked.

The atmosphere became increasingly amicable as she offered him tea, motioning for the constable to bring it. Her questions meandered in a spiral, gently drawing closer to her target.

So that when she suddenly slipped in. "So, Mr Burton, could you tell me where you were between eight am and five pm yesterday?"

His response slipped out unhesitatingly. "At home, playing my computer game."

She spoke quickly now, firing back another question after each of his replies, all of them seemingly innocuous, but each providing her with useful information.

"Oh, that's interesting. Which game are you on? My nephew's got the new time-travel one."

"Oh yeah, I did that one last year. I just got a zombie one. It's awesome."

"Was that what you were playing yesterday?"

"Yeah."

"What sort of car do you drive?"

"Volkswagen. Why?"

"Lovely cars. They have satellite navigation don't they? I'm always getting lost, so I need to get a new car with sat-nav."

"Yeh, they're cool. Sat-nav's OK if you need it. Mine's always on but I never use it. I don't get lost." He smiled at her patronisingly. "Aye, but you're a woman; you're always crap at directions."

He looked almost obscenely proud of his basic skill and Julia smiled. He'd just given her what she needed. The sat-nav was always on.

Suddenly she pulled herself bolt upright, fixing him directly in the eyes. He hadn't even noticed her triumphant look, until her sudden shift of posture surprised him into jerking hastily upright to match.

"Mr Burton, you've been most helpful. May we check your car and your computer game, to help eliminate you from our enquiries? And we need a blood sample for DNA. Is that OK?"

She was speaking so quickly that Gerry could see Paul Burton struggling to catch up from her relaxed conversational style two minutes earlier, to the confrontational abruptness now.

"What enquiries?"

"Your wife's death, Mr Burton. It wasn't an accident. She was murdered."

"What? Murdered? I thought she was killed at work."

His small eyes widened for a moment in some type of emotion, and then almost as quickly they narrowed again, into a hard squint.

"Anyway, so what? Even if she was, what does it have to do with me? I didn't shoot her."

Interesting. He assumed she'd been shot: true or bluff.

"She wasn't shot, Mr Burton. She was raped and beaten to death."

Julia pushed past his open-mouthed shock without taking a breath, continuing and accelerating.

"So if we check your computer's timing, and your car and your DNA then we'll be able to rule you out. Shall we proceed with that? You're fully entitled to legal counsel, but of course you're innocent, so why would you want it?"

They watched the emotions flitting across Burton's face: shock, competing with suspicion and denial. He was either a good actor or telling the truth; the DNA would tell them which. The room fell completely silent except for the whirring of the tape, and Julia held her breath, willing him to agree to the test. She could feel her body leaning forward in encouragement. Say it, say it, say it.

Paul Burton screwed up his invisible eyes in thought, his face folding into a wet pillow of flesh. His short, fat fingers were spread palm down on the table, leaving their sweaty likeness on its shiny surface, and he breathed in and out heavily through his mouth, wordless in what passed for deep thought. Finally he opened his eyes and stared dully at Gerry, nodding acquiescence. Julia exhaled softly, only then realising that she'd been holding her breath for the whole time.

She kept her voice steady, retrieving the friendly tone of five minutes earlier. "Could you say it please, Mr Burton, for the tape?"

He shrugged, in a couldn't care less way. "OK, I've nothing to hide, I'll give you blood." He was either stupid or honest and her money was on both.

Julia nodded sharply to the constable as she clicked the tape off, and Paul Burton was led out to the medical examiner for his DNA test. Much good it would do them. She was convinced that the DNA would only confirm what she already felt – Burton was innocent.

Slugs like him didn't kill, not unless pressing the key on a computer would do it. The DNA would swop their best lead for a countywide murder hunt, and leave her with a very grumpy D.C.S.

****

Craig already knew that the twelfth floor of the C.C.U. was very different to the tenth, but it still surprised him every time. It had a plushly carpeted centre framed by the outer offices of five Chief Superintendents, and an air of hush that said 'we're very important,' echoed by high-level fittings and soft-toned lights. The spacious offices were set far apart, as if anything said in them should never be overheard by their rivals; or worse, by the mere mortals in the waiting area.

The twelfth floor P.A.s wore their bosses rank, in clothes and shoes that said, 'remember, I'm important as well'. Craig found it hard to imagine that Nicky's radical fashion sense had ever fitted in there, even allowing for her one hundred words per minute typing speed.

Yet she'd been Terry Harrison's P.A. for five years before his post had split between Belfast and Limavady and he'd tried very hard to keep her. Nicky's ten-year-old son had given her the perfect excuse for staying in Belfast. She'd told Craig she'd been glad to get away and had found Harrison the perfect replacement in Susan Butler.

Susan Butler was a suitably groomed grey-haired, fifty-something woman, maternally plump, with grown children. Her beige Jaeger suit toned perfectly with the carpeted background. If Nicky was a sparky Mazda, then Susan Butler was a sedate Bentley of a woman. She'd been Mrs Harrison's choice for P.A. as well; the perfect antidote to office sexual tension. Mrs Harrison knew her husband's proclivities very well.

Butler was sitting now outside a door bearing the name 'D.C.S. Terence Harrison' bowed over a shiny desk that was angled across the door like a barrier. Craig imagined her dying rather than allow an unauthorised entrant. She split her time equally between Limavady and Belfast, travelling with the D.C.S., willingly living the split-time existence it caused, hinting at a back-story of loneliness at home.

She was looking busily through some files on her desk as Craig approached, and she glanced up at him with cool friendliness. "Ah, Detective Chief Inspector Craig. Good morning." She enunciated each syllable of his rank perfectly, as if it gave her pleasure.

"Good morning, Mrs Butler."

"Detective Chief Superintendent Harrison will see you in one moment," adding importantly but irrelevantly, "He's on a call with the Metropolitan Commissioner. Please take a seat."

He was gestured to a small coffee area of low leather armchairs and a central marble slab. A perfect fan of 'Ulster Bazaars' lay on the table, as if someone had had nothing better to do but set them out, and Craig thought that it would take a very brave man to disturb the design.

"May I get you a coffee? Black with sugar, yes?"

God, she even remembered what he drank. He needed one just like her at home.

"Yes, perfect. Thank you."

He perched on the edge of a chair, knowing that leaning back would sink him into a dip from which he would never emerge, and took the proffered coffee gratefully. Then he lifted a magazine defiantly, less interested in its content than in the disruption the P.A. would feel. He was rewarded by an immediate arch of her eyebrow.

Her large phone console was showing a red call-engaged light, with another yellow one flashing call-waiting. Craig gave in and sank back into the leather, resigning himself to a long wait. She finally lifted the receiver twenty minutes later, said 'yes' into it quietly and then nodded at him regally, indicating that he could go in.

D.C.S. Terry 'Teflon' Harrison was so named because he was one of the smoothest political operators in the police, with the hair to match. Craig hadn't had many problems with him so far, although his predecessors had warned him that it was only a matter of time. They'd also warned him never to let Harrison meet Lucia. He had an eye for pretty women twenty years his junior and once he saw them, his pursuit was relentless. If that happened, Craig's protective urges would do Harrison serious damage, boss or no boss. It would be career ending and he would do it anyway.

Harrison was relaxing in an identical coffee area in one corner of his office, and Craig groaned inwardly, certain that the low-slung chairs were for the short chief superintendent's deliberate inconvenience of taller men. He beckoned Craig over to sit.

"Ah Marc, good morning. Have a seat. Coffee?"

He indicated a silver sputnik that was already gurgling, so Craig accepted, grateful after his heavy night's drinking with John. Harrison talked as he poured, pushing the milk and sugar towards him, his uniform buttons glistening and flashing, like the maître D's at a high-end Milan café. His voice was higher than was comfortable in such a macho world. His gravitas compensating or overcompensating, depending on your cynicism.

"Well now – two things. First, the case you caught yesterday, I need you to brief me on that. And then this." Harrison reached across to the desk behind him, lifted a sheet with the familiar header of 'press release' and pushed it towards Craig. He scanned it while sugaring his cup heavily.

Harrison sat down, pulling his trouser legs up in a self-conscious attempt to avoid creasing. Then he lounged back in his chair with the entitlement of seniority, beckoning Craig to do the same.

"The garage case. Update me, please."

Craig launched into a ten-minute monologue that the other man didn't interrupt. Harrison was good listener, except as he listened he stared at him disconcertingly. All of the past D.C.I.s had warned Craig about it. No-one could work out if it was the stare of professional assessment, if Harrison was gazing through them into space, or if he was actually taking in every detail of their suit, tie and shoes for future reference.

One had even ventured that he was gay, but the trail of noisy ex-mistresses dismissed that idea very quickly. Whatever it was, it was bloody annoying. Finally, Harrison interrupted and Craig took the opportunity to sip at his now-cold coffee.

"Definite abrasions on his knees you said?"

"Yes, sir. From where he fell."

Harrison looked thoughtful but excited. "Wire marks on both shins?"

Craig nodded yes and the excited look increased. "And nappy cream in several patches, sir. Plus Liam's witness is certain that she saw a young woman."

"Nappy cream and a young woman? Well, I may be old fashioned, but that shocks even me."

Craig was getting curious now. Why were the wire and abrasions so significant to him? He was about to ask when Harrison continued.

"We caught a very nasty case last night near Limavady; you won't have seen it in the news yet. I believe the BBC only picked it up this morning."

"A young woman pulled out of the Lower Bann at Portglenone. Suspected rape-murder. Was that it, sir?"

He always listened to the radio during his fifteen-minute drive to work. Harrison looked grudgingly impressed.

"Yes, yes, but the Chief Constable will be making a further statement today to say–"

He looked down for an instant and Craig thought that he saw genuine sadness crossing his heavy-boned face. He recovered quickly, lifting his head to look at him again.

"To say that she was a W.P.C. called Maria Burton."

Hell. A female police officer raped and murdered, that threw up all sorts of grief, and not only for her immediate family.

"I wanted to tell you for the general awareness of your female officers. But now, with the detail on the garage case, I also want to pick your brains."

Harrison had some good points and one of them was his willingness to listen to his juniors' opinions. A bad point was then re-packaging them as his own. He answered Craig's questioning look.

"I need you to liaise with Limavady, and the reason is that some of the details of your garage murder seem to match the murder of W.P.C. Burton in Portglenone. Principally the abrasions on her knees and the thin linear cuts across her shins."

Craig sat forward. "She had them as well?"

"Yes."

"Was there any sign of wire? Was she burnt?"

"No to both of those, but then she'd been in the water for at least twenty-four hours when she was found. I'll ask the C.S.I.s to go back and look more closely at the wire aspect. We have her estranged husband in custody at the moment, answering questions." He paused and took a deep breath, seeming genuinely moved by what he had to say next.

"We're hoping for a DNA sample today. There was semen found with W.P.C. Burton." His use of the word 'with' delicately glossing over its exact location; sensitivity unexpected for a well-known lothario.

"Given the similarities I'd like you to liaise with Inspector McNulty on this. Call her today, will you? But watch out, she's a bit prickly. You know the type. Ex-army and still trying to prove herself. So tread softly."

He lifted the press release from the table and made to get up, hinting that Craig was being dismissed. Sure enough, Harrison turned his back and headed back to his desk, opening the office door as he passed. Craig had a sudden thought.

"Sir, any chance this is the Dissidents?"

Harrison swung around to look at him. He hadn't taken McNulty's anti-police idea seriously, but now a D.C.I. was saying it.

He covered his omission slickly. "Of course. Intelligence is already on it. Until we're certain that the husband did it, we have to cover every base."

Craig smiled inwardly. He knew he'd caught Harrison out and he also knew that he would be straight onto Intelligence as soon as he'd left the room. Harrison continued speaking as if the question had never been asked.

"Susan will give you a copy of the press release and you'll see the Chief Constable's statement on the intranet later today. Brief your female officers to take care just in case. Meanwhile, I'll draft a release on your garage case and run it by you this afternoon. Where will you be?"

"I'll contact D.I. McNulty now then I'm going to the lab to meet John Winter. I could ask him to speak to the lab in Limavady if that would help?"

"Yes. Good...good."

Every senior officer in the force was in awe of John, as the youngest ever Director of Forensic Pathology for Northern Ireland, and Craig's life-long friendship with him hadn't gone unnoticed. Its impact amused them both.

"Yes, do that."

Then, like a dismissive headmaster, Harrison waved him out. Susan Butler handed him a warm press release as he walked past and said "It was very nice to see you, D.C.I. Craig" before cutting eye contact, having already allocated him the attention that she felt due to his rank.

She reflected Harrison's image perfectly and Craig

wondered what Nicky said about his. As he walked away, laughing to himself, he noticed that the magazine fan's perfection had already been restored.

When he re-entered the tenth floor, Davy Walsh, their computer analyst, beckoned him across. Davy was a gangly, handsome twenty-something whose height had outgrown his width about six inches before, and whose floppy Emo hair often had him teased for being a 'big girl' in a world of short backs and sides.

He spoke with an occasional stutter on S and W, making the wind-up merchants deliberately give him things starting with the two letters to research. In revenge, Davy cheerfully pointed out the various obscenities that started with both, using them frequently on his tormentors. Especially after a few drinks, when his stutter disappeared completely.

"Liam asked me to run the w...wire through the import/export database, chief. It's only been manufactured from two-thousand and five, in one firm in Russia – Dashevsky's. Only one company here imports it – Turners. Liam's gone to meet them and he s...said he'll call you later."

"That's brilliant. Anything similar on the murder across GB?"

"Nothing yet, but I'm looking. Dr Marsham e-mailed me the info on the hammer and it's really interesting."

"How?"

"It's not a normal hammer. The image and electron microscopy don't fit anything common. The circumference is too big and the end's far too pointed. I'm chasing it up now."

"OK, thanks Davy. Let me know."

Craig turned and walked past Nicky's desk into his office. Just then, she bent down to reach something and he saw her new 'list' sitting on the corner of her desk. He calmly tipped it into the bin then entered his office quickly, lifting the phone and hitting the connecting code for Limavady Headquarters.

"Detective Inspector Julia McNulty, please. It's D.C.I. Craig from Docklands."

Put on hold to the theme of Greensleeves, he turned to the window to watch the lively harbour traffic, wondering again why the police couldn't pay for some decent album music. A sharp tap on his shoulder made him turn around; to see Nicky standing with her arms folded, her list dangling from one hand and her raised eyebrow confirming that she'd witnessed his attempt at sabotage. He smiled in defeat, motioning her to take a seat just as a female voice came on the line.

"McNulty here, what can I do for you, D.C.I. Craig?" Her voice was soft and clear with a mixed Anglo-Irish accent, and its defiant tone was one that Craig recognised in himself every time a senior officer phoned.

He smiled across at Nicky, determined to be collaborative, and started to explain why Harrison thought that they should chat.

She seemed to relax slightly as he gave her the details of the McCandless murder and highlighted the similarities between their cases. In turn, she insisted that she was on top of her murder, that Paul Burton was innocent and that she'd prove it, just as soon as the DNA came back. Craig countered by saying he'd be even more interested if Burton was innocent as it opened up the possibility of their female suspect linking to both murders.

He completely missed the tension re-entering Julia's voice when he suggested that John liaise with her pathologist. At that point, any facade of her collaborating collapsed, and her defensive tone tipped into rudeness.

"Our path lab is excellent, so we certainly don't need any assistance from Belfast on that front."

"I'm offering to liaise, Inspector McNulty. It's to both our advantages."

"We already have the advantage."

He barked back at her "Oh really? Enlighten me" in a brusque tone that made Nicky jerk upright at the periphery of his view. Julia McNulty was still talking, and at some length, and Nicky watched as Craig's grip on the receiver tightened and whitened until he finally snapped.

"Detective Inspector McNulty, if Dr Winter and Dr Marsham wish to engage with your labs, then that's exactly what they'll do. And if D.C.S. Harrison feels that these two cases are linked, which I'm inclined to agree with, then we will work together to prevent another murder. And believe me; your ego will *not* prevent it. Is that clear?"

Nicky watched Craig's face redden and smiled to herself. He was usually scrupulously polite, especially to women, so his phone companion must be a real piece of work. Even so, she knew he'd beat himself up afterwards.

Craig listened for a few seconds longer before ending the call with an abrupt "I'll be in touch." Nicky watched him fight the urge to slam the phone down. Instead he pressed the button sharply to cut the call, then, when he knew Julia McNulty had gone, he slammed the receiver so hard against its cradle that it bounced onto the floor. Nicky bent to pick it up and waited for the inevitable explosion.

"Of all the rude... for God's sake... that woman... she still thinks she's in the army, and she's obviously used to giving orders rather than taking them!"

He sat down heavily and swivelled his chair towards the window, gathering himself for a few seconds before turning back. Nicky put a coffee in his hand as he turned.

"Thank God it's Friday, Nicky. This week's already gone to hell. And that woman is unbelievable." She nodded at him sympathetically, like a good P.A.

"What was it about?"

"Our garage case and her riverside case have similarities The D.C.S. spotted them and he's right, except that she doesn't want any help. Typical military."

He suddenly noticed that her hand was empty and smiled. "Where's your list? Taking pity on me?"

She nodded. "Yes, I am. And I'm also being nice to you because your mum's just called me about Venice and I'm meeting her for coffee next week."

"You'll enjoy it. You're both crazy."

She laughed at him.

"And just for that, we're going to spent at least an hour discussing you."

He knew she was only half-joking.

"What was on today's list anyway?"

"Not much – just planning the direct appraisals you have to do."

He groaned.

"There are only four. Liam, Annette, Davy and me and they'll be easy 'cos we're all brilliant. The rest of it is just time sheets and expenses you have to approve. There are two case reports for the Public Prosecution Service that need tidied-up, plus a sentencing guideline. An hour will do it all, so how does Monday suit you? You've a meeting at eleven but you're free before that...Well, on paper at least."

It was a dig at his tendency to arrange his own diary without telling her, making for constant double-booking.

"First thing, does that suit?"

"Yes, fine. Now chill out and I promise I won't put any more army officers through. And don't forget you're due at the lab at three. All right, sir?"

Craig laughed. "I love it when you call me sir with such sincerity. Then I definitely know you're winding me up."

Nicky smiled, knowing he was already berating himself for allowing Julia McNulty to make him angry. He pictured her as short and fat with a helmet of dark hair and hidden tattoos, and felt better immediately. Then he just felt chauvinistic.

"Can you get the others together for a quick briefing at two, please? By the way, what was Liam's eventual punishment for you doing his expenses?"

"A bottle of my favourite perfume. The perfume, mind you, not the eau de toilette."

"Good for you, but I think you should have gone for more. He can afford it with that fat expenses cheque coming."

She laughed and closed the door softly behind her, leaving him with thoughts of two women, both of whom were determined to ruin his weekend.

Chapter Eight

Wharf House.

The high-sided police van opened and Jessie was led down its steps by a slightly built W.P.C. She stared at the girl for a moment, suddenly feeling bad about Maria Burton, but her remorse passed as quickly as it came. Burton had had to die; her three children's futures were at stake.

She caught sight of herself in the prison-entrance window. Fiona had brought some of her clothes to High Street, and she'd changed out of last night's tart's costume into a jumper and jeans. Now, scrubbed free of make-up, she looked a pale, slight eighteen, instead of a late twenties mother of three. But what she lacked in stamina she made up for in determination, as her next target would soon find out.

The police had allowed her to have her steroid medication when she'd said that it was for asthma. It was on a legal prescription so she knew they'd never check what she'd really been prescribed it for. And she needed it. It was the only thing controlling the headaches that were worsening by the day.

Someday the headaches would kill her, but only after she had finished her work. They'd agreed to wait forty-eight hours before Fiona would bail her out with an expensive lawyer, long enough to complete her task. Then there would only be one last hurdle left before she could rest for good.

After the searches and lectures, she was shown to her room, to share with Becky, a quiet woman in for credit-card fraud. She was scared and silent like the girls bullied at her secondary school and Jessie felt sorry for her, deciding to act as her guardian angel for forty-eight hours. Her newly tough persona could be useful for something other than killing.

The bell would sound for dinner at six pm and then she'd finally see her target again, after five long years.

Poor little prey, hunted in the one place that she thought she was safe. She smiled to herself sarcastically. Sarcasm came easily to her these days, and she certainly wouldn't waste any sympathy on this woman. She was the cause of everything and she deserved what was coming, even more than the others had, or would.

She was going to enjoy killing this one.

****

At two pm, Liam headed back to the squad-room, confident that Ida wouldn't notice his absence. A plump-faced young officer had replaced him in her affections already; the uniform would always win with Ida.

The D.I. loped his way across to Craig's office. The door was closed and as he reached for the handle, he was stopped by Nicky's quick warning look, much more powerful than any 'no entry' sign.

"Give him a minute, Liam."

That suited him perfectly; he could fill the time nicely chatting to her, while she typed. His little crush on her, and he liked to think hers on him, had livened up many a dull day at work. He gazed admiringly at her long pink nails skipping skilfully across the keyboard. The farmers' daughters at his school had never worn colours like that; not functional so why would they? But he always got a thrill from irrelevant decoration on a woman's hands.

Five minutes of banter later Craig's door was thrown open, the smile on his face showing that the coffee had done its job. He beckoned them both in energetically, calling across the floor. "You too please, Davy. Nicky, where's Annette?"

"She's on her way back – just phoned through. She was with Mrs McCandless again."

Just then Annette walked onto the floor, panting heavily and wishing that she was wearing a lightweight suit. The Indian summer they were having meant she dressed for the morning frost in Antrim, and was half-boiled by lunchtime in Belfast.

"Right. Davy, bring in another couple of chairs please and we'll start."

Craig lifted two files of paper from his desk drawer and passed the sheets round, sitting down at his pale-wood desk with his back to the river. The day was bright and clear and two seagulls were diving towards the building so fast that Annette was waiting for them to hit the window. But, as always, they pulled up at the last minute, swooping expertly backwards into the distance, free.

Liam looked down at the sheets unsurprised, updated by Nicky five minutes before. But Annette was new to the information and stared at one of the sheets completely bemused. Davy looked equally puzzled.

"Why are we looking at a North-West case, sir? Don't we have enough work to do?"

Craig glanced at her, nodding.

"That's almost what I said to the D.C.S., but I didn't, because this case shows major similarities to our own."

Annette looked at Liam, registering that he already knew about it, and the knowledge annoyed her somehow. She never thought of herself as competitive, until someone beat her to something.

"Right. The first thing is, the North-West victim was a young female officer." He saw their shock but ignored it, continuing.

"I need you to alert everyone to be careful. We don't know that the murder had anything to do with her job; she wasn't in uniform when it happened. But people need to be vigilant just in case. And all W.P.Cs are to be paired with male officers on patrol for the moment, please."

Suddenly Nicky gasped, reading on to the end of the page. "Oh, she was raped..."

It was a statement of fact, but the way she said it touched him. Without the uniform, they were all still just Joe and Joanna public.

"Bastard."

Liam looked practically homicidal and everyone

agreed with his sentiments, glad of his willingness to say what they were all thinking. Craig continued.

"The pathologist believes that she was raped, murdered and then thrown into the Lower Bann at Portglenone."

"That's a beautiful part of the country too."

"I know...OK, there are some unusual points in their forensics which I'll tell you about in a moment, and Detective Inspector McNulty will get back to me on those later today."

Even as he said it he doubted it, but John was on the job anyway.

He brought them up to date on the similarities with the McCandless murder: the abraded hands and knees, and the cuts across the shins. Then he told them about the abnormal semen sample leading to McNulty's conviction that the husband's DNA would vindicate him. The sound of Nicky's phone ringing ended his summary, and she reached out through the open door to answer it, then nodded and pressed mute. Craig could tell it was for him and gestured her to transfer it.

"Marc Craig."

His lack of words and frequent nods said that he knew the speaker, and they listened in silence until he finished with. "Thanks, I'll see you later" and a slightly puzzled frown.

"That was Des. He's just spoken to the lab in Limavady."

"What did his wife have?"

Craig stared at Annette, confused for a second, before he realised what she was talking about.

"Oh God – I didn't ask. Nicky, can you find out subtly if Annie and the baby are OK, and send some flowers, please." He turned back to the North-West case.

"Des has just told me that the semen sample they found on Maria Burton *is* a DNA match for the estranged husband." He hesitated for a moment, looking slightly confused. "But the sperm were dead and had been for many hours, so he believes the sample could have been frozen."

"Frozen? Are they selling sperm ice-cubes now?"

"Liam!"

Annette thumped him on the arm, disgusted, and even Nicky looked at the D.I. reprovingly. Craig shrugged; he was used to Liam's un-PC-ness by now.

"Liam, that's pretty bad, even for you, but I have to say that Des sounded puzzled as well. He said that maybe Burton had donated to a sperm bank, but even that couldn't be right, because the sperm would be preserved alive there. And it still wouldn't explain what it was doing at the scene."

Davy raised a finger to speak. "Maybe P.C. Burton wanted the baby but not the man? Or maybe s...she'd inseminated herself earlier that day and it was just a co-finding, and everyone just assumed that she'd been raped?"

Craig thought about it. "That's not a bad theory, Davy, but the sperm wouldn't have been dead in that case. Ask Des about it, and see if you can get hold of the full lab-report from Limavady. If there were no signs of violence then rape may not have been the method of introduction. Liam, contact D.I. McNulty and see if there was anything else to suggest rape, and run the self-insemination idea past her. Ask her if Maria Burton had told anyone that she wanted a baby; her best friend or mum maybe? But be careful - D.I. McNulty and I have already had words this morning. She's got a bit of an attitude."

Nicky leaned forward conspiratorially. "That's his nice way of saying she's a real piece of work. It took a whole pot of espresso to restore normal service after they spoke."

Craig smiled. "OK, Liam, update us with what you found out about the wire and your witness, then Davy on the hammer and finances. And finally Annette on the McCandless family, please."

Liam leaned back in his chair. It was rare that he sat at all, preferring to stand, head hitting the ceiling, then spend hours afterwards moaning about his sore back. His claim to suffering for the job.

Davy liked the idea of being a police officer but not the thought of getting hurt, so he often stood as well, hero-worshipping both Craig and Liam by mimicking them in little ways.

Liam's deep Crossgar accent vibrated the air around them. "Ah, well now. The wire..."

"That's the name of an American cop show. Dr Winter told me."

"And he would know, right enough." John Winter's obsession with American television meant that he was inundated with box sets every Christmas and his conversation was constantly peppered with their jargon, to everyone's amusement.

"Aye, anyway. The wire. Well, Davy narrowed it to one importer here, and even they don't have much call for it nowadays. It's vicious 'aul stuff, usually only used to contain large animals, or on secure weapons sites, and thankfully we don't have many of those nowadays. So the list of customers here was short; just three buyers. I've ruled out two of them already, they're Government Units and they've accounted for their wire supplies to the last inch."

"God bless government inventory control – you have to love it."

"Sometimes." Except that it made it impossible to nick an A4 pad for his wife to write her shopping on. "Anyhow, the other buyer was two years back. A farmer in Barnardstown."

"Never heard of the place. Where is it?"

Liam reached into his jacket pocket and withdrew a notebook so small that it disappeared in his giant hand. He flicked through its pages until he found his mark.

"Aye, here it is. Barnardstown. It's up in the North-West. The wire was bought by a dairy farmer called Michael Adams and I'm going up there this afternoon to see what he has to say. The farm's only five miles from Limavady, so I could combine it with a wee trip to see McNulty if you like. Then I can tell you if she really has fangs."

Craig laughed wryly and nodded. "Good thinking.

Maybe she won't view you with as much hostility as she did me. Although why the D.C.S. couldn't just have asked her for details instead of making me call her, I don't know. They live in the same building half the week."

"That'll be Teflon pulling rank, that's why."

Craig knew that he should disapprove of the use of Harrison's nickname, but he agreed so he just smiled instead.

"OK, Liam, follow that up. Right. Davy, the hammer."

Davy pushed back his long hair excitedly. "It's *really* interesting. It turns out it wasn't actually a hammer at all. We'd a bit of trouble finding a match at first, but w...we have now. It's called a captive bolt and it's very unusual; the head is s...sharper at the end."

He couldn't keep the thrill from his voice and for a second Craig thought that the public would view such excitement about a hammer as a bit sad. But then, maybe not. After all, millions of people watched C.S.I.

Davy hesitated suddenly and looked around the group, as if reluctant to go into more detail. He thought that women were of a delicate disposition and should be protected, and they loved him for it. Craig half agreed with him, but he also knew that asking the women to leave for their own protection would earn him a lecture on feminism, and he needed that like a hole in the head. He nodded Davy on.

"W...Well..." He winced visibly at what came next. "Captive bolts belong to a group of tools that were used to kill..." He hesitated again, and then continued.

"To kill cattle. They...they hit them a blow between the eyes and it knocks them out or kills them instantly. But they stopped using them after the Bovine Encephalitis outbreak, because of the possible transfer of brain matter."

Craig understood his earlier reluctance; Nicky looked as if she was going to be sick. It was strange; they heard the details of human murder every day and had learned to distance themselves from the reality by talking about DNA and forensics. But Davy's mention of animals had caught them all unaware.

Craig held a hand up to pause the analyst, but he'd already finished, and the images his words conjured up had already had their impact. The room fell silent for a minute, until Liam finally broke it.

"Farmers, Davy. They would have captive bolts. It fits with Michael Adams again."

Craig grabbed at the lifeline.

"You're right, Liam. Take a photo of it with you and have a good look around the Adams' farm for anything that matches. Well done Davy. Annette?"

They turned towards Annette just in time to see the end of her pallor. But Davy hadn't finished.

"There's one more thing."

"Yes?"

"Dr Marsham told me they found a print on Ian McCandless' Nokia."

"Yes, he told me. And?"

"But w...why?"

They all looked at him blankly and then Liam jumped in. "Maybe the killer touched it accidentally, when they attacked McCandless?"

Craig shook his head slowly. "Unlikely. The phone was inside his jacket. Davy's right and I completely missed its significance when Des told me. Why the print?"

He was puzzled, and the sinking sensation that he'd had when Des had first mentioned the prints came flooding back. He answered his own question.

"The killer needed the Nokia's number. They turned on the phone to get its number."

"What? No way, boss. Who'd take the time to do that? They could have been seen."

"Someone who didn't care who saw them. The killer turned on the mobile and got its number. Then she phoned us, calling herself Monica Gibson. Perhaps she couldn't get the number any other way."

"Weren't the cars advertised? Then the number would have been public."

Annette interjected. "No, they only went up for sale the day before. Joey told me. So the Nokia's number wouldn't have been widely known."

"She wanted to show off."

"No. It's more than arrogance..."

Craig fell quiet, thinking. The killer didn't care who's seen or heard them, or who had their prints. Why? Did they think they would never get caught, or didn't they care? But it was more than that; almost as if they actually needed to show their contempt of the police. Again, why? And had 'Monica Gibson' been working alone, or with a man?

He needed time to work it through, so he nodded at Annette to continue.

"I met with Mrs McCandless again yesterday, and I managed to see Joey separately this morning. That's why I was a bit late. I'm ninety-nine percent sure that Ian McCandless wasn't having an affair, or at least if he was he hid it very well. Although where he'd have found the time beats me; he was so regular in his habits."

She took out her notebook, flicking to its most recent pages.

"He drove his wife to work every morning at eight-forty-five. She was there all day Wednesday, I've already checked. Then he visited his mother from nine to twelve, to help her out, and then went to the local chippy for lunch at one. He worked in the garage in the afternoon or visited a newsagent's shop he part-owned in Dundonald and helped out there, to give the girl a break. Then he collected his wife at five pm and spent the evenings at home. He was a real family man."

"Any grandchildren or babies around the family?"

"No, none yet. His wife nearly choked at the idea of anything dodgy with children, and immediately offered us access to their computers, the house, everything. I've someone over there now. McCandless didn't help out anywhere that he'd come in contact with kids either; no scouts or Boys' Brigade, no church or school activities, and the only sport he played was a bit of golf. He was Mr Family-Man, but we're doing all the checks anyway."

"How did his wife take the questions?"

"Upset but not defensive. She actually said that she understood we had a job to do. She just wants his killer caught."

"OK, good. Follow up on all that and for any possible connections between Maria Burton and Ian McCandless. What about the son?"

Annette looked at him unhappily. "He's a different case. His alibi for the time of the murder is weak. He says he was at college in a lecture hall with sixty other students, but conveniently can't remember who he was sitting beside. It would take a lot of legwork to confirm that he was there. He owns several hoodies but insists that there's no way he was anywhere near the garage that afternoon, and he confirmed everything his mum said about his father." She hesitated for a moment. "Joey wants to be a communications officer with a charity when he finishes his degree, so..."

"So?"

Annette looked reluctant to say what came next and stared straight at Liam, as if daring him to be cynical. "He works in a voluntary capacity with the disabled, sir. So I suppose he would have had access to Purecrem..."

Liam sat back triumphantly, "Well, there you go then. He's our man."

She rounded on him angrily. "God – I just knew you were going to say that! You're so bloody predictable."

She turned to Craig for support. Even years of working with Liam hadn't managed to make him cynical – sceptical maybe, but not cynical yet.

"I'm sure Joey's telling us the truth, sir. I think he's just a nice kid. I really believe that the whole family are clean."

Craig shook his head. "I know you do, Annette, but if Liam put the C in cynical you put the T in Trusting, so check him out further, please."

"But what's his motive, sir? His mum says he and his dad had a really close relationship."

"Sometimes that's exactly the motive." He looked at her kindly. "Look Annette, I'm sure you'll turn out to be right about Joey." And he was. He looked challengingly at Liam, who just shrugged. "But we need to rule him out nonetheless."

She nodded reluctantly, avoiding Liam's eye but determined to prove him wrong. Their work sibling rivalry was getting stronger and Craig could see it.

"OK, good. Well done, all of you. Please follow up on everything. Davy, can you run Maria Burton, Michael Adams and Ian McCandless for any connections please? But don't spend all evening on it. It's the weekend."

"It's fine, chief. I can leave the computer running the s...searches and rig it to alert me on my mobile when it coughs."

The three forty-somethings gazed at each other in amazement, quite sure that he could do it but with no idea how.

"We believe you. Liam, how soon will we have our sketches?"

"Well Ida's fairly getting through them now. I should get copies to everyone before the end of the day."

"Great. Don't forget to get that W.P.C warning out to all stations please. If anyone wants me I'll be at the lab until three-forty-five."

He shot a quick look at Nicky and laughed, remembering her 'list'.

"That's if Nicky gives me permission, of course."

Chapter Nine

The Lab.

Craig was on his third cup of John's strongest espresso and he was feeling more relaxed than he had all week. They were starting to make progress.

"It would be great if you'd speak to the North-West labs, John. There are too many co-incidences between these cases for them not to be linked. But watch yourself with McNulty. She's tricky."

"She's a woman – isn't that part of the job description?"

Craig laughed wryly.

"You've been spending too much time with Liam. For God's sake, don't say that near Lucia, not unless you want the feminist lobby on your back. By the way, I'm meeting her latest man tonight. Apparently he's not her usual tortured artist, he plays piano with the L.C.O."

"Your mum will love that. But can you really cope with two musicians in the family? Just think of all that artistic temperament flying around."

Craig shrugged, smiling. The new man probably wouldn't last anyway. Lucia's men usually had a shelf-life of six months before it dawned on her that they weren't 'compatible'.

"Where's Des? He called me earlier so I thought he'd be here."

"He's back at the hospital, it's a long labour. Thirty-six hours of being sworn at."

"Tell him Davy's narrowed the weapon down to a captive bolt. They use them for killing cattle. A Russian manufacturer makes the razor wire. There are only three users in Northern Ireland – two government departments, both accounted for, and a farmer up near Limavady. Liam's on his way there now."

"Is he visiting D.I. McNulty as well?"

"Yep, and if anyone can handle her, Liam can. The sperm is an interesting twist, isn't it? Des thinks that it could have been frozen."

"OK, I can see that happening. But how did they acquire it to freeze it in the first place?"

"Pass. Limavady have the husband in custody."

"I know. I just spoke to Trevor Cromie, their pathologist. The husband's DNA is a match, so they should get answers very soon. Are you in at the weekend?"

Craig nodded. "And every day until this is solved. Maria Burton is making the brass very nervous indeed."

****

Limavady.

Julia tapped a cigarette repeatedly on her desk and stared at the pink DNA report, as if the semen's owner would suddenly become a different man. But it was Paul Burton's, no question about it. It was definitely his dead semen inside his dead wife's body, and she knew that as soon as Harrison heard about it, he would want Burton charged. She also knew that he would be wrong.

DNA or no DNA there was no way that Paul Burton had killed his wife. He was a wobbling blancmange of a man without the balls or the venom to commit murder, except by games console.

Her thoughts were interrupted by Gerry banging hard on her door. She waved him in and was instantly glad that she had. The triumphant smile on his face meant that he had something to make her happy, he knew better than to smile at her today otherwise.

"What? Tell me."

"The computer game's timings and sat-nav back up Burton's alibi. The big slug was online gaming from nine am to five-thirty pm yesterday, in Templepatrick. He obviously has no work to go to."

There was a slight note of envy in his voice. Julia

looked at him reprovingly and he moved on hastily.

"Anyway, basically there's no way he could have got from Templepatrick to Portglenone, killed her and then got back home in time. The on-line activity was constant and his sat-nav didn't move. He's not our man."

She punched the air in victory. But it was short lived. There was still the DNA. She slumped back in her chair, beckoning him to sit.

"That still leaves us with his semen. How did it get there? He said he hadn't seen his wife for weeks."

Just then, the half-open office door was rapped so loudly that its frame shook, and the doorway filled with the shape of an extremely tall, extremely broad man, so tall that he barely cleared the door. He was sandy haired and so pale that Julia fought hard not to stare. But she did, and Liam Cullen stared right back.

Liam had come to Limavady prepared to do battle with a hefty harridan, so the slim, pretty redhead in front of him was a pleasant surprise. And gave him enough ammunition to wind up Craig for months to come.

Julia had never seen anything quite like Liam, and then he spoke and his voice matched the rest of him, booming and echoing its way around the small, wooden-floored room.

"Inspector McNulty, I'm Inspector Liam Cullen."

He thrust his large hand out so fast that it skimmed Gerry's ear, but the sergeant grinned up at him anyway.

"Well, well, if it isn't Big Whitey. How the hell are you, Liam?"

Liam squinted at him for a second. Then he recognised the now detective sergeant as a young P.C. who'd trailed after him for two years when he was in uniform.

"Ach, Gerry lad, I didn't recognise you. Sure, you're nearly grown up. How are you?"

"Grand, grand. Married with two wee ones now. You?"

"Aye, one and one in the oven."

Julia watched the exchange, amused. It was exactly the interaction she'd have if she met one of her junior officers now, not that that was ever going to happen in Limavady. It made her feel lonely suddenly and she was genuinely reluctant to interrupt their 'love-in', but she still wanted to know what a Belfast D.I. was doing on her patch.

"Sorry to break up old home week, gentlemen, and while it's always a joy to have a visitor from the big smoke...to what do we owe this honour, Inspector Cullen?"

The frosty tone of her last few words reminded Liam of Craig's description of her attitude. Pretty and all as McNulty was, she had a sarcastic mouth on her. He ignored the question just long enough to disconcert her, while Gerry watched and waited, smiling. Liam in action was a sight to behold.

Liam used the pause to gaze very slowly and deliberately around Julia's small office. It was like a private detective's hideaway from a Chandler novel, with its wooden floors and scratched walls; Belfast definitely had the better deal on facilities. But he couldn't have cared less about the décor; his silence was working. He could sense Julia's frustration building, and he could use her on-edge.

Finally he answered her question, in a dry tone.

"And lovely to meet you too, Inspector McNulty. I understand that D.C.I. Craig has already spoken to you about the similarities between your murder case and ours?" Adding, just to put her back in her box. "At the explicit request of D.C.S. Harrison."

She seethed inwardly at the closing of the upper ranks and his alignment with them. "Yes he has, and I told him exactly what I'll tell you – we don't need any help from Belfast."

Her pursed lips and newly folded arms reminded Liam of Annette in a snit and he decided they must learn it at the 'Wimmin's group'. He ignored her words and ploughed on, while Gerry watched Julia's face, knowing she'd met her match and not knowing which side to cheer for.

"Oh, so you don't need any help, do you not? So can you explain the hand and knee abrasions and the shin cuts? And the dead sperm with the husband's DNA? And the unusual wire and hammer? Go ahead then, I'd love to hear it, because we're not proud in Belfast – we'll take all the help that we can get."

Julia glared up at him with such venom that Gerry thought he saw a glint of real hatred in her eyes. Then she rose to her feet and stood facing Liam, the silence thick with unspoken expletives and neither of them giving an inch. Finally, 'Gerry the peacemaker' broke the quiet.

"Do you have anything that explains the forensics then, Liam?"

Julia's glared at him for fraternising with the enemy and he knew that her retribution later would be fierce.

"Aye well...I'm very glad you asked that, Gerry. Not specifically, but we do have a few good ideas."

Liam grabbed a chair from the corner leaving Julia standing, and sat down, stretching his long legs across the doorway.

"Sure, a cup of tea would be grand. Thanks for asking."

Then he launched into their progress so far and his planned visit to the Adams' farm, just as soon as he had had his tea.

****

The police artist's four sketches were spread across Craig's desk. They were exceptional; almost photographic quality.

The postman and paperboy should be easy to climinate, but the 'Spiv' and the 'Hoody' were of particular interest. No matter how hard he stared at the Hoody's features, they didn't look any less feminine. And although the curves were hidden they were still too obvious to ignore; it was definitely a woman. She was small and very slight, and the pallor and dark circles around her eyes confirmed the frailty that Liam had heard in the voice calling Ian McCandless' mobile. Monica Gibson.

The number she'd called from had yielded nothing, as expected; just a pay-as-you-go mobile, bought with cash. And the only Monica Gibson they could find was an eighty-three-year-old living in Londonderry.

Craig was sure now that their caller had been so close she must have seen the C.S.I.s go about their work.

Annette was right; Joey McCandless would turn out to be a dead end. This woman was their killer, he was sure of it. The Spiv would turn out to be a debt collector, after McCandless for money he'd owed. They needed to confirm it, but Meg McCandless had said that they were always calling at the garage.

But they still needed to rule out Michael Adams and his razor-wire, and then there was Joey McCandless' possible link to the Purecrem. They still had a long way to go to close the gaps that some slime of a defence barrister would try to wriggle through in court. Craig had always wondered how they could defend someone that they knew was guilty, knowing that the 'everyone deserves a defence' line would be trotted out in reply.

He beckoned Nicky in. "Can you get these sketches out to uniform please. They're to identify and rule out these individuals."

He gestured to the sketch of the Spiv. "Give this one to Davy and ask him to try the local debt collectors first, please. I'm pretty sure that he'll turn out to be an agent for one of them. Ask Davy if he can find any images for Michael Adams as well. I know it's a long shot, but..."

She nodded and took the sketches, pointing at the wall clock.

"Don't forget the D.C.S. wants an update before the press conference and it's nearly four, sir."

Craig was startled, realising that he'd forgotten to eat all day. Nicky's smile said that she'd predicted it, so he wasn't surprised by the appearance of a sandwich and coffee five minutes later. She was more like his mother than she knew. A sudden thought struck him, and reaching into his jacket, he produced his credit card.

"Nicky – that little lady who helped us with the sketches, has she gone home yet?"

"No, she's downstairs waiting for a free car." She smiled, knowing what would come next.

"Then, would you mind nipping out for a nice bouquet of flowers? And get a photo of a young uniform handing them to her, please. Tell her we'll frame it and send it on. She might just have cracked this case for us."

This was why she loved working for him. All the hours, all the coffee, and even the occasional moods and silence were worth it for this. Her obvious approval made him feel unexpectedly vulnerable and he took an overly large bite of his sandwich, trying to re-instate the reputation for sceptical macho-ness that he aimed for.

Just then his phone rang. It was John.

"I've just spoken to the North-West, Marc. Burton has never donated sperm and there were no signs of violence to indicate rape, so Maria Burton may have simply consented to sex with her husband."

"But if they had consensual sex then why use frozen sperm, when she could just have had a fresh sample? This really doesn't make sense."

"I know. And apparently the husband has a solid alibi for the time of the murder – he was twenty-five miles away in Templepatrick. Also, Des says the wire marks found on Burton's shins match the ones on McCandless exactly. Nice jigsaw you have. Sorry, I have to give a lecture now so it's all yours. See you tomorrow."

Craig rubbed his eyes hard, anticipating his next conversation with Harrison.

"Thanks for that, John. Now I'll have to bull shit Harrison *and* the press."

He'd wasted his sarcasm on a dead line.

****

Julia stared hard at the fax Terry Harrison had just sent from Belfast, praying that it would disappear. It was a draft press release and it was complete crap. Now she had to tell him that it was.

She didn't care what the DNA said, Paul Burton was innocent. She'd always been sure of it and now his computer and sat-nav backed it up. But how could she convince Harrison? Older officers' complete faith in DNA would be almost touching if you didn't have to convince them they were wrong.

She looked at the fax again, hoping that she could interpret its meaning differently. But it was unambiguous. Harrison's desperate desire for impact had removed any wriggle-room.

'Perpetrator under arrest' was written clear as day in half-a-dozen different ways. If she let it go ahead, she would be blamed later, and if she didn't then she would get an earful now. And Harrison think that she was just some dopey woman going on a feeling that Burton didn't do it, despite the DNA.

Why was it when men had hunches they were called instincts, but when women had them they were called feelings and accompanied by a pitying look? But she *still* had to tell Harrison that he was wrong; Paul Burton wasn't their perp. She screwed up her nerve and lifted the phone, preparing to contradict a very senior officer, and not for the first time in her life.

Chapter Ten

The C.C.U.

The soundproofed room was crammed full of journalists, media and press, busily rigging lights and microphones in preparation for the conference. Each perforated sidewall had been hung with sockets and leads, every one of them feeding a different network. All so the public's appetite for information could be satiated twenty-four-seven.

Jeans-clad electricians and cameramen crowded outside, grabbing the courtesy coffee and sandwiches from the catering table. They were too busy talking to notice Nicky handing them their drinks, as she covertly gathered information for Craig, completely unknown to him.

Meanwhile, Craig was upstairs with Harrison preparing to face the lions. Press conferences were the only part of the job he truly hated and Nicky knew that. He'd been trotted out too often as the poster-boy for intra-UK liaison during his years at The Met, and for Europeanism because his Italian side. So five minutes before he entered their den she intended to gift him a list of the fourth estate's most likely questions. Her contribution to improving his crappy week.

****

Craig had spent the last ten minutes arguing with Terry Harrison and it didn't look as if it was going to stop any time soon. The phone call the D.C.S. had received from Limavady two minutes earlier had thrown even more petrol on his flames.

"That bloody woman McNulty keeps insisting that the DNA's wrong. But it's science and science is fact. You can't argue against fact."

"With respect, sir, I don't think that *is* what she's

saying."

Harrison rounded on him angrily.

"Of course that's what she's saying. Paul Burton's DNA was found at the scene and his wife, the wife with whom he was engaged in a very acrimonious divorce, was sexually assaulted and murdered. My officer, raped and murdered, D.C.I. Craig..."

Craig sat forward, even more determined to make his point. "But that's just it. John told me there was no sign of rape, nothing to say that the semen was introduced in an act of violence."

"Well, how else was it introduced, for God's sake? They weren't even on speaking terms, never mind friendly enough to have sex. There's no way on earth that Maria Burton consented to sex with that man."

Harrison's face had turned so deep a red that Craig thought he was about to have a heart attack, so he sat back quickly, deliberately arranging his body language to calm the situation. He hadn't put much stock in psychology until he'd seen it work on the street, but now he relaxed in his chair and half-smiled, and Harrison automatically did the same without realising why.

They sat for a minute without eye contact, and then Craig broke the silence, speaking in a measured voice.

"Let me run a hypothetical case past you, sir."

Harrison's look was challenging, but Craig ignored it, continuing quietly.

"Let's just say that Maria Burton wasn't raped."

Harrison went to argue but Craig held up a hand, halting him without rudeness.

"Wasn't raped and in fact didn't have sex at all. And that there are no signs of resistance because she wasn't raped, but that instead the semen was deposited after she was dead."

The disgust Craig felt at his own words was echoed in the chief superintendent's face, but Harrison remained silent, listening harder now.

"That scenario would explain why there were no signs of violence. Yes?"

Harrison nodded him on grudgingly.

"All right. Then let's say that Paul Burton is telling the truth and that he wasn't anywhere near Portglenone at the time of the murder..."

Harrison spoke in a sarcastic tone. "So how did his sperm get there? Walk on their own?"

Craig half-smiled, acknowledging the bad joke and knowing that it indicated a thaw. He continued carefully, knowing that Harrison was more engaged than he'd been for twenty minutes, and not wanting to break the spell.

"The sperm were dead, and they were dead when they were put there – forensics confirms it. So we can agree that they had left Paul Burton's body some time before. We thought of sperm donation or someone putting the semen there to stage the scene..."

Harrison stared at him thoughtfully.

"But why would Burton need to bring his own dead sperm to the scene where he killed his wife?"

"And why would he deliberately incriminate himself by putting them there at all, sir?"

Realisation dawned on Harrison. "Because *he* didn't bring them! Someone else did."

"Exactly. Someone else planted Burton's dead sperm at the scene."

"But that doesn't mean Burton didn't get them to stage it like that, to throw us off track."

"No, it doesn't. But why would he, sir? It just incriminates him. And with the sat-nav and computer info, it makes it unlikely that Paul Burton had anything to do with the crime at all. And..." He paused for a second to let Harrison catch up with the logic. "With the similarities between this and the McCandless' murder, it also makes it a lot more likely that it was the same killer who committed both."

The D.C.S. nodded imperceptibly, but it was enough. He had agreed and Julia McNulty was out of his bad books.

Terry Harrison's next suggestion almost made Craig wish that he hadn't made the effort.

****

His dad was dead. His dad was really dead. It still seemed too surreal to be true. Maybe it was the suddenness of it, or maybe it was the way that he'd died. Like some terrible scene from a Godfather sequel that he'd studied in media class. So grotesque and over the top that it had to be some scriptwriter's fantasy instead of real life. Except that it was true, and his dad was dead. And their last conversation had been so monosyllabically male and ordinary.

"Don't forget it's your mum's birthday on Friday, Joey."

"OK, I'll get her some flowers. Bye, Dad. Catch you later."

Ordinary.

Ian McCandless had had no idea what his son had really been thinking, and needing to say to him that day. The words that Joey had tried to form a thousand more times than he'd actually seen his father in the preceding months. Words that he couldn't even say to himself, never mind to his dad.

Words that could have created a gap of guilt and shame between them that could never have been crossed. Making every casual conversation tense, changing their one-word, easy exchanges into earnest, stilted conversations of political correctness and reproach. With his mother wedged between them; loving them both but always protecting her child. Just like a mother.

His dad had been a man in the old mould, with big rough hands and a hard day's pay and his 'work hard and look after your family' values making his boy's world safe for eighteen years. Intent on educating both his sons, and angry when his older brother took the easy way to adventure across the water. Investing extra effort in him to compensate, accepting that an arty degree was better than none, and proud to say that his son Joey was at university. So proud of it. So proud of him. And never judging.

He'd laughed uncomfortably at his once-blue hair and Chinese tattoo, even arguing for it against his mum. He tolerated his loud music and strange friends, with their floppy hair and street fashion. He'd even swallowed his macho objections to his pierced ear and occasional cosmetic adornment at nightclubs. Still smiling proudly and laughing at 'kids', citing his own seventies attempts at flares and long hair in comparison. None of his younger son's arty teenage rebellion had managed to cause him disgust.

Except that *this* would have disgusted him. This would have made him angry and confused, and he would have blamed himself. This would have widened the gap and driven a wedge between him and his wife, her siding with her child, always with her child.

It was better that he'd died than hear this. Joey nodded to himself in guilt and justification. Perhaps it was kinder to all of them, better for all their futures? Yes, it was. He nodded to himself again; yes. Nodding all his guilt and blame away, nod by nod.

Now his dad would never know; never be disappointed; never hate him. It had been for the best, for all of them. Successful justification. But that still left him with his guilt.

****

They'd spent thirty minutes arguing. Craig's reasoning that the sketch of their Hoody should be released, being over-ruled by Harrison's insistence that it would drive their killer underground if they plastered her face all over the news. They'd finally agreed to compromise on a paragraph's description of the person they needed to help them with their enquiries. They were just preparing themselves for the onslaught of journalists, when they heard a set of heels clicking towards Harrison's room. Nicky's dark head suddenly appeared and she knocked at his smoked-glass office door.

Harrison saw her first and smiled. His smile always reminded Craig of a shark with indigestion but he recognised the sentiment; he was genuinely pleased to see her, and of the respite from their debate.

"Nicola – how lovely to see you. To what do we owe

this visit?"

She smiled broadly at him, all the petty irritations of working together forgotten in the genuine affection that she always held for old bosses.

"Hello, sir. How are you? And Mrs Harrison?"

Craig smiled to himself, knowing that it was her way of marking Harrison's infidelities, and her loyalty to the woman whose tears she'd heard often through the years.

"Good, good – excellent. Sian's just got a post with Aymes and Boyce Marketing you know."

"That's brilliant, sir. You and Mrs Harrison must both be very proud."

Thirty-Love, Nicky.

Her subtle digs passed completely over Harrison's head and he nodded, smiling.

"Yes, yes, we both are. Very. Well Nicola, was it me or D.C.I. Craig that you wanted to speak to?"

The question was delivered as if it must be him, daring her to say otherwise. Craig didn't mind what she said but Nicky reacted diplomatically, as he knew she would.

"Well actually, sir, it's both of you."

Craig stood up and offered her his chair and Harrison nodded her down, flicking his eyes over her slim thighs, nicely outlined in dark winter tights. She sat down, crossing her long legs elegantly, then began to speak in her growling voice.

"I've just been down at the press room, sir."

Harrison raised a quizzical eyebrow but Craig smiled, quickly realising what she'd been up to.

"And exactly what were you doing there, Nicola?"

That had been Craig's question the first time she'd done it, but despite his objections she'd done it again, insisting that it was her contribution to 'undercover operations'. He knew better than to try to stop her; he'd about as much control over Nicky as he had of Lucia.

"I just happened to be passing that way with some papers, sir. Anyway..."

Harrison stared at her sceptically "Yes ...?"

"Well, I just happened to overhear them talking. And they've a few nasty little questions lined up to ask you both.... Live on air, sir."

Craig's ears picked up. Nicky might just win his argument for him. Harrison was listening intently now.

"Such as?"

"They've made a link between the two cases, and they're planning all sorts of mischief. I heard one of them say that they're going to play up the possible Dissident angle for the evening news. Another one was talking to his editor about a headline that went something like. 'Rape and murder spree against W.P.C.s.'"

A look of disgust flicked across her face as she added. "And he was trying to make it rhyme as well."

Craig would have happily dropped all journalists and defence barristers into a watery grave.

"What did he look like, Nicky?"

"A weasel. But I know who it was, sir. It was Ray Mercer from The Belfast Chronicle. He door-stepped me once last year, remember? When we were doing that Robertson case?"

She smiled, remembering. "Gary thumped him."

Craig grinned; he remembered. Mercer had cried assault so he'd had a few words with Gary over a pint.

The sudden explosion that came from Harrison wasn't completely unexpected, but Craig hadn't quite anticipated its volume. Nicky had been even more effective than usual.

"Those bloody hacks, they should all be put up against a wall and shot. And I don't want that comment going outside this room." He glared at Craig and looked at Nicky as if she was a naughty child.

"Irresponsible, panic-mongering, illiterate..."

Craig had watched Nicky light the blue touch paper, and now they both watched as the rocket launched, treating them to five minutes of Harrison pacing up and down his office. Finally he slumped heavily into his orthopaedic chair and lapsed into complete silence, staring at the floor.

Craig waited barely five seconds before he spoke.

"Sir, with respect, there's a very easy way to diffuse all their headlines and make them look very stupid into the bargain."

Harrison's head shot up and his eyes fixed Craig's fiercely.

"How? I'd love to hear it."

The tone was sceptical but with a hint of desperation, as if he'd consider wire-walking if it would stop tomorrow's bad press.

"All we have to do is release the sketch of the girl."

Harrison opened his mouth to object but Craig pressed on. "No, hear me out." Harrison's lack of reply gave him permission.

"If we say that we're looking for the same person in connection with both crimes that means that it isn't linked to W.P.C.s in particular, so they lose their spree angle. Then we release the sketch and say that our prime suspect is a woman, which will completely throw them. At the same time, we leak that we have strong reasons to believe that W.P.C. Burton's death was staged to look like a rape, but that it definitely wasn't."

Harrison was slightly calmer and nodded to himself. "That's a possibility but...it doesn't take account of the Dissidents."

"No, but no organisation has claimed either murder and they always do. And we've no intelligence to support a Dissident angle. The rape of a young woman is low, so it's likely the Dissidents will come out and deny it very soon anyway. If we argue all those points we can direct it firmly towards two motive-based killings by one person, most probably a young woman."

Harrison rubbed his chin pensively, as if enjoying the feel of his own stubble in some sort of virility-affirmation ritual. Nicky had often said that the habit had creeped her out and now he could see why.

He leaned against her chair while she remained totally still, barely breathing, until eventually Harrison gave them both a triumphant grin.

"I've decided exactly how we'll handle these press boyos."

Nicky smiled and leaned forward encouragingly. "How, sir?"

"I'm going to release the sketch of our prime suspect for both murders. Deride any suggestion of genuine rape, or of a vendetta against W.P.C.s, and firmly link the crimes together as the acts of one warped woman with a personal grudge."

I'm?

"Then I'm going to make it clear that Dissidents invariably claim their kills and to suggest that this is anything to do with any of those groups is completely laughable. That'll make all those journos look like complete idiots."

Nicky smiled at him, openly admiring, but Craig could see her tongue firmly in her cheek. "Oh, well done, sir."

Harrison slapped his open hand down hard on the desk and smiled broadly, standing up to pull open the door. "Mrs Butler, come in please and take a new draft for the press release."

As he dictated the changes, Craig smiled to himself, trying to avoid Nicky's eye in case he laughed out loud. Only then did he realise that she'd deliberately changed into a short skirt from the leggings she'd been wearing two hours before, just to manipulate Harrison.

Her motto had always been 'Whatever works. Within reason' and he thanked something somewhere yet again for the day he'd inherited her from the D.C.S.

****

It was six pm by the time Craig finally returned to the squad-room, exhausted. The press conference had been argumentative but they'd managed to hold the line, and he wondered yet again if the press realised how much police time was wasted dealing with their questions. Maybe they should charge them all with obstruction of justice, except for the headlines it would cause.

Now he was just waiting for the Dissidents to deny Maria Burton's death, outraged, and then play some petty game to re-assert their terrorist credentials, like they did every time they felt they were being disrespected.

It was a Friday evening, but as he walked tiredly past Annette's desk he saw her poring over some papers, still working away.

"Go home, please, Annette. I'll be here until seven if anything comes up. There's no point in you being here as well."

She smiled up at him, knowing that it was only his family's insistence on Friday dinner that was dragging him away at all.

"I just wanted to check through a few things, sir. I spoke to the nursing home where Joey volunteers and he hasn't been there for over a week, so he wouldn't have had any reason to use Purecrem on Wednesday. They did say he's been there a bit less recently so they think maybe he's got a new girlfriend, although his mum didn't say anything about it."

"Maybe he doesn't want anyone to know about her; lads his age are secretive. OK, dig a bit on that and then get him in again. And use an interview room this time, please. Don't make it too cosy for him. I want to know more about his relationship with his father and exactly where he was on Wednesday. That lecture alibi is rubbish."

She nodded. "I know. If it's all right I'll try to crack his alibi, before I waste time interviewing sixty students."

"Fine. Whatever you think." He looked at what she'd been poring over. It was the sketch of their Hoody.

"This sketch is amazing, isn't it? It's like a photograph. Someone is bound to recognise her from this."

The artist had captured the image of a thin woman somewhere between twenty and thirty, but there was another, deeper dimension to the sketch. An awful weariness that stared out from her hollowed eyes, watching the world as if it was a punishment. She looked sick, or an addict. Craig had seen plenty of Heroin eyes like that when he'd worked in Earls Court.

"Let's see if the database knows her. The postman and paperboy will be easy to find, and I think our Spiv will be too. She'll be the real challenge. Speaking of Spivs, have you heard anything from Liam recently?"

She gave a wry smile.

"Oh yes. I've heard from him. He's been on the phone four times since he got there and mostly in words of one syllable. It seems D.I. McNulty isn't too happy to have our assistance. His last call was ten minutes ago on the way to the Adams' farm and it ended with the words 'dead body', and I'm pretty sure he meant Julia McNulty's. He did say he agrees with her on one thing though, he doesn't think Paul Burton did it. Not only was he online at the time, but he ordered an afternoon grocery delivery and signed for it in Templepatrick at two-forty-seven."

She anticipated Craig's next question. "They've corroborated it with the supermarket. The delivery guy recognised his photo."

"So, how did his sperm get all the way to Limavady?" Craig rubbed his temple thoughtfully. "His dead sperm?"

Paul Burton had never donated sperm so he'd obviously never been a starving student like he and John had; the going rate was ten pounds a time when he was eighteen. And John's conversation with the North-West had ruled out rape, so why the dead sperm?

Suddenly Craig had a Damascene moment. He grabbed Annette's phone urgently and dialled Liam.

"Liam, where are you right now?"

He hit the speakerphone and Annette could hear the sudden rush of traffic and Liam's muffled voice, confirming that he was on the car hands-free phone. His loud bass forced its way through the static, but only alternate words were clear.

"...Road..."

"Right, when you get there, call D.I. McNulty and tell her to ask Paul Burton two questions. Did he have sex recently with a woman he didn't know? And did they use a condom?"

The next phrase from Liam was crystal clear.

"You ask her, boss. That one's like a viper and I value my balls. She was eating the head off her sergeant when I left. She needs a good..."

His last word was drowned out by a car-horn but they all knew what it was. Craig made a mental note to give Liam the political correctness lecture again. He had to do it every few months or Liam's natural exuberance led to some W.P.C. complaining, and yet another compulsory course.

"OK, I'll give her a call. Update me when you've spoken to Michael Adams. Nicky's sent the sketches through to your phone so check if he's our Spiv, please."

He cut the call, looking at Annette warily to see if she'd taken offence. She was laughing.

"Don't worry, sir. I was a nurse for years, and medical humour is far ruder than anything Liam could ever say."

Craig smiled at her, suddenly hopeful. "I don't suppose you'd like to earn some brownie points by calling Inspector McNulty with those two questions?"

She stared at him hard, seeing Nicky grin in the background and toying with the idea of making him suffer. She decided to give him a break instead and nodded resignedly.

"OK then, but you owe me. And I intend to call in all my debts someday."

Then she waved him away, picked up the phone and prepared to play her best female solidarity card.

****

Limavady.

Liam programmed the sat-nav and headed for Barnardstown, and the eponymously named Adams'

Farm, swearing hard when he still hadn't found it an hour later. The local farmers obviously considered road names an unnecessary luxury, and everyone he'd asked was convinced that 'down past Anderson's orchard and left at Henry's copse' were acceptable directions for a complete stranger. He remembered tormenting outsiders in a similar way when he was a kid. Any Townie stupid enough to enter their territory and give looks that said 'you're a thick culchie' had been fair game. Eventually he reached a crossroads that looked like a point on the sat-nav called Tohey Road, with the Adams' farm clearly marked at the end of a long lane.

His car was a basic Ford without the traction of a four-by-four, and recent rain had slicked the mud on the farm-track into a slide, so it was hard going. Liam's impatient revving splattered his windows with mud, completely defeating his screen-wash and blinding him when he went above five miles an hour, but his vision of a weekend spent scraping off mud were calmed by the thought of a free valet in the compound. It was long overdue; two of his daughter Erin's year-old gummy bears were still stuck to the car's back seat.

Eventually he turned a blind corner and the lane opened out suddenly, into a gravelled area that led to an impressive double-fronted stone house. It was three storeys high, with leaded bay windows set on either side of a wide front-door.

As he got closer Liam could see that the house's grandiose first impression couldn't hide the neglect of dull brassware and tattered nets. When he switched off his engine, he could almost feel the cold silence that had been hidden behind his revving and expletives. The hairs on the back of his neck stood up urgently, in a fight or flight response.

The whole place was empty. No, more than that. It was deserted, with a terrible pall of sadness obvious even to someone as insensitive as him. It felt as if all the life here had died.

He climbed slowly from his car, casting a quick look around for someone to speak to, but there was nothing in the farm except a funereal air. No sound and no movement, not from the house and not from the grounds. No sounds of machinery running, dogs barking, or workers yelling. He walked to the front door preparing to knock it, but as he lifted the rapper, the heavy door drifted inwards, breaking a spider's web at its edge. Liam entered the tiled hall cautiously, his hand moving to his gun.

In earlier times, the farmhouse must have been immensely beautiful. The entrance hall had a wide mosaic floor and the walls were completely covered in wainscot. The glass chandelier on the ceiling still shone, even through its dust, and the wide sweeping staircase behind it said that this had once been a wealthy farm, and Michael Adams a very wealthy man.

"Mr Adams. It's the police." Liam's loud voice echoed back to him once, dying against the wooden walls and returning the hall abruptly to silence. He walked slowly in and out of the rooms, their contents revealing a once-full family home, with toys belonging to more than one child, and all hinting at girls. The style of the toys told him that wherever they were now, these children were still young. He shuddered involuntarily, thinking of his own small daughter. What had happened here?

When he'd finished exploring the house he wandered outside, into the outhouses and around the near-grounds. He opened shed doors and bunkers, until he reached the worn wood of the largest barn.

Entering the barn's already open door, he was greeted by cattle pens and instruments, some resembling implements of medieval torture. The captive bolt that Davy had described would fit perfectly here, and he was sure they would find razor-wire somewhere in the grounds as well. There was no question that this place had something to do with their two murders, but where was Michael Adams?

Liam walked quickly back to the house and lifted the abandoned post. M. Adams and J. Adams. The postmarks hinted that M. Adams' post had stopped nineteen months before, but J. Adams' only in the last year.

Liam had seen enough. He pressed dial on his mobile, looking around one last time as it rang.

"Gerry. It's Liam. I'm at the Adams' Farm and I think I've found something interesting. You'd better get McNulty and the C.S.I.s out here now."

****

"When I want your help, Sergeant McElroy, I'll ask you for it! Just who the hell do you Docklands' lot think you are? First, I have Craig barking at me, and then the Incredible Hulk drapes himself all over my office. Now *you* ring me doing the old girls' act, telling me which questions to ask my suspect, *my* suspect. This is bang out of order and you know it. This is *my* investigation, so for the last time, will you all please butt out!"

Julia wasn't in a good mood and Annette was paying for it. She was holding the phone receiver as far away as she could to still be able to hear it. Julia's mood wasn't improved by the fact that Craig's questions were exactly right, and that she hadn't thought of them herself. In fact so far, his labs and his questions had moved her case along far more than her own had. Bugger. Now he'd asked a junior officer to call her, using female solidarity as the game. Well, sod that.

Annette now knew exactly why Craig hadn't wanted to call Julia McNulty himself, and although McNulty was an Inspector, after two minutes of being yelled at she really didn't care anymore. She'd had enough and she blew.

"Look, I really don't care if you're used to shouting at your own sergeant, Inspector McNulty, you won't do it to me. You're obviously too stupid to realise that the D.C.S. *asked* Chief Inspector Craig to help you, and that our two cases are linked. If you could put your giant ego to one side just long enough to think of the two grieving families and the other female officers out there who'll feel vulnerable until we catch this killer, then maybe together we could solve both cases. You stupid, ungrateful woman...ma'am!"

Annette slammed the phone down and had banged the case file hard against the desk several times, before she'd calmed down enough to realise that someone was watching her. It was Nicky. She looked at her, embarrassed. Annette rarely lost her temper, but she'd make an exception for Julia McNulty.

"God, Nicky, I've done it now. She'll report me."

"No, she won't. Not unless she's completely thick. She's in the wrong and if she has any sense, she'll ring you back and apologise. And you were absolutely right anyway, she is a stupid woman."

Nicky glanced at Craig's door, knowing that he'd heard everything. "And don't you worry; he'll back you one hundred and ten percent. Just tell him what happened before she does."

She was right, so Annette was just walking towards Craig's door when he emerged, trying hard to stifle a grin. Finally he gave up and burst-out laughing.

"Well done, Annette, she needed to hear that. Her ego is coming before her investigation. Don't worry, even if she says something to the D.C.S., I'll say that I overheard the whole thing. And that you were perfectly polite and didn't use a single word that you shouldn't have." He looked embarrassed suddenly.

"It's my fault for being a coward anyway. I should just have called her myself, and I will now. But, before I do." He bowed in mock-admiration and Annette blushed and smiled.

"Wait till Liam hears about this one."

****

The C.S.I.s were working throughout the electricity-free farmhouse, hoping that the daylight would hold. Liam was leaning against the front door talking to Gerry, who was on his way to relieve him.

"Can you see any signs of violence?"

"Nope. Nothing. It's weird. The place is like that Marie Celeste ship. Do you know anything about the family?"

"Eamonn Ross at Barnardstown Station will know them, if anyone does. He's been desk sergeant there for twenty years. He's off till tomorrow, so I'll call him then."

The C.S.I.s had just finished with the outhouses. They'd found a set of captive bolt guns and a sample of razor-wire; the weapons that had killed Maria Burton and Ian McCandless had definitely come from the farm. But was the killer M. or J. Adams? Or both of them? Were the Spiv and the Hoody that Ida Foster had seen working together?

Gerry was still talking.

"Look Liam, this traffic's dire so don't wait for me. Head on home and I'll call you as soon as I know anything."

"OK. We're in all weekend anyway. I'll catch you then."

****

Stranmillis. 9 p.m.

Craig was stretched out on his settee when an insistent ringing jolted him awake. The living-room of his apartment was in complete darkness and for a second he was confused, certain that he'd switched on a lamp when he'd arrived home. He looked around him quickly, his hackles rising, but there was nothing more threatening to find than a blown bulb. The case was making him twitchy.

The ringing stopped abruptly and then started again. It was coming from his landline, and it was suddenly joined by a vibration in his pocket. Reaching into his suit, he realised that he still had on his leather jacket. He must have fallen asleep as soon as he'd got home. The landline would be his mobile-phobic mother, and his mobile call was probably Lucia. Oh hell, *now* he remembered; it was Friday and he'd promised to go for dinner.

He flicked on the mobile, preferring thirty seconds

of English bollocking to five minutes of Italian, and he spoke quickly, before Lucia could.

"I know I'm late, Luce, sorry. I'll be there in ten minutes."

She could hear he was half-asleep and laughed. "Calm down, it's fine. We've just arrived, so Mum's ranting at me as well. Take your time, the last thing we need is you killing yourself on the motorway. I'll deal with Mum, see you."

She cut the call so he didn't have to and he smiled. Lucia could handle their mother as well as his father could; they were both so easy going. But he was Mirella's double, his Latin fieriness only tempered by the discipline of his job. They'd had some flaming exchanges throughout the years, while his father and Lucia had just ignored them both and watched TV.

He reached for the lamp and changed its blown bulb for a new one, then he pulled open his tall, steel fridge and swapped his warm beer for a bottle of chilled white wine. Rubbing a handful of ice-cubes over his neck, an old trick for extended partying, he grabbed his car-keys and cast a grateful look at the suddenly silent landline. Lucia had done the trick.

He pulled the apartment door behind him and raced down three flights of stairs to the carpark, then he drove to his parents' house, in leafy Holywood.

****

Wharf House.

Jessie shivered violently in the cool evening air, pulling her thick hoody tightly around her overly thin frame. She was exactly where she needed to be, and it wouldn't be long before the guiltiest of them all was dead.

She could feel her six months of waiting and planning nearing its end. Only one more of them would be left after tomorrow, and he'd be dead as well in three days' time. Then she, Fiona and the girls would leave Northern Ireland forever.

She gazed through the window of the centre's small television room, out at the country night-sky. It was pitch-dark, with no city lights and no stars. It reminded her of home. The night's damp was seeping into her bones and she reached into her pocket for the new blister pack of tablets, preferring them in a bottle. Somehow, the challenge of the child-lock made them seem more potent.

She stared around the darkened room at the other women. All eyes were fixed blankly on the huge screen ahead, some blanker than others and tomorrow's target's the blankest of them all. Jessie thought contemptuously that the girl should pay special attention to this evening's programmes; after all, they'd be the last that she'd ever watch.

She slid down into an old armchair and shut her eyes, letting the mixture of tablets and TV wash over her. She counted the hours until the next day's execution and her bail the day after, as her pain gradually eased away against the backdrop of an old movie, in their brief free time before bed.

****

Holywood, County Down.

His unexpected nap, compounded by heavy airport traffic on the motorway, meant that Craig arrived just as Mirella was serving coffee and liqueurs.

Only the dog and his dad smiled at him. Lucia was too busy staring doe-eyed at her latest candidate for husband to even notice that he'd arrived. Murphy's barking informed him that they'd already left the warm comfort of the large country kitchen for the marginally greater luxury of the living-room. Luxurious except for the areas of carpet and upholstery that the Labrador had ripped apart. Craig smiled to himself. No matter how bad his behaviour got, Murphy's would always be worse; they'd been in the doghouse together many times over the years.

He dumped his coat over the weathered oak

banister and slipped in as invisibly as possible, his cover blown by renewed barking and the cheerful, "hello, son" that followed it. His father was sitting in the armchair he'd had since they were kids, worn into complete comfort despite his mother's many refurbishments. The compromise between its eviction and survival was Tom Craig's willingness to allow its reupholstering, to match whatever luminous colour scheme Mirella was inflicting on them that year. Subtle home décor had never been her thing.

This year the room was a riot of cherry and aubergine. Its bright cosiness echoed in the flames of the real log fire that his mother insisted on burning for six months of the year, still unable to bear the British cold despite forty years away from Rome. Ornate lamps lit every corner of the room, casting their light towards the fire and the grand piano, where his mother practiced every day for the charity concerts she still gave.

Mirella looked up at her son from the drinks she was pouring, her jaundiced look only tempered by her immediate joy at seeing him. "You are ve-ry late, Marco. This is not good." He could see her finger mentally wagging at him, knowing that only the presence of a guest actually prevented it happening for real.

"We 'ave guest."

She gestured towards a chair dramatically, its occupant half-hidden behind Lucia's massive head of tawny-blonde hair. Craig detected a pair of long male legs protruding behind his sister.

"This is Richard. He is pianist like me." The pride in his mother's voice almost made Craig laugh. Richard could have been a mass-murderer as long as he could play the piano well.

He walked over and ruffled his sister's hair, smiling as a fairer, finer version of his own face grinned back at him.

"Hi Marc. This is Rick."

From behind Lucia's hair appeared the face of a fair-haired man, handsome but not in the arty way

Craig had expected. He was strong-framed and tanned like a sportsman, and as he stood up to shake hands his height and demeanour reminded Craig very strongly of someone else. It only took him a second to realise who, and to realise that he could be looking at his future brother-in-law.

He turned towards his smiling father, knowing that he'd seen the resemblance as well. Lucia, the family's little rebel, had just conformed completely by falling for a man like dear old dad.

Chapter Eleven

Wharf House. Saturday.

The soft morning light breaking through the curtains woke Jessie painlessly. It wasn't so bright that it hurt her eyes, but bright enough to cast soothing shadows across the small, cool room. She smiled to herself, still unable to believe that everything had come together so well. If she'd believed in a benevolent God she would have called it divine intervention, except that she didn't believe in anything any more.

She gazed around the room, and not for the first time she thought that prisoners had it better than many pensioners. There was no justice in a system that was more humane to the criminal than the innocent.

She'd pretended to listen sympathetically to the women's moans over dinner, bleating on about their loss of freedom and how 'it wasn't fair, locking them up'. But she'd only heard every third word, her eyes fixed on a young, blonde woman across the canteen, laughing and talking as if she had some sort of right.

Lynsey Taylor's sallow skin and premature lines gave her away as a smoker, and Jessie already knew about her other vices. She wasn't alone. There were so many women wearing long sleeves in the warm dining room that she knew there must be a roaring Heroin trade going on behind the guards' backs. Or maybe they knew. Some of them certainly seemed more concerned with being popular than with any discipline.

Maybe it was because it was a women's unit, or maybe male prisons were just the same. Guards matey with the inmates, as if it was some grey-walled summer camp and they were the hosts, there to make each day more tolerable for their guests.

But it *shouldn't* be tolerable; it should be hell for them every single day. Like the hell they gave their victims. She could never tell Fiona how easy life was here, now that equality and human right's campaigners had removed the hard from hard time.

If she had ever had any doubts about killing Lynsey Taylor, which she hadn't, the luxury Taylor had lived in for the past five years while she and Fiona had lived in hell would have killed them stone dead. There had been no justice for either of them for years, but today she'd make damn sure that some of it was delivered in full.

****

The C.C.U. 9.15 a.m.

"Michael Adams wasn't the S...Spiv at the garage. He's dead."

Davy had been in since eight o'clock, chasing the searches he'd left running. His little electronic friends hadn't disappointed him; he had driving licence and passport photos on his screens.

"Here he is."

He pressed a button and the image of a slim, blonde man no older than forty appeared on the large screen by Nicky's desk. Michael Adams was grinning, even though he shouldn't have been in the regulation photographs; but even if he hadn't been, the look in his eyes was one of amusement. He looked like a happy man, so what could have happened to make his farm so sad?

Gerry had been as good as his word and the sergeant at Barnardstown had phoned Liam on the dot of nine, with everything he knew about the happy Adams' household. Happy until nineteen months ago that is, because that was when the people at Adams' farm had seen it all go to hell.

Michael Adams' family had farmed the same two hundred acres of land for one hundred and fifty years, crops and cattle mostly. As the eldest son he'd taken over the farm and it had all gone brilliantly for a while. He'd married a local girl and they'd had two little daughters; it had been their toys that Liam had seen abandoned in the house. Then three years ago encephalitis had hit their herd, followed by crop blight, and the Adams had fallen into debt. They'd struggled until finally the farm had ceased production.

Michael Adams' younger siblings had blamed him for running the farm into trouble and things had spiralled downwards. Until finally, nineteen months before, when the farm had been circling the drain, Adams had hanged himself in one of the outhouses, leaving his young wife to find him there. It had been a real local tragedy, garnering inches in the local paper, The Neutral Recorder.

His children were two and four when he had died and, after a few months trying to deal with their creditors with no life insurance to help because of his suicide, Jessica Adams and her children had simply disappeared and no-one had known where they'd gone.

Davy flicked the control and a marriage certificate came up. Jessica Margaret Adams nee Atkinson, aged twenty at marriage and twenty-seven now. That would fit the Hoody's age. But the wedding photo that Gerry had sent from the local paper showed a sweetly beautiful girl with long dark hair; healthy and blooming. It was definitely the same woman, but the gaunt figure in their sketch looked like a mere shadow of this bride. Could her husband's suicide have made her ill? And what had been her motive for killing Maria Burton and Ian McCandless?

Craig pulled up a chair and nodded everyone to sit.

"Morning, Liam. Did you hear about Annette's meltdown at D.I. McNulty yesterday? We should have sold tickets."

Annette blushed and shot him a murderous glance.

"No, what was this?"

"I'll tell you later, but let's just say that they crossed swords and the inspector lost."

"Good for you, girl. All those 'find yourself' workshops must've taught you something."

Annette ignored the wind-up, thinking of

something more important.

"Sir, if Jessica Adams is our killer, and she still might not be; the farm was pretty open so anyone could have lifted the bolt-gun and wire. But if she is, then shouldn't we send her photo and the sketch to Limavady, to show to Paul Burton, just in case. If he has slept with a stranger in the past few weeks, it might have been her."

Craig thought about it. "You're absolutely right, Annette. If Jessica Adams slept with Paul Burton and used a condom, then she could easily have taken some of his semen to place at Maria Burton's scene."

"But why do it?"

"Playing for time perhaps? Trying to send us in another direction?"

"OK, but why play for time, sir? If she'd already killed McCandless she didn't need the time for that, so maybe she was just trying to escape being caught?"

Craig closed his eyes in sudden realisation. Of course.

"We don't know that she killed McCandless first. Maria Burton had been in the water for at least a day, so she could easily have killed her first in Portglenone on Wednesday morning and then made it to Belfast in time to kill McCandless on Wednesday afternoon."

Annette thought for a moment.

"Could their deaths be something to do with her husband's? Maybe the victims both had something to do with his debts, after all Maria Burton lived near the Adams farm and McCandless was in debt as well? Maybe Mrs Adams blamed them for her husband's suicide."

"I don't think so, Annette. We can't rule anything out yet, but Maria Burton wasn't in business, she was a local W.P.C. And McCandless' business was all in Belfast, Davy checked that already."

Davy shook his head.

"Don't dismiss Maria Burton just yet, chief. S...She only became a constable this year. Before that she lived on her dad's farm, two miles from the Adams'. She w...would have been living there when Michael

Adams killed himself."

The room fell quiet for a moment then Craig spoke again.

"OK, that's worth following up. Maybe Jessica Adams is just trying to evade capture, or maybe it's because she hasn't finished everything yet? And if she needs time to kill more people then who and why? If we find out one then we'll have the other. Davy, run McCandless, Maria Burton and both the Adams through every database that you can think of. See if there are any links. There's something connecting them.

Liam, follow up the findings from the Adams' farm. And Annette, I want you to find out everything there is about Jessica Adams, including showing her photograph to Ida Foster, and to Meg McCandless and Joey when you get him in. Watch Joey's face carefully when he sees her picture, please."

Davy tapped his computer urgently.

"S...Something's just come through on the man at the garage, chief. He works for a local debt-collection agency called Mercury. His name's Adrian S...Smith."

"OK, great work, Davy. We've already eliminated the postman and paperboy, so Liam, have a quick word with Mr Smith and rule him out completely. If he's clear then that leaves Jessica Adams as our prime suspect." He glanced at his watch.

"Sorry everyone, I know this isn't much of a weekend, but we need to meet again at three."

"Aye. And in the meantime, just think of the overtime."

Craig made a face.

"And you can pity me. I have to call D.I. McNulty now and tell her that she needs to ask Paul Burton even more details about his sex life."

****

Limavady.

Gerry wasn't quite sure how to tell the D.I. this one,

not without getting his ear in a sling. But there was no question. Paul Burton had taken one look at the sketch of the woman that Belfast had sent through and smiled lecherously; his wet, puffy lips folding into the smirk that men reserved for their sexual conquests.

At least Julia would be spared the full details of the encounter, only hearing his sanitised version. He honestly wished that he could say the same.

But no, he'd had to sit opposite slug-man, hearing how "There I was, just standing in the Triffic Takeaway Friday night two weeks ago, picking between double pasty and chips and deep-fried Pizza, when this really fit ho comes in and stands real close to me, like. An' she just gives me that look. You know, the one that says 'you're mine tonight son'."

Gerry had wanted to throw up by the word 'ho', so by the time Burton had got to 'mine' he was thinking of oceans and mountains and anything else that would distract him from what he knew was coming next. It hadn't worked.

"So I said, come back to ours and I'll show you my moves, luv."

That was it; it was all Gerry could listen to. He'd suspended the interview and headed outside, not sure whether to laugh or bang his head off the wall. Opting for the former, he'd laughed for a full five minutes and then resumed his customary deadpan and re-entered the interview room.

Now he was bracing himself to tape the statement that he just knew was going to be ten very long minutes of Paul Burton giving him every detail of his 'moves'. He could already hear the Barry White CD.

Chapter Twelve

"Crap, crap and more crap. How did Belfast know that she'd been Burton's one-night stand, and why didn't I?"

Julia was staring at the sketch printout, positively identified as the woman who had picked-up Paul Burton and had sex with him two weeks before. She couldn't believe that Burton hadn't questioned his luck, but he just acted as if attractive women threw themselves at him every day!

Harrison wasn't going to be happy, but they had no option now but to release him. The local uniforms would keep an eye on him, but somehow she doubted that he'd stray far from his Templepatrick armchair. She was furious with herself for not working it out before Belfast had; she'd been playing catch-up every step of the way.

Gerry had tried to be supportive.

"Maybe their minds have been cynically corrupted by years of policing in Belfast, ma'am. While you were fighting in noble defence of your Queen and country."

She nodded at him, completely missing his tongue in his cheek, and tapped her un-lit cigarette so hard against the desk that its end split and crumbled on the veneer.

"In other words, experience, Gerry. I might have the rank, but I don't have the experience people expect from a D.I."

He nodded inwardly, the words 'graduate entry scheme' forming on his lips but never reaching the air.

"Ma'am, may I humbly suggest something?"

He was taking the piss now and she knew it; he must have heard about her run in with Annette McElroy. She didn't have the energy to bollock him so she shrugged assent.

"When someone offers you free help in future, for God's sake, grab it. This isn't a competition between you and the rest of the force like some inter-regimental cup. It's a competition between all of us and the bad guys."

He was right, but she wasn't going to tell him that. Not today and probably not ever, so she continued as if he hadn't said a word.

"Burton had sex with a woman who matches the sketch Belfast sent us of their Hoody. They may have an I.D. on her but they aren't sure yet. Burton said her name was Monica something. Such a gentleman. He didn't even get her full name."

Gerry instantly looked embarrassed; he'd had a few un-gentlemanly moments of his own before he'd got married.

"And Monica was the name D.I. Cullen got from the caller at the garage, ma'am. Monica Gibson – except that she doesn't exist. Well, there is a Monica Gibson, but she's an eight-three-year-old nun from Derry. Anyway, whatever her name is they used a condom and she stole his semen."

Julia shuddered at the thought.

"I'm not sure stole is the word I'd use, Gerry, but her motive was dodgy that's for sure. I don't know which surprises me more, the fact that someone was desperate enough to sleep with Paul Burton or the fact that he had the sense to use a condom!"

Gerry laughed. "He said she insisted. He'd have preferred to go bare-back riding, as he so delicately put it."

"God, now I'll never watch a Western without that image in my mind."

Just then the phone rang and she grabbed it, glad to be rescued from a fuller discussion on the subject.

"Yes? That's brilliant. Where? OK, bring it to my office right now, please."

Gerry's silent query was answered a minute later when a young constable entered with something dark and square inside an evidence bag. It was Maria Burton's handbag. Julia donned a pair of gloves, opening the clear bag gently. The red-plastic handbag inside had been found half a mile downstream from Maria's body, with the badge and warrant card identifying its owner still inside, although not intact.

Maria Burton's warrant card had been cut in two, and her badge broken into several pieces, very deliberately. As if it hadn't been enough to steal her life but all trace of her office had to be destroyed too.

The only other article in the bag was a half-full bottle of cheap perfume, and suddenly the remnants of a young life loss overwhelmed Julia. Tears pricked urgently at her eyes and she stood up quickly, gesturing brusquely at Gerry to follow her outside, intent on using cigarettes and the weather to conceal her upset.

It was a gusty, drizzle-filled day and they huddled in the small alcove outside the back door. Julia turned her back to cover her tears, clicking repeatedly at her lighter against a wind that seemed determined to make her quit smoking. Finally, the cigarette caught light and she put it in her mouth, sucking gratefully at it in silence for a moment, only drawing it out reluctantly to breathe, her eyes streaming in the wind.

Finally, she turned to him.

"OK, so our killer is Belfast's killer and although she called herself Monica Gibson she's most probably Jessica Adams, married to Michael Adams. Michael Adams killed himself nineteen months ago over debts and his farm failing." She thought for a moment. "Have the C.S.I.s found any sign of the wire at the river yet?"

"No, but there's sixty kilometres to search."

She eyed him grumpily, not wanting to hear excuses.

"Jessica had access to the bolt-guns and wire found on the Adams' farm, the same type as the ones used in Belfast's case, and probably used on Maria Burton. OK?" Gerry nodded yes, knowing it was his only role in the conversation.

"She had access to Paul Burton's dead semen to frame him, but I don't think that was about incriminating him, I think it was about delaying us. I always said Burton didn't do it, remember?" She looked at him, needing reassurance, and he nodded.

"You always said he didn't do it, but why is *she* doing it? And why with so much violence? She could have just shot them. She has to be seriously warped to kill them in this way."

"Damaged, Gerry. She has to be damaged in some way. But I still can't see a motive. We haven't found any links between Maria Burton and the Adams' farm, and there's no link between McCandless and W.P.C Burton, or Adams. Has Belfast found anything?"

He shook his head, "No, not yet." She smiled, pleased, at least Craig hadn't beaten her to that.

Gerry decided to chance an opinion. "Setting up the rape might just have been staging, but it felt like hatred as well. And now with her warrant card..."

"Hatred." She thought for a moment, then her mouth fell open in realisation. "Of course."

"Of course what?"

"You're right, it *was* hatred. But it wasn't just hatred for Maria Burton. Gerry, you saw her handbag, that's why the badge was broken and her warrant card was cut up; it was as much hatred for her uniform as for her." She smiled smugly, "I bet Belfast haven't thought of that."

"So? What? The killer hates law and order?"

"Or maybe she feels it failed her somehow, failed her husband?"

Julia drew heavily on a new cigarette, blowing the smoke out in a funnel. Then completely without precedent, she threw the barely smoked stick on the ground. Ignoring the rain, she walked straight to the parking lot, clicking her car open as she walked.

"Come on."

"Where are we going?"

"To see if Maria Burton's family had anything to do with Michael Adams' death. And you're driving; I need to make a call. Belfast doesn't know it yet but they need our help."

****

Wharf House. 1 p.m.

Jessie's head was throbbing, and the noise from Saturday's Coronation Street's catch-up wasn't helping. She took a handful of the strong painkillers that Fiona had smuggled in that morning and looked at the photograph in her hand. The image danced in front of her, doubling at the edges so that Pia's face ran into Anya's arm. She shook her head hard, trying to focus. Her vision was definitely getting worse, but she couldn't stop now.

What had started as money for the girls had matured into something much deeper, and she had to get this right, to safeguard all their futures. She held her head in her hands until the edges of the photo sharpened and the room stopped spinning. Then she rose slowly, gripped the side table and pulled open her room's unlocked door.

The sound of the television blaring in the recreation room had drawn inmates and guards alike to the other end of the corridor. Becky had innocently told her that the place was always empty between one and one-thirty on Saturdays. Except for the few cool cynics who stayed in their rooms to do who knew what, while the guards allowed themselves to be distracted. That meant she had a maximum of thirty minutes for her task.

She moved as quickly as she was able, crossing the main lino-covered hall to the rooms on the other side, searching for the door bearing Lynsey Taylor's name. It was already half-open and as she walked casually past she could see the tired blonde from last night's meal sitting on the bed. She was sorting through a small tin box that Jessie immediately recognised as 'works'; an addict's box of tools.

The easily identifiable spoon and heater sat ready on the bedside table, and a thin rubber tourniquet was already wrapped around Taylor's upper arm.

Jessie walked past the room and reached into her pocket, extracting the plastic bottle of perfume she'd taken with her to the club. She very deliberately sprayed the glass eye of the floor's only camera from behind, playing for time not anonymity, and then turned purposefully, back towards Taylor's room.

The addict looked up suddenly as Jessie's blonde crop appeared at her door. She snarled aggressively and yanked down her sleeve. "What the fuck do yee want? Get outa here. Piss aff."

The words' hard edge gave Taylor's origins as Belfast, and rough Belfast at that. Jessie's country youth wouldn't allow her to pinpoint it any closer, but she knew that the woman in front of her definitely hadn't gone to finishing school.

Jessie ignored the barked order and grinned widely, pulling two small plastic bags from her pocket and dangling them tantalisingly in front of Lynsey Taylor's face. Fiona had surpassed herself; she should have been a smuggler for the amount of stuff she'd managed to bring in that morning.

As soon as she'd seen Taylor at dinner, she remembered her cruel insolence from years before. Her hollow eyes and long sleeves had confirmed Heroin as her drug of choice, so getting it into Wharf House was just the next, small step. Fiona had used the sources and hiding places that her husband had told her his school-kids used. They were always at it apparently; such a nice school he'd been a teacher in.

Jessie put on the hardest Belfast voice and grammar she possessed, with a look that she hoped was street enough, and moved un-invited into the small room.

"Soon as I seen you last night I knew."

Taylor glared at her.

"Knew what? Get out ya stupid bitch, yee'll have the screws down on us. I'm outa here next week and I'm not losing it for yee."

Jessie continued, undaunted. "I knew you was into smack, like me. So I brung you a sample to try. It's good stuff, honest ta Gawd."

"Fuck aff, it could be any 'aul shit. I'll stick tee my own. What's in it fer yee anyway?"

"You can do me favours on the outside. Spread the

word about my gear."

Taylor looked at her cagily but Jessie could see her curiosity taking over, so she laid the bags flat on the table, careful to keep one of them to the left. Then she reached into her pocket, withdrawing a tin box just like Taylor's, and sat down on the bed, pretending to hunt for veins in her own thin arms.

The thirst that drove all addicts focused Lynsey Taylor's eyes greedily on the bags. They were pillow-full of white, odourless powder. She looked at the brown mess already on her spoon, knowing that there would be no contest with the high that Jessie's smack would give.

"Is that 'fit'?"

Jessie nodded and watched the other woman's eyes glittering with excitement. 'Fit' meant top-grade Heroin, the ultimate high, and Jessie laughed inside at what she knew was coming next.

"Shut thon door an' pull the bolt across."

"How'd you get a bolt?"

Taylor grinned, showing yellowing, stained teeth. Jessie could feel revulsion welling-up in her throat, but she had a job to do.

"My friendly little screw. I scratch her back ..."

The image of all that meant flew through Jessie's mind but she shut it down immediately, focussing only on the two bags. She quickly grabbed the sugar–filled one on the left that Taylor was just about to reach for, ignoring the short, angry query in her eyes.

Hunger killed Taylor's questions in seconds and she drew the Heroin from the other bag onto her spoon, completing the ritual of preparation with a reverence that Jessie was sure she'd never shown at church or school.

Jessie watched her intently, her eyes urging her on but careful not to look too keen. The needle steeped itself in the warm liquid, the vacuum sucking it up into the clear, slim, syringe, while Taylor's vein bulged forward, eager for penetration and not disappointed in its wait.

She loosened the rubber tie and fell back onto the

bed as the chemicals hit her brain, her eyes immediately losing sight. The tourniquet fell off her arm, leaving the needle dangling over a stream of bloody liquid that leaked from her pale loose skin. Jessie held her breath, afraid to break the moment, only leaning forward gently to watch her victim's demise.

Taylor's breathing slowed and her pinpoint pupils fixed into small, black discs, filling her eyes with absence. Jessie watched for minutes that seemed like hours, until finally the air stilled, Taylor's pupils grew again and her pulse was gone. She quickly gathered the bags, re-instating the brown mess in her own clean spoon and removing all signs of the pure-grade death that Lynsey Taylor had just enjoyed, still feeling that it was too good for her.

She wiped the more obvious surfaces then, with one last look around the room, she pulled back the bolt and left the door as she'd found it, slightly ajar. She stared at the dead woman with a mixture of rejoicing and disgust and then walked calmly down the hallway towards the music of 'The Rover's Return'.

****

The Lab.

"Have you seen today's papers, Marc? You came off pretty well considering there've been two dead bodies in one week."

"That was Nicky's doing."

Craig answered John's quizzical look by relating how Nicky had saved his neck the day before. The pathologist laughed and turned back to his X-rays, pushing the Chronicle's morning edition across the desk.

The sketch of their Hoody was the paper's leader and Craig quickly scanned the three pages of story that followed. He lit on a paragraph where a 'senior Dissident source' denied that they would ever do anything as heinous as rape a young woman; as if blowing people apart somehow wasn't as bad! Still, at least they'd managed to get their message across.

"The problem is, John; what's the motive? If it is Jessica Adams doing the killings, then why?"

Craig didn't require an answer, just an audience. He was wandering around the large dissection room like a caged animal and John had seen it before during a case. It was as if he couldn't answer the why, or who, or what, unless he took some sort of physical action. And in the absence of someone to compete against, the athlete in him had to create movement somehow. So he prowled.

It had been the same at school. John reading quietly, while Craig, the school's golden boy in sport, and charm, and pretty much everything else, ran around the rugby field holding a book. It still amazed John that anyone could run and read but Craig's grades had proved it was possible, and thirty years later he was still prowling.

"Why are you here, John?"

"Is that an existential question, or do you mean why am I here on a Saturday?"

"Saturday."

"Catching up on paperwork, until you arrived."

He hit the switch on the coffee maker, grabbed his sandwich and sat down again at the desk, knowing that Craig would join him when the smell became strong enough. The perking and gurgling grew to a crescendo and just as the heat knocked the light off, Craig returned to his seat, as if he'd heard the faint click sixty-feet away at the end of the lab, which was impossible.

He continued talking as if they were still on the same sentence.

"Of course, if it *is* pure revenge, then why the need for such violation of both bodies? The petrol pump and the mock-rape were real overkill. Do you think the methods had any specific significance?"

John looked up from his cheese and pickle thoughtfully, wondering what Joe-Public would think if they knew how often crimes were solved over lunch.

"There was a case on C.S.I. once..."

Craig groaned and looked for something to throw at him.

"No, hear me out. It was a case where the killer wasn't killing for his own revenge; he was acting as some sort of hit-man, doing the Moscow Rules thing."

"Moscow what?"

You know, cold war assassins; two shots to the chest and one to the head. It's called the Moscow Rules and if you watched less sport, you'd know that. Anyway, maybe that's what this one's doing? Maybe she's a hit-woman?"

Craig rolled his eyes. "Great, thanks for that. Now we have a woman who, for no particular reason, decides to kill a man and a woman with no apparent links to her, but we don't know why anyone else wanted them killed either. And, by the way, she's about five-feet-four, skinny as hell, possibly ill and doesn't use a gun. Some hit-man. Tell me, if you wanted someone taken-out would that be your best bet?"

John refused to be deterred by Craig's sarcasm and kept going.

"Well, it's better than anything you've come up with. Have a coffee, there's a spare sandwich, and for God's sake Marc sit down – you're making me feel sick walking round in circles. Or go and find a football pitch."

Craig laughed and slumped in the proffered chair. John was right as usual and if he wasn't a mate that would be really irritating. Craig couldn't make any sense of things, so he supposed some sort of contract killing was as logical as anything else. John continued his theme between chews.

"Do you remember during The Troubles when they used to rent guns from the paramilitaries and use them for contract kills?"

"It was called 'signing out' and the going rate was five hundred quid."

"Allegedly. Anyway, I often wondered how many domestic killings were written off as sectarian. Five hundred pounds for a quickie divorce. You'd really have to hate your ex to do that, wouldn't you...?"

He stopped, suddenly realising what he'd just said, and bit harder into his sandwich while Craig fell silent. When they'd been kids, he had often offered academic solutions to Craig's occasional moods and confusions. But he'd learned years before, through a series of arguments and silences, that the best answer to anything personal was almost invariably: listen, say nothing and watch from a safe distance while Craig sorted it out himself.

He would take professional input gratefully, but personal advice, no-way. It had got ten times worse after Camille.

John had watched his friend's career trajectory closely over the years. Targeted by The Met's high potential scheme as soon as he'd joined up, Craig had made D.I. at twenty-seven and D.C.I. by thirty-five. Then, just as he should have been going for superintendent, Camille did her worst. Now, no matter how many times the Chief Constable pressured him, he wouldn't go for promotion. Camille had put out every spark he'd had.

Time to change the subject.

"Des says the wire matches the stuff Liam found at the farm. By the way, Annie had another little boy. They've called him Rafferty. Great name, don't you think?"

Craig nodded, glad of the change of theme. They descended into five minutes of banter that had Rafferty alternately growing up into James Bond, or the dashing artist, writer or adventurer that his name would undoubtedly force upon him. Craig imagined his first day at school; Marco had been a hard enough to cope with in Belfast, but Rafferty...

Suddenly his mobile rang, making them both jump. He answered it, staring at the screen. It was a number he didn't recognise.

"D.C.I. Craig?"

The voice that came through was female and hesitant, and not one he recognised. For one distracted second he thought that Jessica Adams was calling him, just as she'd called Ian McCandless' mobile. Then "it's Julia McNulty" came through and his heart sank even further. He didn't need grief from her today.

"Yes."

John's quick look told Craig that he was being brusque.

"Oh, sorry. If you're busy?" Too late, she'd realised that it was a Saturday, and that not everyone kept her hours.

"No, it's fine. What can I do for you?" Her hesitance softened him and his voice.

"Well. Perhaps it's a small thing, but Maria Burton's handbag has just been recovered and..."

She was having second thoughts and Gerry's old-fashioned look wasn't helping. She turned his chin back round to face the road.

What had seemed exciting back in the smoking area didn't seem quite so important now, until the sudden eager tone in Craig's voice said that perhaps it was.

"Yes?"

"Well, her warrant card was cut in two and her name badge was broken into small pieces, and it definitely wasn't trauma from the river because her perfume bottle's unbroken. I think they were damaged before the bag entered the river and...well, I just thought, they're symbols of the job and maybe justice somehow?"

It sounded weaker aloud than it had in her mind, but she kept going.

"As if they hated the police... maybe?"

Of course. Why hadn't he seen it? This was what everything was about. The badge, the warrant card, calling them at the garage on McCandless' phone. Hatred, contempt for law and order, all of it.

"Yes, D.I. McNulty. Yes!"

He was excited and it showed. At that moment he could have hugged her. "Thank you, that's very helpful – very."

John's puzzled look reminded him of something

else.

"Has your lab had a look at the bag yet?"

"No, it was only found this morning."

"Right, would you mind if we looked at it first then? We've a particular forensic trace that we'd like to match."

"Yes, absolutely." She was relieved and excited. He was taking it, and her, seriously. She was back in the game.

"I'll get it up to you this afternoon."

"Thank you." They clicked off at the same time and he turned to John. "You heard?"

"Only half of it. What?"

Craig filled him in quickly and then left for the C.C.U., praying that the single forensic trace he was hoping for would be all over Maria Burton's bag.

****

The C.C.U.

"I've talked to Jessica Adams' General Practitioner, but he w...wouldn't give me much. I just got the usual confidentiality clause, but he did drop a big hint that she doesn't have any contact w...with either of her parents."

Craig looked up from the file he was reading, interested. "Any idea why, Davy?"

Annette stood up at her desk and peered over her cubicle wall at them.

"Yes, why? They're definitely alive; they live in Spain somewhere. Wouldn't she have automatically taken the children to them after her husband's suicide?"

"Didn't s...someone else comment that she hated them?"

"You're right, Davy. It was the Barnardstown sergeant, Eamonn Ross. He said that there was no love lost with her parents, but Liam didn't say why. Right, Annette, ask Liam why and then follow it up with the local station. We need to know why Jessica Adams hates her family so much. Then call them in Spain and get their side of the story.

We'll have a final catch-up at three and then everyone can go home and come back fresh on Monday. I'll take anything else until then. We're all getting too tired to be effective."

He laughed dryly. "And for some strange reason it comforts me to believe that some of you have a life, even if I don't."

****

Wharf House.

The major incident alarm sounded just after Coronation Street ended and the women in the recreation room stared at each other glumly, knowing that it signalled hours of lock-down, no matter what the cause. Jessie had been playing cards with Becky and she threw down her hand in mock-disgust, grinning to soften the action.

"I was winning and don't you forget it. That's a lip-gloss you owe me."

Her charge smiled at her in hero worship, safe from the bullies while Jessie was nearby. Becky really wished that she wasn't being bailed tomorrow, but she seemed to have wealthy friends.

"Can we play again later...please?"

Jessie nodded, gazing at the younger woman. She'd defrauded some credit card company to escape a boyfriend who had hit her. Probation or helping out in an old folks' home would have been fair, not locking her up in here with addicts and murderers. Good old British justice, an all-round cock-up.

"Yeh, we'll play later. I need to win some mascara as well."

They laughed and shuffled out to join the lines of women already leaning against the four walls of the main floor. Jessie turned to the guard beside her, whispering. "What happened?"

She whispered back conspiratorially, half-smiling,

"Lynsey Taylor's overdosed."

Jessie feigned surprise and glanced down the line. The information had reached everyone quickly and no-one looked even slightly sad, one brave soul even venturing a muttered "good riddance."

Taylor had bullied the smaller girls and annoyed the guards by boasting how she'd played the system in court. Well, the system had caught up with her now all right. Even Becky felt brave enough to speak out.

"She was always picking on me and I'm glad she's dead. She hooked two of the younger girls on smack."

A vision of someone starting her own daughters on drugs flashed through Jessie's mind, and she'd happily have killed Lynsey Taylor again just for that. Her death felt like a personal bonus now.

An abrupt quiet fell over the room and the guards suddenly straightened up, tidying their hair. That meant only one thing; the Governor was on the floor.

The grey-metal outer door unlocked noisily and a strong-jawed woman strode into the centre of the gathering. She glared silently along the lines of women, the eyes of all but the most defiant dropping to the floor as she did. Satisfied of her complete control she turned towards Lynsey Taylor's room, standing just inside the door staring at the bed. She touched nothing and said nothing until she emerged, turning to face the restless women.

"Lynsey Taylor is dead. Her next of kin will be informed and there will be a post-mortem. It has been alleged that she was a Heroin user but we will be investigating this fully. I want anyone who saw anything unusual in any way today to inform the guards. In absolute confidence, of course."

Then she stared at them all for a moment, like a zoologist trying to name their species, before turning on her heel and walking off the floor so fast that Jessie bet she was rushing to disinfect herself.

As soon as she was out of sight, the once-timid girl beside her stepped forward, waving her arms above her head. "Taylor's dead." The floor erupted with whoops and hollers of celebration, so genuine that even a guard allowed herself a grin. Lynsey Taylor wouldn't be missed much by anyone at Wharf House.

****

The C.C.U.

"There were allegations that the father abused Jessica when she was young, sir, and the mother stood by him. There was nothing definite proved; child protection not being what it should have been back then. But it seems like a case of thirteen-year-old Jessica accusing Daddy, and Mammy telling her that she had a dirty little mind."

Davy sat forward, chipping in. "I called her parents and her father called her a liar. He said that they didn't care what happened to her, but they're determined to go for custody of her girls after s... she's caught."

Craig drew a hand down his face despairingly; child abuse was a story they heard with terrible frequency. This time it wasn't a member of the clergy involved, but it was just as bad in a different way; a mother who chose the father over the child, a crime against nature as well as a crime against Jessica Adams.

"What happened to her after she made the accusations, Annette?"

"As far as I can find out Jessica moved in with her best friend's family at fifteen and continued living locally until she left school. The friend was called Gemma Orr. Then she got a job in SuperMark in Limavady, met Michael Adams and the rest we know. The G.P. wouldn't say anything more. Do you want me to get a warrant for the records?"

"When did he last see her or her children?"

They all jumped suddenly as a loud klaxon sounded; a signal that information was coming through on Davy's system. He turned to the screen excitedly while Liam screwed up his face.

"What's that bloody noise, Davy? I know I asked you to get rid of the dog barking, but not to replace it with that. It's even worse."

"Sorry, Liam." The complete lack of contrition in Davy's voice almost made Craig laugh, but the analyst's obvious excitement cut through the urge.

"What have you got?"

"OK, you know I've been looking for anything that could give me Jessica Adams' recent movements and I've been hitting a brick w...wall. There have been no hits on her cards and her bank account's been completely inactive. I've been trying to find the children too, they're usually easier to trace; doctors records, immunisations, that type of thing. I reckoned that if s...she was as good a mum as everyone told us, then they'd have had every check."

"But surely she could have changed their names."

"It's actually not that easy. There's nearly always a trail in the U.K. and I've just found it. And interestingly, s...she *didn't* change their names. Maybe that goes along with her not trying to disappear completely, maybe just long enough to kill."

Craig waved him on. "What have you got?"

"Jessica Adams had another baby fourteen months ago. Pia Adams, born 5th August 2011." He said it triumphantly, with a well-deserved look of pride on his face.

"Oh God." Annette's voice broke and she looked horrified as the full depth of Jessica Adams' pain suddenly hit her.

Liam nodded slowly.

"That means she was already four months pregnant when the husband hanged himself, boss, which makes him an even more selfish bastard in my book. It certainly explains why she's gone off the deep end."

Annette agreed "It would be enough to push me over the edge. Poor girl, if she wasn't a murderer I would feel really sorry for her."

Craig nodded. It was typical; when nice people murdered there was usually some personal devastation as the trigger. But it was still no excuse.

"But she probably is a murderer, Annette. Although..."

He turned to the others.

"I still want Joey McCandless interviewed. He's hiding something. And let's find Gemma Orr. She might be able to throw more light on Jessica Adams' thinking."

Liam leaned over Annette's desk partition, looking as thoughtful as he ever could.

"Here, did the G.P. not mention the baby, Annette?"

"No, nothing. He only mentioned two children, and even then we had to drag it out of him on the basis that we needed to know in case they got hurt. I really don't think he even knew she'd had another baby."

"Well, she must have seen someone before this one was born. Danni's never away from the flipping antenatal clinic."

Craig nodded. "Liam's right. There must be a record of the birth, and the baby must have been registered. Davy, where did you find out about the baby?"

"S...She took her for vaccination last Tuesday, at Farren Lane baby clinic. It's in Belfast, about a mile away from McCandless' garage."

"OK, forget the G.P. for now; we can come back to him if we need to. Good work, Davy. Now see if you can get more on the baby. Antenatal, postnatal, birth registrations, earlier immunisations."

Liam nodded in sympathy. "Aye, they have about four immunisations in the first year alone – poor wee things."

"And you've done nothing but moan about your tetanus from Mrs Foster's cat, you big baby."

Craig continued. "Anything that gives us a clue where she's been in the past year. And if you can find us a home address then I really owe you."

Davy smiled; that meant something big; Craig paid his debts ten-fold.

"I'm going to speak to D.I. McNulty again, Liam, in the spirit of entente."

"But without very much of the 'cordiale'."

****

Stranmillis. 8 p.m.

Craig took another drink of his beer and flicked on the television, still thinking about the case. He'd been disappointed by another tense conversation with Julia McNulty, picking up where they'd left off about the handbag. He understood her hostility but he'd already had to bollock her twice this week, the second for her treatment of Annette, so he really thought that she would have learnt by now. She'd been marginally more polite, although as Liam had anticipated, still not cordial.

He was curious about her but he didn't know why, except that something must have happened to make her so aggressive; no-one was born fighting the world that way. He contrasted McNulty's macho approach with Lucia's sunny younger-child cool. If he hadn't been ten when Lucia was born, he'd have been tempted to say that personality was nurture not nature, but he remembered her being the same in the cradle. Even as a sulky teenager he'd hardly resented baby-sitting her. No, D.I. McNulty definitely had some issues.

He shrugged, not really caring, and surfed the channels until he found some football. Then he switched off his thoughts completely, to spend a blissful Saturday evening undisturbed by murder, or women.

Chapter Thirteen

It was Sunday afternoon by the time Jessie's bail was posted. She gathered her few possessions together and waved good-bye to a smiling Becky, far safer now that Lynsey Taylor was dead.

She stepped out through Wharf House's open gate, her hands full of written warnings about breaching bail, and walked slowly towards Fiona's newly purchased Prius, parked at the end of the driveway. Two fair, tousled heads were clearly visible in the back seat.

Her left leg had been dragging slightly since that morning so she climbed awkwardly into the passenger side, kissing Fiona lightly on the cheek and answering her hopeful glance with a single nod. Fiona relaxed visibly, taking her hand in gratitude. "Thank you, Jessie."

Jessie half-turned to face her three pretty daughters, relaxing into her own soft accent after days of pretending harder Belfast vowels.

"Have you all been good girls for Fiona?"

The high chorus of "Yes, Mammy" made any memory of her recent mission disappear.

"And did Fiona tell you where we're going now?"

"No, Mammy." Anya's eager six-year-old face gazed up at her, smiling; her imagination of sweet shops far surpassed by Jessie's next words. She smiled gratefully at Fiona for letting her tell them.

"Well... you know Fiona has packed your little travelling bags, just like Mammy's?"

"Yes, yes. Where are we going, Mammy? Where are we going?"

"Where would you like to go, pet?"

It was directed at Anya, but she looked at her four-year-old sister for guidance, always deferring to Ruby's stronger personality. Ruby was a natural leader, just like Michael had been, so when she yelled, "Disneyland, Disneyland," the two of them jumped up and down, bouncing Pia's rocker in unison. Pia laughed, enjoying the game.

"We'll go to Disneyland soon, pet, but not for a few more days, because ..."

"Yes, yes, where, where?"

"This weekend we're going to... Sunny Days Play Camp.

Excited squeals and chants of "Sunny Days, Sunny Days, Sunny Days" filled the car as Fiona drove down the gravelled lane, turning left for the journey south and intent on breaking Jessie's bail.

Jessie looked at her. "Can you bear a bit more noise?" Fiona nodded, awaiting the next explosion.

"And then in a few more days... we'll really be in... Disneyland! All thanks to Fiona."

Her last three words were completely drowned out by squeals of pleasure, as their high voices and Pia's gurgles jumbled into a tangle of 'Snow White', 'Mickey Mouse' and 'Sleeping Beauty' for the next few miles, until they finally sat back, happy and exhausted.

Jessie handed them the books hidden earlier in the glove box, so they could colour in pictures of all the things they were soon going to see, and they headed for the motorway. She rested her head back against the seat for the long trip to Dublin, remembering happy times with Michael and letting the tension that she'd been carrying for the past week seep out of her. Then she fell into a deep dream of her final target and the life beyond him. But before that, she dreamt of the next two days when she would get to be a mother again.

****

Limavady. Monday.

Julia scrolled through her Monday morning e-mails, trying to focus, but she still couldn't clear the image of Maria Burton's mother from her mind, after a weekend of trying. No matter how tough they all believed the job had made them, it was a lie. A lie they told themselves to be professional, and as protection to deal with their guilt when they didn't catch the bad guys. But it always collapsed when you had to tell a parent that their child was dead, no matter what age that child was, and that had been her job just days before. She could still hear the screams.

What do you say when someone screams "Why, why, why?" for ten minutes. Not pausing for breath and with thick tears streaming from their eyes so fast that they drip into their mouth, making them choke, as if they might suffocate in their own pain. What do you say when they ask you. "How did they die?"

Do you say "Please don't ask me, because you'll never forget the words I say" or "it's better if you don't know, because the images will haunt you to your grave?"

Better not to know. Better only to see the face of your child clean and calm in the viewing room, and believe they had a peaceful end. Not the skull-crushing, air-gasping reality of it. Not the indignity and violation of it. Not the fact that even if we catch their killer, nothing will give you justice or compensate. That no form of execution, even if it existed here, would ever hurt them as much as they've hurt you, or condemn them to the hell you're in.

Please don't ask me to tell you how they killed your lovely daughter by the water that she loved to walk beside, her love of nature engendered by the way you brought her up. So that you're going to ask yourself every day "What if we hadn't owned a farm? Then maybe she would never have been outside admiring the morning, walking by the river that drowned her?"

Please don't ask me.

But those were her needs, not theirs, so she had answered whatever they'd asked her, however many times. Now she would help them to deal with the images that her words had created, images that would live with them for the rest of their lives.

****

The C.C.U.

"Right. OK, I want to go over everything again."

They were crammed into Craig's office. Craig pacing, Annette and Nicky sitting at the desk, and Liam and Davy leaning like bookends against the wall.

"We have someone, most probably Jessica Adams, who killed Maria Burton and framed Burton's husband for rape. We know she was the woman who slept with Paul Burton and took his semen, using it at Maria Burton's scene to mislead us. Burton's got a solid alibi so they've had to release him, but he gave us a description of a very thin female about thirty years old, with long brown hair and no distinguishing marks except for a pierced navel."

"Trendy farmer's wife."

Nicky leaned forward, agreeing with Annette. "That's exactly what I thought. Piercings are more East Belfast than East Derry."

Liam was about to say something rude, but Craig ignored him and moved on.

"Maria Burton was definitely tripped up, as confirmed by the same knee and hand abrasions as those found on Ian McCandless. She also had the same razor-sharp cuts on her shins that he had. And although no wire has been found yet at any point along the river, the cuts on both Burton and McCandless' shins match exactly with the sample of flat razor-wire that Liam found at Michael Adams' farm.

Their skull damage and the location of their head injuries also match. Both fractures match a captive bolt, and a bolt-gun of the same type and manufacturer was missing from the set that the C.S.I.s found at the Adams' farm. Both victims were hit where the skull-bone was thin and the blow was most likely to kill them. Which thankfully it did immediately with Maria Burton, but unfortunately, it didn't with Ian McCandless who eventually drowned in petrol."

He paused for a sip of coffee then restarted.

"But I believe that McCandless' petrol pump and fire scenario was just as much staging as Maria

Burton's rape – done purely to misdirect and delay us."

"Although bloody vicious, boss, so that tells us something as well."

Craig nodded at Liam in agreement. Yes it did.

"I don't think the killer delayed us just to evade capture. They delayed us to play for time. They didn't really mind us finding their fingerprints because, although they haven't finished yet, I believe that our killer feels that they have nothing to lose, which makes them very, very dangerous. There's a link between Maria Burton, Jessica Adams and Ian McCandless, I'm sure of it. But even if Jessica Adams *is* our killer, her choice of victims may not link them directly to her."

They stared at him, puzzled, until he told them about John's throwaway hit-man remark, and one by one, they slowly nodded agreement. Annette was the first to speak.

"That makes sense, sir. Just imagine that you're a young widow with no money and three children to feed, you've no family to turn to and you're only skilled as a wife and mother. Remember that Adams only worked for two years before she got married so she had no real work experience or training in anything else. How do you get a job that pays enough to feed them? Then you see a way to make money by killing people on someone else's behalf, sort of a gun for hire. She'd already lived on a farm where they slaughtered cattle, so maybe killing didn't seem so bad to her?"

A sudden thought struck Craig. "Davy, did anything come through on the searches at the weekend?"

Davy shook his head, embarrassed, as if his computers had let him down like naughty children.

"Nothing yet. They've covered their tracks pretty w...well so far."

Liam asked a question.

"If she's really a hit-man then why not just use a simple weapon like a gun, boss? Why all this violence? Could it be mental illness?"

It was a valid point. Why *not* just use a gun? Or did she need the victims to suffer more than a gun would cause?

"And just say she needs money to support her children, then what happens to them if she's caught? She will be eventually. She's not covering her tracks very well, just enough to play for time, so she doesn't seem to care if she's caught in the end. Then the children will end up in care and that definitely doesn't fit with her being a loving mother."

Annette nodded furiously.

"Or her parents might claim them, and if she has three little girls she'll be desperate to keep them away from her father if he's a paedophile. And all the money in the world couldn't guarantee that the courts wouldn't give them custody."

Craig topped up everyone's drinks, thinking.

"You're all correct, there's something more here. One possibility is that we have Jessica Adams, a mentally unstable killer, killing for money to protect her kids. But for some reason needing to inflict severe pain and suffering as well as kill, so she doesn't use a clean weapon like a gun, even though it would make much more sense given her small stature.

And if she's really killing to protect her kids then why leave prints that might lead to her being caught eventually, leaving the kids she loves to grow up without her, possibly even with a paedophile grandfather? Of course, if she's unstable she may not be thinking this through as logically as we are."

He raked his hair. "Or else this hit-man theory is all complete rubbish."

Liam jumped in.

"The suffering was an important part of the hits, boss, I'm sure of it. Someone, maybe Adams and maybe not, wanted the victims punished as well as killed. Yes, it also helped to send us in the wrong direction for a while, but they could have done that some other way. I'm certain the torture was part of the kill. Maybe Maria Burton wasn't meant to die instantly. Maybe Adams had even more suffering planned for her – like drowning her in the river. And maybe McCandless' drowning was intentional. Either way she's not finished yet."

They all nodded in agreement; Liam was right.

Craig summarised. "OK, if we find the link between her first two victims, hopefully we'll find her next target in time to stop her. Davy, find that link please. I want you to run two searches together. One just for links between Maria Burton and Ian McCandless. Leave Jessica Adams out of that one in case she's killing on someone else's behalf, and you're already running the second search with her included.

Annette, you interview Joey. Liam, chase up on Adams' parents – it's a long shot, but see if they can think of anyone she cared enough about to kill for."

Just then Craig's mobile rang. He picked it up quickly, listened, and then clicked it off with a quick "Thanks, John" turning back to them with a triumphant smile.

"OK, what I didn't tell you was that Maria Burton's handbag was retrieved from the Bann on Saturday and they sent it to us for forensics."

"Here, why didn't they just do it themselves? They have a lab."

Craig ignored the remark, knowing that Liam was just winding him up.

"I asked them to send it up." He paused for a second. "Maria Burton's warrant card had been deliberately cut in two and her badge broken into several pieces."

Annette gasped, this was real hatred. Davy just looked puzzled.

"By the river current?"

"No, not the river – her perfume bottle was unbroken and the river couldn't have cut the warrant card. It was deliberate: disrespect, anger, something."

"Against the police?"

He nodded. "Or against authority, justice, whatever. Anyway, I asked John to look for one particular forensic trace and he's just found what I hoped he would." His look was almost smug.

"What? Put us out of our misery, chief."

"He found Purecrem on W.P.C. Burton's warrant

card."

The looks on their faces said it all.

"The river hadn't washed the cream away. The handbag was plastic with lots of compartments, so the water didn't get at the inner ones as much, and that's where the warrant card was."

"That means Burton's and McCandless' killer is definitely the same person. Jessica Adams."

"Yes, and I want you to run a new cross-check, Davy. This one should include links to anything and everything to do with the Criminal Justice system."

****

The Oaks Hotel near Dublin.

Jessie opened her eyes slowly and stared sluggishly around the large, expensively furnished room, disoriented for a moment. They changed location so often these days that she had to rely on Fiona to keep her straight. But it definitely wasn't Wharf House and that was all that really mattered.

Slowly she remembered that Fiona had booked them into a hotel two miles from the holiday camp, so that the girls could enjoy the games and rides, without her having to cope with the noise at night.

She smiled down at her feet. Ruby had made her bed at the bottom of hers last night and Fiona had wisely left her there, covering her with a warm blanket. She was lying across the duvet with her thin pyjama arms wrapped protectively round her shins. As Jessie reached down for her, the daylight illuminated tears streaking her small cheeks.

Jessie gazed at her middle daughter sadly, wondering how much these little girls really knew of what lay ahead. She drew her numb fingers gently through Ruby's fair curls, as fine and soft as Michael's had been. She was perfect, all of them were, and she knew again that she was doing the right thing. She would kill again to protect her children, as often as she needed to.

****

Limavady.

Gerry smiled and started his elevenses. The boss had been in a better mood since D.C.I. Craig had taken her seriously on Saturday, despite their second visit to the Burton's farm showing that Maria Burton definitely hadn't known Jessica Adams nee Atkinson. She'd never even issued her with a littering fine.

There was no connection between the two women but the chief was still grinning like a Cheshire cat, and smoking less as well. He'd just put Belfast's lab through to her, so he sincerely hoped that this morning's good mood wouldn't be killed off by the call.

Her office door flew open noisily and he heard her high-heeled footsteps tapping down the hall towards him. "Gerry –where are you?"

He stuck his head out of the coffee-room's door, almost colliding with her.

"What are you doing in there?"

"Fixing my car."

Julia ignored his dry wit but he could see from her face that she'd had more good news. Happy days. At least that meant fewer cig breaks. It was bucketing down outside and he could do without catching another cold.

"Belfast has just rung to thank us."

She paused as if waiting for a round of applause, so he shot her a quick question to keep her happy.

"Really, ma'am–what did they say?"

"They said that Maria Burton's handbag contained traces that conclusively linked her murder to their man in the garage; it's some sort of nappy cream." She looked as puzzled as he felt.

"And..." Cue silent drum roll. "That they will be liaising with us extensively in the next week. So what do you think of that?"

Gerry knew better than to take the piss, although the urge was truly enormous. Instead he said.

"Well, I think that between his sperm and their

nappy cream, we've finally bottomed out." Before she could say anything he quickly handed her a mug.

"And that calls for a cup of tea."

****

"Liam, I've got Joey McCandless arriving in ten minutes. Tell the boss that I'll be back for the briefing."

Just then, the phone rang and Annette answered it, listening and ending with. "Room three, please. Give him a cup of tea and I'll be down in five."

She turned quickly to Davy. "Davy, that's Joey in now. Just before I see him, was there anything on his father's computer linking him to children?"

"Nothing, completely clean, and nothing on his background checks either. I really don't think there's anything there, Annette."

"Thanks, but Joey's still lying about something."

And she left to find out what.

****

Wharf House. 1.30 p.m.

"This is a shambles, Agnew. I can't have people using drugs in my prison and I certainly can't have them overdosing." Governor Elizabeth Steele was glaring at the guard standing in front of her, her forefinger prodding angrily at the open file on her desk.

"The pathologist's report clearly states that Taylor suffered respiratory arrest, due to a massive overdose of high-grade Heroin. The powder found in her room was almost ninety percent pure! Where in God's name, did a twenty-one-year-old from the Demesne council estate get the money to buy that? And how did it get past five guards and three visitors' checks into her veins? Not to mention where did the syringe and needles came from. Well?"

Beads of sweat had gathered on Eve Agnew's forehead and were now dripping gently down towards her brows. She brushed them away hastily with the back of her freckled hand and swallowed hard.

"With respect, ma'am; you know the prisoners are very adept at concealing things. And even with all our checks, visitors can be tricky, and..."

"Yes? What?"

"Well..." she hesitated.

"Well, what?"

"There's some word amongst the women that Taylor wasn't well liked, so..." She swallowed again, deciding whether to be hung for the whole sheep or not, then she shrugged inwardly, continuing.

"There's also some feeling that this might not have been an accident, ma'am."

Steele stood up abruptly, throwing her full size-sixteen frame into focus against the window behind her, her powdered, round face darkening with anger.

"Are you suggesting that she was murdered? In my prison?" Her voice rose with every word until 'my prison' was almost shouted across the desk at the hapless Agnew. She continued at the same volume.

"You'd rather believe that Taylor was murdered than accept you were negligent. It's your job to see that they don't conceal things. It's your job to see that rooms are searched regularly, so that even if things do get into the prison, they're found before they can do any harm. And it's your job to identify addicts and get them into rehabilitation, not to turn a blind eye to their habit, allow them bolts on their doors, and enable high-grade Heroin to kill them!"

She paused, sucking in breath for her next onslaught.

"And it's my job to get answers, and answers I will get, Officer Agnew, make no mistake. Like her or like her not, Lynsey Taylor was twenty-one years old, due out next week and she was in our care. Her family have lodged an official complaint and heads will roll."

She fixed her narrowed eyes directly on the sweating woman in front of her.

"And I can tell you, that Governor or no Governor, it certainly won't be mine."

****

They'd been sitting looking at each other for the best part of an hour, while Joey McCandless answered each of Annette's questions with silence, or lies, or guilt. If she hadn't seen all sorts of grief-reactions in nursing, she'd probably have just left it at that and charged him, on his lack of alibi for the time his father was murdered. Except that she had seen them.

She knew that the boy in front of her couldn't have murdered his father; he'd loved him too much. Her maternal instinct told her he didn't have it in him to murder a spider, never mind a human being. He'd have been a 'lift them out the window to freedom' type of little boy, like her own son.

But he was lying about where he'd been and Annette knew it, and she'd absolutely no intention of interviewing sixty students from his bloody improvisation class just to prove it. She was already losing the will to live even imagining all their luvvie drama during the interviews.

Maternal instinct or not she'd had enough of Joey's silence now and she was gasping for a cup of tea, so she pressed the tape-machine button so hard that he rewarded her by jumping. It was a real interview now.

"For the benefit of the tape, this is Monday the twenty-second of October two thousand and twelve, interview commencing at one-fifty pm. Present are Detective Sergeant Annette McElroy and..."

Silence.

"For the tape please, Mr McCandless."

Joey looked across at her with wet eyes and nodded. "Joey McCandless."

"Please acknowledge your full name and address for the tape, Mr McCandless." Her voice had hardened with each word and he suddenly looked so frightened that she felt a flicker of guilt. Suppressing it, she held her severe pose through the next short silence, while Joey McCandless stared first at her and then at the machine, as if they were both his enemy.

Finally, in a high tenor voice, he croaked, "Joseph

McCandless of twelve a River Road."

"Mr McCandless has kindly agreed to have an informal chat with me. No charges have yet been brought and he has waived his right to counsel or companion. Could you please confirm this for the tape, Mr McCandless, and confirm that you're content to have this meeting recorded."

"Yes..." Then, even more quietly, as tears started to flow freely down his cheeks. "I'll tell you everything. I really can't hide it anymore."

And Annette was as certain as breathing, that what he was about to reveal wouldn't be a confession of murder, but something that he imagined was even worse. It would be the real source of everything: his false alibi, the guilt that she'd heard in his voice, and the guilt that he was even more ashamed of admitting now. That he was almost glad his father was dead, so that he would never know the truth about his youngest son.

****

3 p.m.

"Where's Annette?" Craig had emerged from his office and was perched on Davy's empty desk, ready to start the briefing. It was Liam who answered.

"Downstairs with Joey McCandless. She'll be back soon. Here, there's some interesting stuff on that bolt-gun, boss."

"Hold that until Annette gets here, Liam. We'll stay out here. Everyone grab a coffee and let's start."

Just then, Annette hurried in, dropping the file she'd been carrying on her desk. She quickly lifted a cup of tea and a biscuit before sitting down heavily beside Craig.

"You look as if that wasn't fun?"

"No, it wasn't. The reason Joey's been so cagey is because he thinks he's gay, that's why he hadn't told anyone at the nursing home about his 'girlfriend'. He was off at some counselling session when his dad was killed. Personally, I don't see what his problem is. If he's gay, he's gay. It's twenty-twelve for goodness sake. But actually, I don't think he's gay at all. I saw him checking out the secretary on the second floor and he wasn't admiring her fashion sense, not unless she keeps it in her breasts."

They all burst out laughing and Annette realised what she'd just said, suddenly embarrassed.

"I can't believe I said that! Working here is turning me into a bloke. But you know what I mean? I think Joey thinks he might be gay because he's arty. Anyway, he definitely felt that he couldn't talk to his dad about it."

She looked at Craig and Liam thoughtfully.

"Maybe one of you two could have a word with him?"

Liam leaned forward eagerly.

"No. Better not, Liam. You'd just hand him a copy of Loaded and a pack of condoms."

She turned towards Craig. "Sir?"

Craig swallowed so hard that he nearly choked; sex counselling a teenager was definitely beyond him. "I'll ask John to have a chat." He blushed and changed the subject quickly. "Right, Liam, what do you have on the bolt-gun?"

Davy had just joined them and he leaned forward curiously. "W...What did you find out?"

"Just a wee thing. The bolt isn't actually meant to kill cattle."

Craig scanned the room quickly for Nicky, relieved that she wasn't there.

"OK, quickly. Before Nicky hears about the cattle again."

"Well, it's not supposed to kill them, just stun. Then they're secured in harnesses or pens for their throats to be cut."

"Oh God, Liam. That's way too much information."

"No, but don't you see, it's better. That means that maybe Jessica Adams thought she was throwing Maria Burton in alive, to drown..."

"Which is worse if anything."

"No, but it means that she really doesn't know her own strength. Instead of placing the bolt lightly against the skull to stun her, she pressed so hard that she fractured Burton's skull and killed her. McCandless' skull was fractured as well, but maybe he didn't die immediately because it was thicker?"

Annette stared at him incredulously. "Exactly how is this better?"

"Yes, Liam, that means she *meant* to drown them, so Maria Burton was just lucky that she died before she drowned. It's still evil, in fact more so."

Davy came to the D.I.'s rescue. "Liam, do you mean that this demonstrates the killer didn't know her own s...strength?"

Liam looked confused for a second and then realised he had a lifeline. "Oh...aye, Davy, aye. That's exactly what I meant."

Annette gave a sceptical snort, but Craig was interested now, and he'd also decided to save Liam's face.

"Whatever way you cut it, she's just plain bad. But this idea of untempered strength is something that John was going to look into for me, and I'd completely forgotten to chase him on it. So thanks, Liam, and all of you, that's a real help."

****

10 p.m.

Jessie cautiously removed the violet-blue leaves from the bag that had held them for months, wearing the extra-thick gloves that Fiona had bought for her. Then she placed them in the small pestle, grinding down hard until they'd disappeared. She squeezed every drop of liquid from their beauty before emptying it into a small phial, then she tied the remnants in several separate bags for disposal, so that no-one innocent could be hurt. That would never do.

Now she had everything ready for her final task. Jeans and trainers and hair clips, the phial and new gloves. And, most important of all, her fake pass. She went to bed and fell asleep quickly, with a last idle thought that her prints would be in the system now. They'd taken them after her arrest and again in Wharf House, so they would match her to the murders eventually, not that it mattered now.

It didn't matter if or when she was caught just as long as it was after tomorrow, although she would rather not be caught at all. But the police couldn't hurt her any more than life had already, and whatever happened to her, soon no-one would be able to harm her daughters or Fiona ever again.

Chapter Fourteen

Wharf House. Tuesday, 10 a.m.

"The Government party is at the front gate, ma'am. You asked me to tell you."

"Thank you, Aoife; I'll be there in one minute. Is Doctor Regan on hand for the meeting after the tour?"

"Yes, ma'am. I've lunch arranged in the board room for one o'clock."

Elizabeth Steele nodded her young assistant out kindly and stood up, straightening her brown suit and smoothing its A-line skirt down with her ringed right hand. She told anyone who asked her that she'd hurt her wedding finger; it wasn't their business that Bill had left her the year before, for a primary school teacher even older than her.

He couldn't cope with her job, or as he'd put it. "I can't cope with the Elizabeth that the job has created." She shrugged; equality of pay and opportunity were one thing, but men's expectations still had a way to go.

She checked her coral lipstick quickly in the small mirror behind the door, then pulled her shoulders back and left her office, fixing on the smile that would see her through. Through the cool looks of the men in grey suits, and the long and pointless tour of the facility; stopping pointedly in silence at Lynsey Taylor's empty, taped-off cell. Through the inevitable grilling afterwards and through the lunch of crust-less sandwiches and awkward silences that would pass for a first enquiry into the demise of an inmate, but which would really start the slow death of her thirty-year career.

****

Belfast.

Jessie stirred the soup slowly and pushed her paper

hat back with her free hand, gazing cynically around the large canteen kitchen. She remembered her Aga and Le Creuset at the farm; she'd held wonderful dinner parties once. Cooking with Michael for hours, preparing everything and then disappearing upstairs to get ready together, but getting naked instead before their guests arrived. She thought of him often and was able to smile at the memories now, finally forgiving him for leaving them. They would have lost each other soon in any case.

She kept stirring, watching as several hot containers were lifted and placed behind her on the long serving counter. She pretended to take care not to burn her hands, as if she could actually feel the heat. The chubby catering manager wandered over to her.

"You wanted to be on hot food today, didn't you, Monica?"

"Yes, if that's OK? I'm a bit cold. It'll warm me up."

"You're too thin, girl. You need some weight on you. OK, everyone, the doors will open in five minutes, so can everybody change your aprons and stand behind there."

She indicated the serving counter with its heated canopy and then walked to the entrance, straightening her apron and unlocking the door of the high-ceilinged staff canteen for lunch.

Jessie fingered the small phial in her pocket, a last little gift from the farm she had loved; then she got ready to serve and waited for a particular man to ask for her hot food.

****

The C.C.U. 1.45 p.m.

"Has anyone seen Liam?" Craig half-shouted the question across the floor.

"I saw him about twelve-thirty, sir. He was going for lunch, then onto the lab to check something with Des."

Davy nodded. "I s...saw him in the canteen queue at

a quarter to one."

"I'm just back from the lab and I didn't see him. By the way, I meant to tell you, Des has a son." He looked proud of himself for knowing. "But he hasn't done him any favours with his name."

"What is it?"

"Rafferty."

The look on Davy's face said it all.

"All I can say is I hope he doesn't have a s...stutter like me. Davy's bad enough but he'd be there all day on that one."

Annette hit him fondly on the knee. "I think Rafferty's a lovely name. He could grow up to be an actor or something famous."

"He'll need to."

"That's just what John said."

Craig leaned backwards over the desk he was perching on and lifted the telephone, hitting the connection for the lab. One ring later, Des Marsham lifted the phone. Craig put it on speaker. "Hi Des, congrats on the baby. A little boy I hear"

"Yes." There was so much pride in his voice that Craig could practically see him standing with his chest puffed out.

"We called him Rafferty. It has a certain something, hasn't it?"

Annette put her hand over Davy's mouth while Craig diplomatically agreed.

"Yes, it certainly does." He wasn't going to be drawn on what that certain something was.

"Des, is Liam with you?"

"No, in fact he was due here at one-thirty but he hasn't showed. I assumed he'd been called to a new scene or something. He wanted to discuss something about the bolt-gun and wire matches."

The mood in the office suddenly changed to one of alert. There was no new scene.

Annette grabbed the phone on her desk and immediately rang Liam's mobile, shaking her head at Craig as it rang out. Des was silent for a moment, noticing Craig's sudden change of mood.

"Has something happened, Marc? Where's Liam?"

There was no need to take away from Des' new-father joy, so Craig fudged his response, intent on ending the call cheerfully,

"Oh, you know Liam; he'll be following a lead and forgot to tell anyone. I'll get him to call you and rearrange your meeting. Thanks, Des, and congratulations again." He dropped the line quickly, desperate to get away.

Annette was already calling Danni, formulating a question that would locate Liam without terrifying her. "Hi Danni." They couldn't hear her response and Craig motioned her to put it on speakerphone. Annette made her voice as casual as possible, keeping the tone conversational. The last thing Danni needed at six months pregnant was to be frightened.

"Is Liam there, by any chance? Only he said that he might pop in to collect something he'd left."

"Hi, Annette. No, he's not here. How are you?"

"Fine. And Erin?"

"Into everything as usual. Liam didn't say anything to me about coming home today. Mind you, he might have and I've just forgotten. My head's like a sieve with this baby. He must've decided he didn't need it, whatever it was. Will we see you and the kids for the Halloween party? I've promised Erin the works this year, now she's old enough to understand."

"Yes, I'm looking forward to it. And Amy says if you ever want a baby sitter, she's desperate for pocket money, 'cos I'm such a mean mum. OK, thanks, Danni. See you soon. Bye."

Craig nodded as she dropped the phone gently. No answer from Liam's mobile, he'd missed the meeting with Des and he wasn't at home. Something was definitely wrong.

"Right, the last time he was seen was at twelve-forty-five in the canteen. Nicky and I will go down there and start looking. Davy, get the close circuit TV tapes of all exits from the building and see if he left. Annette, go down and speak to the security detail, ask if anyone they didn't recognise came in or out in the past two hours. Check the sign-in logs and get them to start a floor-to-floor search. Liam's here somewhere."

He saw their anxious looks and tried to reassure them, "Don't worry, he's too big for anyone to hide." But it was too late; John's hit-man suggestion was already running through their minds.

****

It had all gone perfectly again, and through her drugged haze Jessie thought that perhaps she'd missed her true vocation in life. She really should have been an assassin. Well, maybe next time round.

The small sensible part that was the old Jessie was horrified by the thought, but she was getting weaker all the time. Drowned in the cocktail of drugs and poison seeping through her system, until the edges of what was real blurred more every day. The only truth she had now was Fiona and the girls.

He'd walked into the canteen at twelve-forty on the dot; tall and ghostly. Her eyes had fixed on him and stayed there. She couldn't drag them away. She had pictured his face for five years, long after the others had faded. He should have helped the victims, he was the professional. But he hadn't helped, letting barrister-engineered sentiment sway him instead.

He'd moved slowly up the queue, a head higher than the others, laughing loudly with the man behind him, obviously liked and unavoidably visible. Several people greeted him with "Hi Liam" and "Hey Whitey", so that even if she hadn't already recognised him, she soon would have done.

But she'd known him all right: that voice and height, and arrogance. She'd planned to enjoy this one. Fiona deserved this one. He had pretended to be on Fiona's side until the very end, and then he'd been just as weak as the rest.

She'd waited patiently, glowing in the heat and smiling, until he'd finally stood in front of her and she had stared straight at him. She'd looked for some sign of recognition in his eyes, some vague idea of who she was, but there was nothing. Just a throwaway "Beef stew... and plenty of chips, love." Signing his own death warrant as he turned his attention to a passing W.P.C.

Ladling the stew carefully into the centre of the plate she'd created a small crater, and then turned away briefly, saying "Just getting some nice fresh chips for you, sir. A fine big man like you needs his food" sickened by his half-flirtatious grin in response.

She'd turned away just long enough to flick the cap off the phial and empty its contents deep into the crater. Stirring it in as she added the chips, so that every morsel on the plate was filled with fatal goodness. Then she'd handed it to him, unable to resist a garnish of extra chips on top.

She'd watched him as he took it, not even looking at his killer. Merely throwing a careless "Thanks, love" over his shoulder, as she'd coolly changed her ladle and gloves and served the next order.

She'd watched him as he ate and talked, deliberately leaving her counter to clear the tables close by. Watching and wiping as he'd started to sweat and then suddenly excused himself. She'd smiled as she'd tidied and folded and scrubbed; clearing his plate, first into a plastic bag and then into her rucksack. Then she'd changed without hurrying and left the other girls with a cheery wave. "See you tomorrow", except of course she wouldn't see them tomorrow, and neither would Detective Inspector Liam Cullen.

****

Liam had never experienced anything like it before. Not when he'd been knocked down by a joy-rider in eighty-four, or shot in eighty-nine and rushed in an ambulance to St Mary's. A young female doctor had pummelled his chest and kissed him then, but he'd been too out of it to enjoy himself.

They'd said he'd died for seven minutes that time, and he vaguely remembered his dad standing there, back from the grave they'd put him in twenty years before. Him and some jazz playing, and he really hated jazz. That was bad, but nothing had ever felt like this. This was a very different sort of trip.

The food had tasted fine but logic dictated now that it couldn't have been. He just knew that he had to get to the bathroom. Cold sweat was dripping wholesale down his face and he could feel his heart beating hard and then slowing, the dropped beats becoming too frequent to count.

He felt sick, but not a normal sickness. This was a deep burning inside his face and chest and a terrible tingling over his arms and thighs, and then no air for breathing.

He collapsed on the hard, frozen floor of the cubicle with thoughts of the mundane; how cold the floor was, how clean the toilet looked, how cubicles were so much bigger nowadays. There were small explosions inside him; each tiny cell swelling and bursting, pouring their contents out like acid, corroding each muscle and vein. Turning the walls and ceiling and lights above him into one stream of white. Until Liam finally stopped thinking and a dark peace descended, forcing him to rest.

****

Julia had been composing her speech all the way up the M22. "I realise we may have got off on the wrong foot, D.C.I. Craig."

No, that was way too grovelling.

"I think there are ways that we could help each other with our investigations."

Maybe – at least it was less subservient, more like equals. But then, he was a D.C.I. and she wasn't, so they weren't equals. And she respected rank, grudgingly, but she did, so maybe a bit of grovelling wouldn't go amiss.

Oh bollocks, she'd decide what to say when she got there. With a bit of luck he'd be out anyway and she could just leave a message. Then he would have to contact her.

****

"Annette, anything from security?"

"Nothing, sir. No-one but the usual staff in or out all day."

"Any temps?"

Hell. She realised that she hadn't asked. "Give me a minute and I'll get back to you."

Craig clicked his phone off and continued looking around the third floor. Liam hadn't left the building; the CCTV was clear on that. He was in here somewhere and he was hurt, he was sure of it. He was so sure that he'd already called an ambulance; it was downstairs waiting and armed officers were searching every floor. If their killer had got to Liam, there was nothing to say that she wouldn't kill someone else trying to escape.

Annette called him back. "There were temporary kitchen staff – four of them. I'm pulling their photos now." Then it dawned on him; Adams would never have got a recognisable weapon into the building, but Liam had been in the canteen.

"Annette, tell the ambulance we have a poisoning. They need to put the poisons unit on alert. I'm going back to the canteen, Nicky's already there. Find me with those photos."

He ran to the lift and pushed hard on its call button, refusing to remove his finger. Suddenly the walkie-talkie in his pocket crackled into life.

"We've found him. Sixth floor toilets and he looks bad. It looks like he's been poisoned."

"Get him down to the ambulance and I'll meet you there."

He raced down the flights to the ground floor, passing Annette at the lift. She caught him at the side entrance by the ambulance, handing him four grainy photographs. There was no question about it; one of the photos was of Jessica Adams, blonde now and calling herself Monica Gibson again. Attacking a police officer inside a secure building! She really believed she was flameproof.

"They found him on the floor below the canteen, Annette. But brace yourself, it doesn't look good. I'm going with him in the ambulance. Go and collect Danni and meet us at the hospital." For a second, her stricken face halted him, but they didn't have time for personal feelings.

"They'll do everything they can, the poisons unit's ready."

Just then, four black-suited officers appeared, carrying the dead weight of Liam Cullen's limp body. They pushed past them to the ambulance, and Craig jumped in. The ambulance's urgent siren was joined by a chorus of blues and twos, ready for the two mile trip to the hospital.

Then suddenly they were gone, leaving Annette and Nicky alone.

Chapter Fifteen

St Mary's Healthcare Trust.

Craig was outside the intensive care unit staring out a window when John arrived, hurrying breathlessly down the corridor. The detective was aware of the familiar steps but he kept staring, focusing on the strange normality of a delivery-van six floors below.

"God, Marc, I've just heard! What happened?"

"Poison."

The word fell flatly on the air, its two syllables covering hundreds of possibilities and thousands of scenarios, from instant to slow, mild to irreversibly fatal.

"How?" John stood alongside him, while Craig still stared ahead.

"In his food. By a temp worker in the canteen. It was Jessica Adams, no question." He half-smiled but didn't move his gaze.

"Some of his lunch was on his lapel. That's Liam. Always the messy eater. This time it might just have saved his life." His voice cracked slightly, but John knew to stay where he was, an arm's length away.

"The doctor said it was aconite, fatal in a hundred percent of cases where twenty mls or more has been ingested."

John nodded. He'd written a paper on it years before. It was one of a group of plant poisons, easily accessible and usually lethal. Craig was still talking.

"They said the only reason he didn't die instantly was his size, and the fact that he only took a tiny amount. Apparently he was too busy chatting up some W.P.C. at the next table to eat." He half-laughed. "If he survives, Danni will kill him just for that."

He leaned forward, his breath misting condensation on the glass. John knew that he felt responsible. There was no reason for it and it wasn't logical, but he did. Liam was part of his team.

"What you said, John."

"What was that?"

"About Jessica Adams acting as a hit-man."

"I was only talking to hear my own voice, Marc. You know me, it was just theoretical rubbish."

Craig turned slowly to look at him.

"No...no, I don't think it was. I think you were right. She has a list of people that she's killing, and the reason we can't connect them to her is that it's not her list. She's killing to order, maybe for one person or for several, and there's some reason that a loving wife and mother has done this. Something more than money."

"A breakdown after her husband's suicide?"

Craig shook his head, frustration in every muscle. "No, that's not it. Everyone we've spoken to says Jessica Adams was a wonderful mother. Her daughters were the centre of her life. They would have kept her going even after her husband had killed himself. There's something else here that we're missing."

"She can't hide forever," John's voice became softer as Craig's got angrier.

"Well, she's done a bloody good job of it so far! She's not in the system anywhere; Davy's been on it for days. There've been no hits on her prints or her cards, and her bank account's completely inactive. There's nothing, nothing."

He turned away again and leaned hard on the windowsill, staring out at the van. "She's just another woman walking the streets of Belfast."

"Murdering people."

Craig nodded. He looked thoughtful for a moment, and then pulled his mobile out hurriedly, excusing himself to the stairwell. He returned two minutes later, looking calmer.

"OK, I've spoken to Harrison, and as far as the press and the world are concerned, Liam Cullen is now officially dead."

"What? Why?"

"If these *are* hits and it gets out that Liam survived, she'll try again. So as far as the world is concerned he has to be dead."

John rubbed his eyes and then gave a small laugh, breaking the sombre mood. "Imagine if people start sending wreathes."

They looked at each other for a second and then laughed so loudly that the door at the end of the corridor opened, and a young P.C. put his head around it questioningly. He disappeared rapidly at the sight of Craig, but his quick disapproving look made them laugh even harder.

Eventually their laughter tailed away and the analysis started again.

"What about the children? They must be traceable, Marc. Doctors' records, schools, immunisations – if she's a good mum she'll have been taking them for everything."

Craig nodded, "Davy's on it. He found a bit of information but she could have changed their names to anything by now. Her parents retired to Spain and haven't heard from her for years. There was a charge of abuse against the father so she left home at fifteen to live with a friend."

Disgust flickered across John's face and Craig nodded. "I know. But Davy did manage to find out one interesting thing."

"What?"

"She had another baby fourteen months ago. She was already four months pregnant when her husband died."

"God, if she wasn't a murderer, I'd actually feel sorry for her."

Craig nodded, but any sympathy that he might have felt for Jessica Adams had completely gone now. This was a woman who'd nearly put Liam in a box.

****

The elderly gate officer waved Julia on, indicating an empty parking bay on the left. She reversed into it very cautiously, taking four tries. Parking had never been her strong point.

She smoothed her skirt down, psyched herself into

best humble-pie eating mode and then climbed out, walking towards the man, who cast an appreciative eye over her curves.

Julia could feel her hackles rising after years of sexist army officers, but the gate officer's advanced age and benign smile indicated that he was being more appreciative than sexist, so she decided to let it pass...this time.

"I need to get to the Murder Squad. Could you tell me which floor that is, please?"

He peered at her over his glasses, as if about to say something, then he shrugged his thin shoulders slightly instead.

"Who are you seeing, ma'am?"

"D.C.I. Craig."

"That'll be the tenth floor then, you'd best take the lift. It's just over there."

He pointed to the far corner with a finger twisted by arthritis, like her father's. She softened and smiled him a warm thank-you then crossed the concrete expanse towards the lift.

The lift's slow arrival and even slower journey gave her time to run through four different speeches, and she eventually emerged on the tenth floor more confident in her final choice. Her momentary surprise at the silence that greeted her passed at the sight of a dark female head bent over a corner desk. She walked across and stood in front of her, gently coughing to signal her arrival.

Nicky looked up slowly, rubbing at her eyes with a sodden hanky, to be greeted by the unexpected sight of a visitor. At any other time, she would have chatted brightly to her, but not today. Her tears shocked Julia into silence, with her first thought 'Is this how they treat their staff in Belfast?' and her second 'I'm not surprised, the way Craig spoke to me'.

When Nicky gradually explained, Julia knew that this wasn't the day to talk to Marc Craig. So instead she sat with Nicky, until eventually she dried her eyes, lifted her bag, and declared that "she wasn't going to sit here answering stupid phones when she should be at the hospital" and they left the squad together, heading for St Mary's.

Chapter Sixteen

St Mary's. Midnight.

The PVC doors at the end of the corridor opened noisily and John woke with a jolt. He yawned, covering his mouth at the last minute in deference to his mother's years of nagging, and reached forward to the low table his feet were resting on. He rifled through the detritus in search of food and emerged disappointed. He was starving and a look at the clock told him why; it was midnight.

Just then Craig's lean figure appeared, carrying white paper bags whose oozing scent signalled Chinese food. John cheered up instantly, clearing the table in grateful preparation.

"Good man yourself. Which Chinese did you go to?" Long years of bachelor-hood had rendered him something of an expert on Belfast's takeaways.

"Don't worry, it was your favourite – I know better than that."

Craig nodded towards the ICU door. "Any movement?"

"Sorry, I fell asleep. I was on call last night and even if you aren't called, you never sleep properly. But no-one came and woke me up if that's any help?" Craig nodded and opened the cardboard containers while John talked.

"Hey, I meant to tell you. Nicky said that inspector, the stroppy one from Limavady, came to see you today. But you were here, so she had to shuffle back home."

Craig glanced up from the boxes, curious. "Did she say what she wanted?"

"Nope, not exactly. But I got the impression it was to apologise."

"You're kidding. This I have to hear."

He took out his mobile and John pointed to the no-phone signs, so he walked into the stairwell and called

Nicky at home.

"Hi, Nicky."

"What's happened? Is he dead? Please tell me he's not dead."

Craig suddenly realised what time it was. "Oh God, no. I'm sorry, I should have thought before I phoned you so late. No, Liam's not dead. That's not why I called."

"Yes, you should have thought...sir." But the relief in her voice was a reluctant thank-you anyway.

"He's holding his own. You know Liam; he's a big ox, and if anyone can survive this, he can. I'm sorry to have upset you, Nicky. I'll speak to you tomorrow."

But she was curious now so he wasn't getting away that easily.

"Why did you call?"

Craig wasn't actually sure why, but he suddenly felt embarrassed asking her about Julia McNulty.

"Well, John and I are still here. We'll be here all night so it's Chinese takeaway time of course." He knew that he was babbling. "But...well...John said...D.I. McNulty was looking for me earlier and..."

He gathered himself, finishing briskly. "I just wondered if it was anything important? About the case."

Nicky smiled at the other end of the line.

"Now, sir, you know I'd have told you if it was." He knew she was right. "But, as you've called. I think she came to apologise for being stroppy."

He was astounded. "Did she actually say that?"

"Not in so many words, but it was definitely in her manner. She's actually very nice you know."

Craig greeted her comment with the snort that he felt it deserved, and she snapped back at him.

"Don't be rude. She was very nice. I was upset about Liam and she made me tea, and sat with me for nearly an hour."

He was surprised by the kindness, but he didn't trust it. "Was this before or after she knew I was unavailable?"

"Oh, you're far too cynical these days. It was after.

And she could have just got on the road home and left me there, but she didn't. She stayed, knowing she would hit the traffic back to Limavady. Then she dropped me up to the hospital. And another thing..."

Craig smiled to himself; she was on a roll now. "Yes Nicky."

"You know the way you thought she'd be short, fat and have a helmet for hair."

God, Liam must have told her he'd said that. He'd kill him when he was better.

"Well, she's not. She's gorgeous. Slim, red-hair, and a real looker. So if I were you, I'd let her come back and apologise. Or... if you were feeling like a gentleman..."

"Yesss, Nicky..."

"You might even take a trip up to see her. Good night, sir."

She ended the call before he had time to argue back...

Forty-Love.

****

Wednesday. 9 a.m.

The two little girls gazed up at their mother tearfully, sure that they wouldn't see her for a very long time. It would actually only be twelve hours, but it felt endless to Jessie as well, and she turned away quickly wiping her eyes, careful not to let them see.

Fiona was waiting outside, affording them a few private moments before they parted – they couldn't let tears draw attention to them at the airport.

Jessie stroked her daughters' cheeks in turn, tracing the shape of their faces as if it could imprint them on her brain. Who knew, with her brain maybe it could? Her numb fingers denied her their softness, but her vision was still un-blurred enough to see their white smiles.

"Now, you know you must be good girls for Fiona, don't you?"

"Yes, Mammy." Their duet was echoed by the baby's gurgles.

"And you know that we're playing a game and we all have nice new names now, don't you?"

Ruby's strong voice spoke out first. "Yes, Mammy. I'm not Ruby any more, I'm Rosa."

"And I'm not Anya, I'm Ambra."

"Good girls. And remember Pia is Pietro. Tell me again. When I point to you, tell me your new name."

"Rosa."

"Ambra and baby Pietro."

"And what's Fiona's new name?"

"Fina Morales."

"And my name?"

"Juan...Juanita Morales."

"And remember those names *whoever* asks you, even a policeman, until Mammy tells you different. Fina is your granny, you live with her and you're going on holiday. Can you both remember that?"

They nodded vigorously, making their shiny hair fall in loose tangles. Jessie gently pushed the curls behind their ears and straightened their coats, hugging them tightly, unable to bear their loss even for a day. Then she deposited them into the mess of car-seats and toys in yet another new car that Fiona had bought for anonymity, and they started their final trip to safety.

Chapter Seventeen

The doctor's crumpled scrubs and stubble said that he'd been up all night saving lives, one of them hopefully Liam Cullen's. The team had gathered in the ward's tiny rest room, waiting for Danni to arrive.

Annette gazed around the warm room. She'd nursed on intensive care once and she knew that relatives often lived and slept in these rooms, afraid to leave in case their loved one's next breath was their last. She idly noticed that someone had placed red and white flowers in the corner and she was surprised; in her day, red and white had meant blood and death, and was only ever seen in wreathes. Things changed.

Just then the door swung open and Nicky entered with Danni, who she'd met on the stairs. Craig had a fleeting, incongruous thought about who was answering the phones before he realised they would be diverted, and that he didn't much care anyway. He stood up as the women entered, then they all sat again as the doctor began to speak.

"Mrs Cullen, would you like me to speak to you privately?"

Danni looked around the room at all of them, her large green eyes and blonde hair in bright contrast to the tired pallor of her skin. She looked fifteen and frightened instead of thirty-seven and the strong woman she really was. She shook her head decisively. "Liam would want everyone to hear."

She indicated Craig and John. "They've been here all night, poor things."

The young doctor nodded and began to explain, in as un-technical a language as Liam's condition and ICU procedures would allow, exactly what the poison was, and how it had affected Liam's body.

"As you know, Mr Cullen ingested approximately ten mls of aconite, a neurotoxin derived from plants. Principally a plant called Monkshood, common in northern temperate zones like the U.K."

He paused, gazing at them kindly before delivering the most frightening piece of information. "The fatality rate for ingesting twenty to forty mls of Monkshood is one hundred percent."

Danni opened her mouth in a silent scream and Annette squeezed her hand, as the doctor realised what he'd just said and moved quickly to reassure them. Like John, his people skills were a bit on the thin side.

"The good news is that Mr Cullen only ingested a small amount, less than ten mls, and that he's physically a very strong man. Both of those things saved his life. He's not completely out of the woods yet, but thanks to D.C.I. Craig getting the ambulance and poisons unit alerted, and thanks to hemoperfusion with charcoal and the use of cardiac drugs, he's stable. The rest is being dealt with by his considerable powers of healing."

He turned to face Danni directly, with a tired smile.

"Without making any promises, Mrs Cullen, we're cautiously optimistic. We should know more this evening. Meanwhile, the very good news is he's awake and asking for some 'decent food'." A subdued laugh rippled round the room.

"For some reason he thinks the enteral feed we're giving him is pig swill – although it certainly doesn't say that on the bag."

Craig laughed dutifully. John had told him that when the doctors started telling feeble jokes, it was a sure sign that the patient was recovering.

They waited behind as the others went in to see Liam, and John saw a new glint in Craig's eyes, knowing exactly what it meant. Now that Liam was on the mend, he would hunt Jessica Adams down relentlessly.

In a strange way, Liam had also given Camille her rightful importance. If Craig *did* agree to see her, John had the impression it would be completely on his terms now. As the others returned, Annette's thumbs up said that Liam could be subjected to some well-deserved banter about his messy eating, and whatever other handy ammunition sprang to mind.

****

The traffic noise was rendering Craig's hands-free phone nearly inaudible, but he thought that he'd better tell Nicky where he was heading, if only to save a lecture about always disappearing.

"Nicky, I'm heading up to Limavady. I've arranged a meeting with Inspector McNulty at one pm."

Nicky could hear that he was already on the motorway. He was keeping his own diary again and she raised her eyebrows but bit her tongue hard.

"Ask Davy to phone me with any results as soon he gets them please. I'll be back about eight tonight if you need me."

"OK, sir. But Dr Winter mentioned something about the theatre tonight, just in case you'd forgotten?"

Oh, crap – Camille. He had forgotten.

John had bought two tickets to her play last week and he'd promised, grudgingly, to go with him, worrying it to death all weekend. That was before Liam, but he still couldn't believe that it had slipped his mind so completely. He wasn't sure what that meant.

"OK, leave it with me. I'll call him on my way."

"All right, sir. But just to warn you, we're doing diaries first thing tomorrow morning..."

****

Belfast City Airport.

The car pulled off the M3 into Belfast City Airport and Jessie gathered their things quickly, trying hard not to cry. She was desperate to grab Pia and get out of the car, so she started unfastening her seatbelt as they drove into the drop-off zone, hurriedly refastening it at the sight of two police officers at the barrier. The last thing they needed was some eagle-eyed constable stopping them.

She needn't have worried; the policemen were too busy checking out a pretty flight attendant running for a departure. Thank goodness for human nature.

Fiona pulled in, idling the engine as if not actually turning it off would make their parting easier. Jessie turned round to the back seat, quickly kissing each older girl with her fingers, before she climbed clumsily from the high front seat onto the ground, and lifted Pia out. Then, with a single wave behind her, she walked quickly towards the terminal, hot tears running down her cheeks, as Fiona pulled out through the barrier and accelerated towards the motorway south.

She turned on the tape of fairytales and started two hours of storytelling and singing to Dublin airport. A grandmother and her two granddaughters heading off on holiday; what could possibly be more normal?

****

Craig sped up the M2, thinking. He knew that he should call John, but he dreaded the inevitable questions about his convenient memory lapse about the theatre. So instead he took the route of male resistance and put on a Snow Patrol CD.

If Craig ever admitted to obsession, which he didn't, it took two forms. Sport of any description; especially Man. United playing anywhere, Ulster Rugby playing at home, and any Northern Irish golfer hitting a ball. And Snow Patrol, not because they were home-grown but because they were the best.

Turning up the volume to maximum, he attempted to block out his thoughts, and he had half-succeeded, managing to get through one side of the album before the phone rang. John's voice cut through Gary Lightbody singing Chasing Cars and to Craig's relief he launched immediately into a thesis on poisons.

"Aconite's clever stuff, Marc. It's a neurotoxin – acts by paralysis of the heart and respiratory centre. Liam's bloody lucky to be alive, although you'd never believe it from the moaning he's doing. I've just left him and he was ready to make a run for it down the corridor." Craig laughed, imagining Liam shinning down the ICU's drainpipe.

"Well, he needn't think he's getting back on this case, it's far too personal now. I wouldn't trust him within ten miles of a suspect, and we're not losing a conviction just because Liam says the wrong thing."

"True enough, that mouth is hard to control. Where are you?"

Craig hesitated, feeling bad about the theatre, but knowing that he could cover all lapses with the job.

"On my way to Limavady to liaise. I've just passed Maghera."

"What time are you back? I have tickets for tonight, remember? Camille."

John thought halfway up the M2 was a safe enough distance to mention her name, but the silence that followed almost made him reconsider.

"To be honest, John, with all this going on I haven't given it much thought."

He paused for a moment before continuing. "Did I tell you she called my folks on Friday?" He laughed awkwardly. "Apparently my mum gave her hell."

"Yes! Way-to-go Mirella. I wish I'd heard that conversation."

"Dad had said she'd called and given me her number, but..." He was considering the damage that Camille could still do to his heart, and whether the call would be worth the pain it would cause. John changed the subject diplomatically, already knowing that he'd be going to the play alone that night.

"Are you off to view the beauty of the North-West then?"

Before Craig could pretend to misinterpret the question, he added, "And by that, yes, I do mean the lovely Inspector McNulty. Liam told me she's a real looker."

"Well, we only have Liam's word for that, and he's probably winding you up."

"Not true. Nicky confirmed it."

"Well, whatever they told you, I don't care if she *is*

good-looking. She was bloody rude on the phone. So whatever romantic thoughts you're thinking, don't bother. You're getting worse than Nicky."

"Give her my number then. I don't meet many live women down here. Speaking of which, the budget manager's coming to give me an earful in thirty minutes, so I'd better look at the books. I'll have those final reports for you tomorrow plus a short one on Liam. And I'll give you a full review of tonight's play. Bye."

The phone clicked off and Craig hit the CD again, accelerating up the motorway. He was more curious about Julia McNulty than he'd admitted, and surprisingly, less curious about Camille than he had been in years.

****

St Pancras Station, London. 2 p.m.

The flight to London had been no problem. Despite having her forged passport ready, Jessie hadn't been asked for I.D., normal for some intra-UK flights. Fiona had said it might happen. She just hoped that the Dublin to Paris leg was going as smoothly for the others.

They'd agreed zero contact until they met in Gare de Nord station, so all she could do for now was hope. She and Pia were sitting in Carluccios waiting for the Eurostar from Paris to arrive. Soon they would be on board, and in a few more days no-one would ever find them again.

She spooned apple puree into Pia's eager mouth, thinking. The joint part of their journey from Paris would be tricky, but security outside the UK wasn't half as bad as inside. And once they were in Paris, it would be Disneyland and then only two day's sunny drive to their final home; where the girls would become fluent in their new language, and she would prepare for the final step that would protect them forever.

****

Limavady.

Craig pulled into an empty space in the small police car-park and walked quickly towards the double door of a low, brick building, only the police logo distinguishing it from a Victorian grammar school. It certainly had character. He thought of the steel and chrome of Docklands, uncertain which he preferred, until the river finally clinched it.

The desk officer rechecked his pass and indicated the lift, but running up the three flights would be good exercise for him. He got little enough of that nowadays, remembering the sports kit he'd abandoned in his office. He headed towards the stairs, readying to take them two at a time, when a voice behind him called out his name.

"D.C.I. Craig. Hello. I didn't expect to see you here. Liaising?"

He turned, expecting to see Terry Harrison, and he was right. He was standing there in all his shiny-buttoned glory with Mrs Butler a respectful two steps behind.

"Take the lift and we'll talk."

Just then, the lift doors opened, rendering excuses useless, and they all crammed into the small steel cage. Harrison pressed the seventh floor button, ensuring that Craig would account to him before he did anything else.

"That was a bad business with D.I. Cullen. How is he?"

"Improving, sir, but it was a close call."

"Bloody ridiculous how they managed that on our property. I've ordered a complete review of security. There are far too many temporary staff floating in and out, and they cost us a fortune as well." From his tone, the cost appeared to concern him more than Liam's health.

"Aconite or something obscure, wasn't it? What is that anyway?"

"John said it's derived from a plant called Monkshood that's common on the farms round here. That's what I hope to confirm this afternoon."

The lift shuddered to a halt on the seventh and Craig made to get out. But the conversation had obviously already satisfied Harrison's need for control and he waved him goodbye, walking off grandly with Mrs Butler in hot pursuit.

Craig pushed button three gratefully, leaning against the lift's cool wall. One minute later, he was in a narrow, windowed corridor lined completely on one side by doors. He scrutinised each of them for a sign that Julia McNulty lived inside.

He struck lucky at the fourth and knocked on its glass panel, less confident than he should have been but not sure why. A quiet female voice beckoned him to enter, so he pushed the door open and stepped into the small office. A titian-red head was bent over a desk directly opposite the door, and the woman who owned it was writing vigorously in an old-fashioned copperplate. Her small hand gripped tightly at an elderly fountain pen, her head not lifting an inch from the page as he entered.

"I'll be with you in a second, please take a seat."

So he sat, unsure whether she was game-playing or in complete ignorance of her visitor's identity. The latter was confirmed when she eventually lifted her head, her surprised look indicating that she had no idea who he was. He reached his hand quickly across the desk. "Marc Craig."

She flushed, suddenly embarrassed, as if she hadn't expected him, despite confirming the appointment time. For a moment, she looked genuinely puzzled, just time enough for Craig to cover his own confusion. He didn't know what he'd expected from their brief conversations but it certainly wasn't this.

She was beautiful; genuinely, unselfconsciously beautiful. And not beautiful in any cold, aristocratic army officer mould, but like some nineteen-forties starlet, with soft ruby-gold curls and cornflower-blue eyes. Pale freckles were scattered liberally across her small nose. He thought they made her look like a strict cherub.

Craig was surprised and suddenly shy, then angry with himself that he'd imagined her plain, just because they had argued. Lucia would hang him up by her feminist banner if she ever heard that one.

Julia stood up and he moved reflexly to match her, unsure why either of them was adopting the pose. Until her straight-backed declaration came rattling out.

"Sir, I would like to apologise for what I said on the phone."

He recognised years of army discipline and, somewhat embarrassed by her apology, he nodded her to sit down. She looked at him as though still expecting a bollocking, until he smiled. Then she smiled back, involuntarily.

"Is there any chance of a coffee? I've been caffeine-free for hours and it's not good for my health."

She laughed at his weak joke, a clear, half-English sound that reminded him of how much he missed London. Then she turned to an old coffee-maker in the corner, pressing the button and moving crockery around on a tray until it perked, before arranging some biscuits on a plate and re-joining him.

"Did you get any lunch? I can offer you half a cheese sandwich?"

"Thanks, but tempting as that sounds, I'll pass." They were laughing together now.

"How's Inspector Cullen? Your secretary was very upset." The genuine concern in her voice echoed Nicky's description of her, and he liked her more by the minute.

"On the mend. Complaining about the food and harassing the nurses, so he'll be out soon, I'm sure. Although, as he was nearly one of our killer's victims, he's on the bench for the rest of the case."

Suddenly an idea hit him but his self-discipline nearly dismissed it, until an image of Camille loomed and he decided to go for it anyway.

"I was just wondering... As our cases are obviously

linked, and we're a man down now, I was wondering..."

"Yes?" Julia knew what he was about to say, or hoped that she did, and she fought hard to stop herself saying yes too soon.

She'd sneaked a quick look at him while she was making the coffee and his combination of mixed accent and dark good looks had piqued her curiosity. He was more attractive than any man she'd met in years, without looking as if he was sure of it. She wanted to know more about D.C.I. Marco Craig, including the origins of his unusual first name.

Craig was still talking. "I think our teams should work closely together on this one. We have excellent lab and analyst support, and Liam and McCandless are Belfast victims. While you have W.P.C. Burton and the fact that our main suspect comes from this area. So what do you say, Inspector McNulty? Truce?"

Julia liked that he hadn't ordered her to agree, when he so easily could have done. She liked that he hadn't used Harrison's clout when he also could have done. And she liked his side-burns. But more than any of that, she liked his addiction to caffeine; it might make him more understanding about her own to cigarettes. Might...

So she half-smiled at him, looking at once like a very un-strict cherub. "It's Julia. And yes. Truce." Then they finished their coffee in amicable silence, before setting out for the Adams' farm.

****

The C.C.U.

"No, this isn't right, it can't be."

Annette was sitting quietly at her desk, marvelling at how peaceful the place was. Liam was off, Craig was in Limavady and Nicky was sipping cappuccino somewhere with Mirella Craig, hearing about the best shops in Venice. It was lovely and she was getting lots of work done; they should all disappear more often.

Only the occasional sound of Davy talking to himself was disturbing her peace and quiet.

"It can't be right. Honestly, I don't believe this."

She could tell that he wanted an audience so she stopped typing and took the bait.

"OK, Davy. I know you're dying for me to ask you what you don't believe. So...OK...what don't you believe?"

"Come here and look."

She knew that she'd get no peace until she did. So, with an exaggerated sigh, she saved the document that she was working on and picked her way past a pile of notes propped precariously beside Liam's desk. They were outstanding public prosecution reports, and death's door or no deaths' door, there was no way *she* was doing them for him.

Davy was almost hopping off his chair with excitement now, his thick Emo hair flopping into his eyes.

"Calm down for God's sake or you'll end up next to Liam. What have you got?"

He turned the computer screen towards her and sat back triumphantly. "There."

"There, what? All I can see is a set of court papers."

"No." He leaned forward and jabbed the screen with a pale, black-nail- varnished finger. "There."

She peered at it, her aging short-sightedness defeated by the vanity that refused glasses. "I give up. Just tell me."

He smiled to himself, careful not to let her see. Annette was good-natured to a fault, unless you pointed out that she was forty-odd and needed glasses. Then she'd get grumpy on sixpence.

"Aye, right enough, the font *is* tiny." She squinted at him, looking for any signs of sarcasm but detecting none.

"It's a list, and Liam's, Maria Burton's and Ian McCandless' names are all on it."

"A list of what?"

Davy leaned back in his chair as if he was on Mastermind.

"A court list from two thousand and seven. They w...were all on a jury panel."

"That has to be wrong. Liam can't possibly have been on a jury, he's in the police."

He glanced at her impatiently.

"No, Liam wasn't on the jury; he w...was the arresting officer. The other two w...were jurors. And guess who else?"

"Hang on, Davy. Maria Burton was a W.P.C. so she can't have been on a jury either,"

She was deliberately delaying his punch line just to wind him up. He rolled his eyes in exasperation.

"I know, but she hadn't joined the force then. The answer is..."

"Jessica Adams."

He glared at her, annoyed that she'd guessed correctly, and even more annoyed that she couldn't have pretended not to. He lapsed into a sulk until she apologised.

"Sorry, Davy." She tried to look suitably contrite, but he sulked for a while longer, unconvinced.

"OK...I know it w...was only a lucky guess. But yes, Jessica Adams w...was a juror too."

Annette was interested now. "What was the case?"

"The murder of a man called Brian McNamee that year. He was a teacher at Constitution College in Glengormley. Have you heard of it?"

She thought hard for a minute, cases flicking through her head like index cards, then she slowly started to recall the details.

"Yes...yes, I do actually. I didn't work it, I was in the Rape Unit then, but I remember it being on the news. Wasn't there an uproar because one of his killers only got five years? The other was twenty-one so he ended up with life in Maghaberry, but the other, a girl, was only sixteen so she was sent to the holiday camp."

"The holiday camp? W...What's that?"

"Wharf House – and if you'd ever been there you'd know exactly why it's called that. Prisoners wear their own clothes and make-up, they even have theatre outings. It's just like that Sunny Days place near

Dublin. It was originally for non-violent offenders so it was a bloody disgrace when she was sent there. I'd be surprised if Liam didn't kick up about it."

She perched on the desk beside him, thinking. There was more to find out before they bothered the boss with this.

"Davy, can you get onto Court Records for me; I need you to dig a bit deeper. I'm going to talk to Liam."

****

St Mary's.

"God, Doc, when can I go home? This place is doing my head in. And D.C.I. Craig needs me urgently; we've an on-going investigation."

The slim thirty-something that passed for his consultant, completely ignored Liam's pleas. Instead she wrote furiously on his chart, while an escaped twelve-year-old masquerading as a medical student scurried around behind her, handing her sheets of differently lined paper for measurements and drugs. And people said you felt old when the coppers started getting younger!

"Why Inspector Cullen... don't you like us? I'm hurt. And to think that only yesterday you couldn't wait to get in here."

She smiled down at him in a way that reminded Liam he was wearing pyjamas. He never wore them at home and they made him feel five years old again, even though they weren't covered in cowboys nowadays.

"Aye well, sure it's been lovely and all that, but I've work to do. Whoever tried to bump me off is still out there, and that offends me. So you'll understand why I'm a bit hacked-off lying here?"

He grinned up at her, flashing his best winning smile. It always worked on Danni. But the doctor just ignored him, immune after years of male patients.

"And maybe *you'll* understand, Inspector Cullen, why *I'd* be a bit hacked-off if, after all our hard work, you ended up dying because I let you home too soon? Besides which, your wife told me it's very peaceful at home and the house is much tidier without you. Your observations are stable so we'll move you onto a ward this afternoon, but I think a few more days of peace will do her a power of good."

With years of practice, she handed the charts to her minion without looking, and smiled Liam a goodbye of exaggerated sweetness. Then she turned on her heel, muttering the words "bed bath" to the first nurse she walked past, and not for the first time Liam understood the urge to kill.

****

Café du Trésor, Marais, Paris. Wednesday, 10 p.m.

Jessie's and Fiona's eyes met incredulously over the girls' sleepy heads. They were free! After six months of meticulous planning and fearful execution, Fiona finally allowed herself to cry. They were hot tears, streaming silently down her cheeks and she covered her eyes with a paper napkin so as not to upset the girls.

They'd done it. Brian was finally avenged, Jessie's children were safe and Fiona would get the chance to be their grandmother; the grandmother that her own grandchildren would sadly never know now.

The weight of five years of loss and injustice finally lifted from her and she smiled at Jessie gratefully, clasping her cut, swollen hands. She knew that she couldn't feel her touch, but hopefully her smile said enough.

Fiona watched her as she fed the baby, her slim, pale blondness making her look like a teenage nanny instead of the mother of three. Jessie was only a girl, only six years older than her own daughter, but she'd already suffered so much. They both had. But while her pain was ending, there would be no relief for Jessie.

Jessie read her thoughts and smiled at her, and there was so much joy in her large hollow eyes that Fiona stopped feeling sorry for her immediately, vowing not to ruin another moment of their limited time together with sad thoughts. There had been enough of those for both their lifetimes.

So she lifted the spoons and distributed them, watching as eager little hands dug into their late-night bowls of ice-cream, smearing it on their mouths, cheeks and jumpers in equal proportions. The girls giggled happily in the warm evening air as they did so, while the two women watched them, almost at peace.

Chapter Eighteen

Belfast.

Craig had been fighting the urge to call John since he'd left home that morning, managing to get as far as the C.C.U.'s car-park before caving in. Now he wished that he hadn't. John's glowing review of last night's play reminded him of Camille's talent, and of the hundreds of happy evenings he'd spent helping her learn her lines. Why did she have to come back into his life now, breaching the defences that it had taken him years to build?

He slammed his car door so hard that the elderly gate officer left his warm cubicle to peer over, anxious not to miss anything. Craig lifted his hand in apology and muttered something inaudible, striding heavily toward the lift. He was still striding when he crossed the squad- room floor ten storeys up.

Nicky heard his mood before she saw it and handed him a coffee as he passed, his mobile clamped to his ear. He grunted his thanks and headed straight for his office, still listening to his mobile's messages.

"I wouldn't bother listening to those, sir. It'll just be me and Annette updating you."

"OK, tell me what you said then."

"The short version is that Davy has made a breakthrough on the case. He's found a link between the victims. He and Annette can give you the detail."

She continued without inhaling, her curiosity acting as oxygen and making her foolishly brave. "How was Limavady? And D.I. McNulty?"

She watched his face carefully for any flicker of personal interest, but he was too good. Years of policing had taught him to hide his cards well. Judging by his heavy steps she'd thought there would be total silence in response to her question, but instead he smiled, pleased at the diversion from his thoughts of Camille.

"It was useful, we..."

Her ears pricked up and she smiled coyly at him. We, was it?

He caught her amused look and ignored it, continuing. "We visited Adams' farm and it was just as Liam had said. I confirmed that Jessica Adams, or Jessica Atkinson as she was, went to court and made herself legally independent from her parents when she was fifteen. She cited abuse by her father, which would explain why they have no contact now."

"She divorced her parents? Like they do in America. In Limavady?" Nicky said it incredulously, as if the idea of it happening in America was unlikely enough, but in the rural North-West of Ireland...

"Yes, I know. Believe me; I was as surprised as you are. But she did it, and then she moved in with her best friend's family – a girl called Gemma Orr. She stayed there until she got married to Michael Adams.

We met Gemma Orr's mother yesterday and she said that Jessica was a very determined, but very loving girl. She only ever wanted to marry and have babies, and she was very happy with Michael Adams. But she said that they'd lost touch with her after he died. Hardly the usual profile of a killer."

"Which brings us back to the idea that this is all about protecting her children, sir? There's no other explanation for it."

He nodded. "I accept that. But we still need to know how she thinks that what she's doing is going to help them."

He scanned the room, half-expecting to see Liam's long legs stretching across the floor. It was too quiet there without him, so he beckoned the others into his office.

"Gemma Orr lives out on Lear Island now, so we've got the local bobbies interviewing her today – hopefully she'll give us something recent on Jessica. And I found a few plants that looked like Monkshood for Des to have a look at."

"Where's Lear Island?"

"It's off the North-West coast, near Portstewart. It's tiny; only twelve miles across with about fifty inhabitants, plus the blackbirds."

"I bet it'd be hard to commit crimes there without someone noticing."

Craig smiled. "Maybe I'll apply for a job there—I might get some rest. OK, what else have you got?"

"Davy's found a case where Maria Burton, Ian McCandless and Jessica Adams were all on the jury. And guess who the investigating officer was?"

"Liam..." Annette nodded and Craig knew that this was it; the reason for all the murders.

"Well done, Davy. Annette, give me the details."

"It was the murder of a forty-five-year-old teacher called Brian McNamee, by one of his sixteen-year-old pupils, Lynsey Taylor, and her boyfriend. It was tragic. He'd always gone the extra mile for the girl. She'd had a drug problem and he'd got her into rehab, worked with her parents etcetera.

Anyway, he was the technology teacher so he was checking out the computer room before going home one night and he heard a noise. Instead of calling for help, he went to investigate. Some of the teachers who gave evidence said that was typical of him. He would have tried to help whoever had broken in, instead of handing them over to the police."

"Kindness. Was that what got him killed?"

"Yes, basically. He went in and confronted the girl, but she kept him talking while her boyfriend grabbed him from behind. Then she stabbed him with a kitchen knife they'd brought with them. They were both high as a kite on drugs. They got away with five laptops and left McNamee bleeding to death on the floor. If they'd even called an ambulance he would have lived, but he wasn't found for hours, until the night watchman did his rounds. He had no hope."

She shook her head sadly, continuing.

"Liam was the arresting officer, but because the girl was only sixteen, she went to Wharf House under section ninety. She's due out on parole next week. The boyfriend got life in Maghaberry." The tragedy of the story was compounded by the killer walking free in seven days' time.

"Did he have a family?"

"Yes. Two children, late teens at the time, so I suppose they would be working or at university now. And a wife, Fiona, also a teacher, forty-two then. She lives out in Glengormley."

Nicky leaned forward eagerly. "Tell him about the jury vote, Annette."

"Well, it took a while for the court to give us the details. Davy nearly had to get you onto the judge, sir. Anyway, they finally let us have them. It turns out that Maria Burton – she wasn't an officer then, she was still working on her parents' farm. Anyway, Maria Burton and Ian McCandless were the two jurors who asked for leniency for the girl. They wanted her to get probation because of her age. I bet she would have changed her mind after a few years on the job, seeing victims.

Anyway, the judge refused but everyone thought that they'd managed to sway him, because Lynsey Taylor got early parole after five years. And she was allowed to serve her sentence in the holiday camp; Wharf House.

"Why there, sir?"

"Because some optimist a long time ago believed that women didn't commit crime, Nicky, so we only have one prison for women. Medium security Wharf House, designed for non-violent offenders."

"And Jessica Adams?"

"She registered an objection against the leniency of the sentence, but it was just noted and filed. She even complained to the press, but that was all we could find on her. But why would she kill them, sir? After all, it wasn't her husband who died. And why now, five years later?"

He shook his head. "Something else triggered this, Annette. Adams would never put her daughters' welfare at risk. That's why she's kept them away from her own father, and why she didn't start killing when her husband died. Which means that her reason for this killing spree has to be something much more recent."

"Maybe it's Lynsey Taylor getting parole?"

Annette jumped in. "That's not personal enough to Adams, Davy, and why not just kill Taylor and leave it at that?

"Because she's in prison, Annette?"

She huffed back at Craig. "She could still do it, sir."

He nodded at her, conceding.

"You're right. If it was Lynsey Taylor she wanted, then why not just wait until she comes out next week and kill her then? And why so many deaths for Brian McNamee, a man that she's not even related to? We're nearly there, but we're still missing something. What did Liam remember about the case?"

"Actually, that's really interesting. It seems our old cynic actually went soft. He felt sorry for Taylor because of her age, so he pushed for leniency as well."

Everyone stared at her, astonished. Nicky was the first to speak. "Liam? Our Liam? Hang-them-all Liam. Soft?"

"Yes, I know, that's exactly what I thought, but he admitted it. Then he said that he'd wised up now."

They all laughed, imagining Liam admitting his leniency in the same way as an alcoholic does the twelve steps.

"Well, there you go, pigs *do* fly. That gives us serious wind-up material when he gets back."

Craig nodded briskly.

"OK. This is great work, Davy, but let's go further. Nicky, can you contact Wharf House and set up a meeting for me with the governor this afternoon please. And while I'm doing that, Annette, can you get Fiona McNamee's address and pay her a visit. We'll brief here again at four."

He glanced down, slightly embarrassed by what he was about to say next.

"Inspector McNulty's team have offered us any help or support we need on this, so please make use of that resource." He looked up defiantly; ready to deal with the smile in Nicky's eyes, but there was none.

"Everyone OK with that?"

They all nodded yes, completely deadpan, and he left his office quickly, before they could start.

****

Annette programmed the sat-nav for Poynton Avenue, Glengormley; Fiona McNamee's home. She pulled out onto Pilot Street, and followed the M2 for the nine-mile journey and after twenty minutes, she checked again. Poynton Avenue was a left-turn three streets further on, so she called Nicky to touch base, everyone on thirty-minute contacts after Liam then s drove on, turning into a long, wide street of detached houses.

The street split halfway down, branching off to Poynton Heights, leaving the Avenue to end in a square cul-de-sac, with an impressive Tudor style mansion as its end. Annette turned her car ready for a quick getaway, and then got out, looking for number thirty-six, in a street where every house was named instead of numbered.

Suddenly, a small blue Fiat reversed out of the driveway beside her, its open windows and heavy bass giving the occupant away as male and young before she even saw them. She crossed to the car, showing her badge, and the teenage driver turned-off the music quickly, the look on his face saying he was searching for reasons why the police might want to talk to him. As soon as she asked him where number thirty-six was he relaxed visibly, suddenly eager to help. "It's that one, officer." He indicated the mansion and she stared at it surprised; some teachers must earn more than her husband. She realised the boy was still talking.

"But she's been gone six months or so. Died abroad, I heard."

"Died? Do you know where?"

He shook his head. "No, sorry, but the estate agent might – he was showing people around the house last week. The number's on the sign."

He pointed at the pole attached to the gatepost and she noticed that his nails were painted black, like Davy's. She had images of her son Jordan doing the same in a few years' time, shuddering to herself and knowing that she had no right to mind. She'd had purple hair herself before she'd turned sensible.

"My mum used to be friendly with the owners. I knew the kids a bit, but they were older than me. Kirsty's twenty-one and Pete's twenty-two now. I think they're away at Uni in England, but my mum could tell you more."

"Thanks...?" She paused until he offered his name.

"Joe... Hanratty."

"Thanks, Joe, you've been really helpful."

He drove away basking in the glow of civic duty and Annette walked up the short drive of number thirty-six. Five minutes of door-knocking and window-peering told her that he'd been right; the house was empty. She took out her phone and rang the agent, arranging to meet him in twenty minutes. Meanwhile she tried the surrounding houses with no answer.

It was an almost wasted viewing; there were barely enough personal items left in the house to show who had lived there. The agent confirmed the memories had been too hard for Fiona McNamee to bear after her husband's death. Annette knew she would feel the same in her position.

He also confirmed that the children were in London and the house was mortgage-free, paid off by Fiona's life insurance: and that all proceeds of the sale were to go to them. He'd never actually spoken to the McNamees, just to their family solicitor, so he couldn't be of any more help than that.

Annette left the house feeling sad for the family, but with serious doubts that they were blameless in everything that was happening now.

****

Nicky dropped the phone and stared at it, then she knocked and entered Craig's office, slumping on a chair with a look of complete astonishment on her face.

"What's wrong?"

"I don't know how to tell you this, sir, but there's no point in you going to Wharf House today to see Lynsey Taylor."

"Why? Are they doing something special?" She looked blankly at him.

"What is it, Nicky?"

"Taylor... she's dead."

Craig stood up urgently, but only half-surprised and with the sinking certainty that their killer had struck again.

"When and how?"

"Sunday. From a Heroin overdose. They aren't convinced it was accidental."

"I'm absolutely bloody sure it wasn't! Jessica Adams did this. Somehow she got inside a locked facility and killed an inmate." He knew that someone at Wharf House would be paying for that with their job.

He lifted the Hoody's sketch and grabbed his jacket, swinging it on over his head.

"I'm still going up there. Call ahead to the governor, please. Adams has managed to reach the killer, the investigating officer and both dissenting jurors. There's no-one left to kill now except the judge, and they'll have a close-protection officer, but ask Annette to call and warn them anyway, please.

We need to move quickly. Jessica Adams has finished her killing spree and that means she's looking for a way out now."

He left the squad, throwing "the briefing's still at four – try to get John and Des here as well, please" over his shoulder as he disappeared.

****

Wharf House.

Wharf House sat in the most beautiful part of the North Antrim coast, the Glens between Larne and Cushendall. Nature had designed it for a Narnian fantasy and an engineer called William Bald had made it accessible by a winding road. The motorway branched off at Junction 2 and Craig drove quickly. Until the 'A' roads had transformed into a series of slow curves and turns and then opened out suddenly, into a wide horizon of one hundred metre-high cliffs to the left, and a calm, wintry Irish Sea to the right.

It was a drive that almost hypnotised travellers, like the Amalfi Coast. Drawing them irresistibly towards the water, as if some ancient siren stood on the rocks below, beckoning them down.

Craig could feel his romantic Italian side breaking cover and he shook himself, casting around for directions to the prison. There were none.

He switched on the sat-nav, pleased to find that Wharf House was only two miles further west. Five minutes later, he pulled up an un-signposted gravel track, its narrow anonymity providing the perfect exile for Northern Ireland's most dangerous women. He wondered if the local sheep knew who their neighbours were.

They'd never had an absconder from the centre, and Craig had always thought it must be down to the relaxed regime that had made court officers christen it the 'holiday camp'. But seeing its location now, he was veering more towards the sheer impossibility of escape. Even if an inmate managed to reach the pavement-less cliff road, a speeding lorry would kill them before they could ever hitch a lift.

He showed his warrant card to the young gate officer, waiting while he checked his list, then he was waved a mile further on into a wide courtyard, where a female guard pointed him to a parking space. He thought that he recognised her from somewhere, and the notion was confirmed by her warm greeting as he emerged from the car.

"Hello, Inspector Craig. I bet you don't remember me?"

Craig gazed down at the small, round woman and racked his brains for the context of their meeting. Then he remembered. She'd been the revenue officer on a joint fuel-smuggling case. Denise something. He smiled at her and she saved him from his memory lapse.

"Denise Robinson. We met in Armagh when we

nicked those petrol-stretchers."

"I remember. Good case. When did you change jobs?"

"Two years ago. It's a long story, but I love it here. Instead of locking them up, now I make sure they stay that way." She smiled at him wryly. "Well that's the theory anyway. You're in the Murder Squad now aren't you?"

He nodded. "For my sins. What's been happening up here?"

"The governor will tell you. She's waiting for you in her office, best china and all. But I'd better warn you; she had a visit from the civil servants yesterday and she's not a happy woman. Word is she's hanging on by a thread."

"Is that good or bad?"

She laughed, acknowledging bad bosses from the past. "Bad actually – she's not the worst. A bit hard sometimes, but then who isn't at her stage? It'd be a pity if she had to go."

She grinned. "Don't spread it around but we quite like the old girl – she means well. So anything you can do to help would be welcome. She can fill you in, but there's a feeling that this was no accident.

Lynsey Taylor wasn't well liked; she was dealing Heroin as well as using it and she got a few of the younger girls hooked. So if you're looking for a suspect-list there's about twenty names on it" she jerked her head toward the building, "all of them locked-up in there."

Craig spoke quietly. "We've already narrowed it to one, and unfortunately my money says that she isn't locked up anywhere."

****

"Davy, could you give me a hand for an hour? I need you to chase up the McNamees and find out what's happened to them since the trial. I'm seeing their solicitor at one-thirty."

"OK. Give me the details and I'll get on it. W...What

happened in Glengormley?"

"The teenage neighbour said the two kids went to university in England and the wife moved to Spain. Apparently, she died there six months ago, but he didn't know any more than that. His mother might know more, but she wasn't in, so maybe you could give her a call as well? It's number thirty Poynton Avenue. The Hanrattys.

All the details are on the sheet and the solicitor's number is there as well – John Dunn. If you need me I'm on my mobile, but I'll be back by three."

"Leave it with me."

Nicky smiled, knowing that Annette was asking for Davy's help deliberately. He loved feeling like a detective so they gave him telephone enquiries to deal with when it wouldn't affect due process. Annette left the analyst as happy as a sand-boy and went to see Mr John Dunn.

****

The car's hands-free was crackling so much that Craig was shouting.

"Can you hear me, John?"

"What?"

"I've just come from Wharf House."

"What were you doing up there?" He answered his own question. "There's been another death hasn't there?"

"Yes. Hang on, I'm pulling over. "Craig pulled off into a small picnic area and lifted the phone.

"Are you still there?"

"That's better, I can hear you now."

"A girl called Lynsey Taylor died in Wharf House on Sunday. Do me a favour and check the pathologist's report. I'm sure it's fine, but I need to keep this tight. I showed Adams' sketch to the warders and they identified her as an inmate on remand calling herself Kate Rogers. She was in for assault and I'm sure she staged it deliberately to get arrested. The prints will confirm it was the same woman."

"You've got her then. Well done."

"No, we haven't." Craig sighed heavily. "She was bailed on Sunday by a woman calling herself Susan Daley. We've got her photo; mid-forties, short brown hair. We'll circulate it, but ten to one it won't give us anything; she looks just like a million other women – probably deliberately."

John pictured her; forties, short brown hair. It was a ubiquitous description.

"Any idea who she actually is?"

"None, but we're following up some new leads at the moment. We've a briefing at four, could you and Des be there?"

"We'll try. How did Taylor die?"

"Looks like an overdose but I want to make sure. They found white powder at the scene. The forensics should be back on that later if Des could have a look."

"Well, at least she died happy, whether she deserved to or not."

Craig gave a hollow laugh at John's dark medical humour. "Could you check something else for me as well?"

"What?"

"Adams was admitted on some medication and they're going to fax the names to you. Unfortunately, there was no G.P.'s name on them – just some tablets in a blister pack. But maybe they'll throw some light on things."

"I'll do my best. See you at four."

****

The Offices of John Dunn, Solicitor.

"Is this really all you have on Mrs McNamee, Mr Dunn? A death certificate from Spain and a Will that says 'sell the house and give the money to the children?' Isn't that a bit sparse after forty odd years of life? Weren't there any insurance policies or a pension when her husband died? Other properties, maybe?"

It all seemed too tidy for Annette and she had a

seconds thought that maybe she was being cynical; maybe this *was* everything. If their choice of solicitor was anything to go by, the McNamees certainly hadn't been loaded.

They were sitting in a small office whose heavy brown curtains had missed several cleans. The office's beige flock wallpaper could have been trendy mock-Victorian, except for a tear beside the door giving away its original colour as cream. The elderly man facing her looked as worn as his décor; there seemed nothing affluent about John Dunn, or his clients.

"I didn't handle Mr McNamee's death myself, you understand. It was my son Andrew. But it does seem that the family lived a fairly simple life. Mr McNamee was a teacher, so there was a pension and a lump sum of course, and the house was paid off when he died. Otherwise, nothing else is mentioned, just whatever money was in the bank. I do know that Mrs McNamee only taught part-time because of the children, so their income was always limited."

Annette wasn't giving up. "So how much did she inherit when Mr McNamee died? Approximately?"

John Dunn stared at her with distaste, but she held his gaze steadily. Even if there was no more money, she knew there was more information to be had. The solicitor hesitated, considering whether or not it was ethical to reveal the secrets of the dead. Annette could see him veering towards a 'no', so she decided to give him some encouragement, fixing his eyes solemnly.

"You could be helping us to save lives, Mr Dunn. This is a very serious murder investigation."

Either his sense of public duty, or the fear of his perfect layer of dust being disturbed by a hairy big policeman, prompted Dunn into action, and he stood up laboriously, reaching into his drawer for a key. The solicitor moved so slowly that Annette could almost hear his joints ache, but eventually he reached the back of the office and lifted up a rug to reveal a well-hidden safe. It creaked open like something from a Hammer Horror film, and Annette almost laughed aloud at the surreal feel to her day. Liam would love this.

Dunn returned just as slowly, carrying a large brown envelope. He placed it on the desk and considered for a few seconds longer, before opening it to reveal a single sheet of A4.

"Well...yes..."

Annette wanted to leap across the desk and snatch the page from his hands, but instead she sat patiently, waiting while the lawyer played out his full show of ethical reluctance. When he finally spoke, it was in a surprised voice.

"It appears that Mrs McNamee inherited...from the proceeds of two life insurance policies, the pension and death benefits...Well..."

"Well, what?"

"A...a sum of two and a half million pounds sterling, plus the proceeds of the sale of the family home." He quickly set the paper face-down on the desk, ever the solicitor.

"Well, I must say...I hadn't realised. As I said, Andrew handled the estate."

"Where did all the money go?"

He pursed his thin lips, openly disapproving of her now.

"I'm afraid that was Mrs McNamee's personal business. Although according to this there are still five hundred thousand pounds in Northern Ireland Bank to be divided between the children, in addition to the proceeds of the house."

"That means she spent two million pounds in just over four years?"

"I believe Mrs McNamee did do a great deal of travelling after her husband died."

She would have had to visit the moon for that amount!

He stood up, replacing the papers in the safe, and then walked quickly to the door, his arthritis miraculously cured. He held it open pointedly.

"I'm sorry, but I really can't help you any further, Sergeant McElroy, and I would be obliged if this meeting was kept confidential. I'm very sure Mrs

McNamee's children would not like their financial business known."

Annette was so shocked by the amount that he'd quoted that she'd allowed herself to be ushered onto the street before she even realised. It hadn't been a wasted visit; she was going straight back to examine Fiona McNamee's bank accounts.

****

The team had decamped to the basement briefing-room; its high ceilings and neon strips more conducive to serious thought than the cosy familiarity of Craig's office. John had arrived but Des had gone home on Rafferty-watch, so Craig decided to start.

"Over to you, Davy."

Davy projected a screenshot onto a whiteboard on the wall.

"Right. The checks reveal that Jessica Adams basically dropped off the face of the earth nineteen months ago. A call came through earlier from Lear Island, and apparently s...she lived there with Gemma Orr last year, and gave birth to the baby, Pia, there. That's w...why there isn't much information on her on our s...systems. The Island's records aren't linked with the mainland so the other girls' immunisations didn't appear either.

They left the island when Pia was four months old and kept in touch with Ms Orr until about five months ago. But there's nothing at all after that."

Nicky nodded to cut in.

"Go ahead, Nicky."

"Well, I was thinking, sir... what would I do if Gary was dead? What would make me kill? I don't think it's just lack of money, because she could have claimed benefits. And she wouldn't risk going to prison and losing her girls just for money. There has to be something else."

"What then?"

"I would do it to protect Jonny, if I couldn't guarantee protecting him myself. Like if I knew I wasn't going to be around..." John leaned forward, interjecting.

"Nicky's right, Marc. These murders were very well-planned, but in each one she let herself be seen, and sometimes even caught on CCTV. Agreed?" They all nodded.

"So, she didn't care if we saw her and we know that she didn't care if we found her prints. That makes it look like she really doesn't care if she's caught and separated from her children. But we know she loves them and really wants to be with them, which must mean that she knows she's already going to be separated from them for some reason anyway."

Craig nodded slowly, saying nothing, so the pathologist continued.

"I believe that the methods of killing, the frenzy at the scene with Ian McCandless and the mock-rape with Maria Burton show that Jessica Adams may be ill."

Craig's eyes widened. "Why do you think that?"

"This is a previously normal wife and mother, Marc. But the deliberate damage to Maria Burton's warrant card and badge, the mock-rape, the viciousness with which the petrol pump was pushed into McCandless' throat and the sheer power behind it, are very abnormal. And given the feeling of invulnerability that let her enter this building in broad daylight to kill Liam, and to probably enter a prison to kill Lynsey Taylor..."

Annette gawped at him. "Taylor's dead?"

Craig brought them up to date on Taylor's overdose and Davy nodded. She'd been the last one on the trial list alive other than the judge.

"Go on, John."

"It all points to a killer who has a sadistic and high-risk taking attitude. So... either they have a pure mental illness, or they have a physical illness that's affecting their rational thought and inhibitions. Adams is completely fearless." A mutter of agreement went round the room.

"And what she also has is enough strength and loss

of sensation to drag a grown man across a forecourt, push a petrol pump down his throat, and twist razor-sharp wire with her bare hands. She left Purecrem and fingerprints everywhere, so she was definitely barehanded for at least part of Ian McCandless' killing."

"But, how-?"

John forged on. "Marc asked me to look for causes of sensory loss while retaining power so I made a shortlist. And today I've received some additional information from Wharf House. Adams has been taking high-dose steroids."

He looked around for any signs of realisation, to be greeted by blank faces, all except Annette's.

"Jordan takes them when he's bad with asthma."

"You're right, Annette, they are used for asthma, but not in these doses. In doses this high, there are only a few illnesses that fit, like organ transplant, but then they'd be on other anti-rejection medication. The most likely illness and the one that fits completely with a change of character, poor co-ordination and sensory loss is..." He continued more quietly. "A brain tumour with systemic effects."

They stared at him blankly.

"It fits. It's as rare as hell but it fits everything. A brain tumour can lead to increased pressure on the brain, causing personality changes and poor co-ordination. It can also make the body's immune system fight back, and eventually lead to a condition called paraneoplastic syndrome. And then in rare cases, an extension of that called neurologic syndrome."

"What does that do?"

"It causes a loss of sensation while retaining normal physical strength. In fact the high-dose steroids used to treat the increased pressure might even have given her extreme strength."

Craig nodded then explained about the nightclub assault. "The officers who arrested Adams said that she was unsteady on her feet but fought them like a tigress. It took four men to cuff her." He shook his head sadly. "They thought she was high on something."

"She was, Marc. On steroids. But they couldn't possibly have known."

The room fell quiet for a moment while everyone took the new information in, then John spoke again, more solemnly.

"I checked and Jessica Adams was seen fifteen months ago at the Cancer Unit. I spoke to her consultant this morning and he faxed this across."

He opened a folder, distributing the sheets within. It was a summary of the medical record of Jessica Adams, aged twenty-seven.

"She's got a brain tumour, a Glioblastoma, and she's terminal. She was given six months to live, six months ago. But there's something else..."

There was more? Whatever it was, it was making John look even sadder. But what could be worse than terminal cancer?

Then Annette did the sums and her mouth fell open. "Fifteen months...but she was still pregnant then... The baby?"

John nodded. "That's exactly it; the baby. Adams refused to have treatment until she was born and..." He turned to Davy.

"She didn't stay on Lear Island just for the immunisations, Davy. She stayed there until she'd finished breast-feeding, and by then she was too late to help herself. The survival rate for a Glio is poor anyway, so she must have weighed up the slim possibility of a few more months of life for her, versus the potential risk to the baby if she allowed them to treat her while she was pregnant and breast-feeding. She chose her baby. They tried chemotherapy this March, but it was too late."

Even Craig was shocked. "My God... That's dreadful, John."

This was what had changed Jessica Adams from a loving mother into a desperate Nikita. The room fell quiet for a moment, no-one sure how to feel. Eventually Craig spoke again.

"You were right, Nicky, it was all about the children. This is the missing piece. She knows that she won't be here to look after them." He shook his head despairingly. "Everything pointed to her being ill – her pallor, her thinness, even her weak voice on the phone. She worked barehanded and left prints, when the pain would have prevented any normal person working without gloves. This is it."

Nicky looked at him, confused. "But I still don't understand. Who *is* going to look after her daughters, sir? The courts will have to get involved at that age and that risks them going to her parents. She would never allow that."

Annette's next words echoed Craig's thoughts exactly.

"She's not killing for her own motives, sir. She's killing for someone else's. In return, they'll look after her children when she dies, financially, and maybe even in other ways. But who's paying her, sir? Fiona McNamee's dead and I spoke to her children; they genuinely sounded as if they knew nothing."

Craig shook his head. It wasn't the McNamee kids.

"The solicitor confirmed that they don't even know how much they'll inherit yet."

"How much will they inherit, Annette?"

"There's five hundred grand and the house. That's probably worth about another four hundred."

"That's a lot for a teacher to leave."

"That's nothing. There was another two million from insurance policies, but she ran through it in the four years after her husband died."

"And she died early this year, Davy?"

"Yes, in April. And I've checked, chief, there have been no hits on any of her accounts from that time. Everything is frozen until the estate has been dealt w...with."

"Cash can be easily hidden, Davy." Craig knew that his next question was cynical, but he asked it anyway.

"How was Fiona McNamee killed, Annette? And where's her body?"

"Sir?"

"Where's Fiona McNamee's body?"

Davy jumped in eagerly, "I can answer that. It's at the bottom of the Mediterranean. The car went over the cliffs at La Venta near Marbella. They never found the car, or her."

Craig sat back, considering, and his next words shocked them all.

"I don't believe that Fiona McNamee is dead. I think she's with Jessica Adams and I think that they intend to take the children somewhere that Adams' parents will never find them." He leaned forward, energised suddenly. "Davy, get a clear photograph of Fiona McNamee and have the airports and ports run it for trips from Spain to here over the past six months. And for all flights out of Ireland over the past few days. If they've saved the CCTV files they can use face-recognition software."

"If it's an inbound flight w...we'll be out of luck; they destroy the files quickly. There's more chance with the outbound journey."

"OK, try outbounds over the past few days then. Look for Fiona McNamee and Jessica Adams out of any Irish airport or port since Tuesday. I think they've been working together to kill everyone who allowed Lynsey Taylor to do soft time."

They all looked incredulous, except John, who nodded in agreement. It made perfect sense. "Adams has been acting as McNamee's hit-man. That's what I said, Marc."

Craig nodded in agreement. "Yes, you did, and she could still try for the judge and Taylor's accomplice, although I think it's unlikely. We notified the judge's close-protection officers, and Taylor's partner is locked up in Maghaberry; too hard to access. I think they've finished and I think that they're leaving Northern Ireland for good. Davy, look for two women travelling with three small girls, one a baby, and widen it to anywhere outside the UK."

The detective dragged a hand tiredly down his face, then he shrugged. "Although I honestly think it's a long shot. I think that they're long gone."

"You really believe Fiona McNamee's alive, sir?"

Craig nodded, "No-one else wanted everyone on that list dead, Annette. She's been thinking about avenging her husband for five years and Jessica Adams was just what she needed. And I'll tell you something else. When Jessica Adams dies, Fiona McNamee is going to be her daughters' new mother."

****

St Mary's.

Liam smiled weakly as John helped himself to a handful of the grapes he'd brought. "Why don't you have some fruit, Doc?"

Even his sarcasm was weak, so John ignored it. Instead, he carried on comforting Liam that he'd only been one name on Jessica Adams' long hit list.

"Great. I feel so much better knowing it was nothing personal."

"You've no idea how lucky you are to be alive, Liam. Twenty mls of aconite is one hundred percent lethal. Chatting-up that W.P.C. probably saved your life."

"I wouldn't be too sure. Danni's promised me hell for it when I'm better. But thanks for telling me how close I was to dying, Doc, you're a real comfort. With that bedside manner, I can see why you chose pathology."

He changed the subject quickly, before John delved even further into his favourite subject, death.

"Anyway, tell me what the boss is up to. It'll give me something to think about, apart from my next bed-bath."

"Oh, you know Marc. Following up the smallest lead. He even went to Limavady."

Liam smiled knowingly. "Oh, did he now? He heard McNulty's a looker then. Pity, I was going to play him with that one for a while."

John was getting fed-up hearing how gorgeous Julia McNulty was, when he'd never even seen her. "If you'd told *me* she was a looker, I could have visited

Limavady last week. Marc always gets the perks."

Just then, a slim brunette sat down by the bed opposite and smiled shyly at John, who quickly smiled back. Liam caught the exchange and laughed.

"I take it you'll be visiting me again tomorrow then..."

Chapter Nineteen

"Anything yet, Davy?"

"The City airport check-in staff recognised one of the photos. They have Jessica Adams on a flight from Belfast to London two days ago, on the twenty fourth. But s...she's a blonde now."

"That fits with the Wharf's mug-shot. Was she alone?"

"No, s...she had a baby with her. It's the right age, but...it's a little boy."

A boy! Of course. It would be easy to pass a baby of that age as a boy; no-one would ever check.

"What names were on her passport?"

"Didn't use one. The airline doesn't request I.D. inside the UK."

Great.

"Damn. OK, check the passenger list; they had to have someone's name against the seat. And find out how she paid for it."

"Give me five minutes."

"What about McNamee and the other two girls?"

"Nothing through Belfast. I'm running Dublin, Londonderry, Cork, Knock, S...Shannon and Galway airports, plus the ferries. And I'm trying to pick up Adams in London."

Craig nodded and headed back to his office to think. Annette was on her desk phone, speaking quietly in the background. She hung up and rushed over to Davy's desk.

"Davy, can you run a name for me, please?"

"Not right now." Then he smiled at her in apology, realising that his tone had been too abrupt.

"S...Sorry, Annette. It's just, I'm buried. Give me ten."

She returned his smile and turned towards Craig's office, knocking once on its half-open door. Craig was standing by the window, looking out at the river. It was raining hard and the wind was howling wildly around the glass-walled building, echoed by a boat horn in the distance. They were ten floors up, and the higher the floor the louder the noise became; Mrs Butler must be deafened upstairs. Below them, the Lagan was whipping itself into a rough, fast moving sheet covered in swaying boats.

He turned and perched on the edge of the desk.

"What have you got, Annette?"

"I've been chasing the McNamee children about their mum's suicide." He nodded her to sit down and made them both coffees.

"I spoke to them both, sir. Kirsty is an intern at Marcheson's public relations company, and Peter has gone into banking. Neither of them chose teaching. Kirsty said she was going to, but she'd lost all her public service ethos after her dad's death."

"Understandable."

She nodded. "Anyway, they were both pretty hostile. The boy hates the police and said there was sod all justice in the UK, and that in the Middle East they'd have stoned Taylor and her boyfriend to death for killing his father."

"He's not far wrong." It wasn't the first time they'd had the capital punishment debate, with Liam throwing in his ten pence worth on the side of the executioner.

"He said that their mum never recovered from their dad's death. She tried to commit suicide twice in the year after his murder, so they weren't that shocked when she finally managed it. She chose the place in Spain where they'd holidayed every year when they were kids. She just couldn't bear life without him, sir."

Craig still didn't believe Fiona McNamee was dead. "Did she leave a note?"

Annette nodded. "In the hotel room. And she posted a copy to the kids from Spain. Kirsty said that she would have known they wouldn't get it for a week, and by then they'd already have known that she was dead. It just said what you'd expect; that she loved them but couldn't live without her husband."

She anticipated his response to her next words.

"They didn't find the body, sir." Craig's sceptical expression didn't disappoint her, but she ignored it, continuing.

"She drove over a cliff into the sea and witnesses saw a woman in the car as it went over. The Spanish police found nothing, but apparently it's a well-known suicide spot and they rarely find anyone. The currents are far too strong."

She looked at him ruefully. Even she had to agree it all seemed too neat.

"I asked them if their mum knew someone called Jessica Adams and Peter drew a blank. But Kirsty said she remembered a young female juror approaching her mother after the trial, and being very sympathetic. She didn't know her name but she said she fitted Jessica Adams' description, so I faxed over the wedding photo from the paper and Kirsty confirmed that it was Adams. Neither of them have knowledge of any contact other than that."

"OK, great work, Annette. Get on to the Spanish police and see what else they have on the suicide please. Let's hope it was a dummy in the car, but ask them about any missing local women just to be safe. I heard you asking Davy to run a name for you. What was that about?"

"Well, it's a long shot, but I've been checking the passenger manifests coming into Ireland from Europe over the past six months, running thirty-five to sixty-year-old women on non-UK passports. I have a hunch that Fiona McNamee might have a foreign passport. She would be forty-seven now, so it would be hard for her to pose outside that age range.

I found ten names. Kirsty said her mum was about five-feet-six so I ran them against heights as well. That narrowed it to three and I spoke to two of them this morning; they don't fit. But there's one woman that I can't find. Her name is Fina Morales." F.M. The same initials as Fiona McNamee. Craig's interest was piqued.

"She flew into Dublin from Paris two weeks ago, on a Spanish passport. The photo is pretty nondescript and it doesn't really look like Fiona McNamee, but then again it doesn't not look like her either, and the initials *are* the same. People often stick to their own initials when they change I.D., don't they? So I thought Davy could have a dig."

"Good thinking. Ask the Spanish police about her as well, but I'm sure you're right."

He yawned suddenly and rubbed his eyes. None of them had slept much since Liam's adventure, and he had no-one to drag him away from work.

Annette changed the topic to cheer them both up.

"Have you heard? Liam's back on active duty next week."

Craig stared at her, astonished. "What? That's far too soon! What are the doctors playing at?"

"Danni says he's giving them hell so they're letting him home today. Apparently, his powers of recovery are superhuman."

Craig laughed balefully. "Now he'll never shut up about how he cheated death. Well, *they* may have agreed he's fit, but I haven't."

Annette sniggered. "Good luck with that one, sir. If it's a choice of home with Danni nagging him, or fighting you to come back, you know fine well which one Liam will choose."

****

They gathered at eleven-thirty for a briefing and Annette led-off.

"Right, here's what I've got so far. Fina Morales doesn't exist, well at least not our Fina Morales. There are twenty-seven of them across Spain that fit our age group, and the Spanish police pulled the passports for us.

Only eight of them even have passports, none of them look even vaguely like Fiona McNamee, and only one of them has been to the UK in the past ten years. She's five-feet-ten and Fiona McNamee was five-feet-six, so that's pretty hard to fake.

So our Fina Morales doesn't exist; the passport was

forged and it must have been a fairly professional job, because it fooled airport security."

She paused for breath and looked at them, as if waiting for a round of applause, but the room remained silent apart from the whirr of computers. Nicky was chewing the end of her pen thoughtfully, while Craig sat with his legs up on Liam's desk, draining his cup. Davy smiled her on encouragingly.

"God, but you lot are hard to please. OK, how about this. There was a woman travelling as Fina Morales on a flight from Dublin airport to Charles de Gaulle, Paris this Wednesday, with..."

She paused for encouragement and Nicky finally obliged her, leaning forward eagerly. She never could feign indifference as well as the others.

"Yes...?"

"Thank you for asking that extremely useful question, Nicky. The answer is, with two small girls. Fina Morales travelled on a Spanish passport that doesn't exist two days ago, with two small girls. They were listed as her grand-daughters."

Craig swung his long legs off the desk and sat forward. "Names and ages?"

"Rosa and Ambra, four and six..."

The names were rubbish but this was their woman. Adams and McNamee were travelling separately to confuse the police.

"Well done. Now where's Jessica Adams?"

Davy had a fleeting thought that Craig didn't bloody want much, but his pissed-off expression was stilled by a quick glance from Nicky.

"S...She flew under the name of Juanita Morales, another woman who doesn't exist, with her baby son Pietro. They were photographed leaving Terminal one at Heathrow at two pm on W...Wednesday, heading for the London underground. The cameras caught them at Earls Court at three o'clock, Rotherhithe at four and finally again at six at Baker S...Street. After that, they're ghosts-"

Annette interrupted him. "We're trying the cameras for mainline trains, and contacting all the local taxi firms, but there's nothing yet."

Craig nodded and smiled at them both. "Thanks, Davy, and thanks Annette. That's brilliant work, both of you. Don't worry about the train stations and taxis; we know where she's gone."

Annette looked incredulous, "Do we?"

"Yes. She travelled all over London trying to confuse us. Rotherhithe's on the opposite side of London to Earls Court, and then she's back centrally at Baker Street. She was zigzagging deliberately. Fiona McNamee's gone to Paris and there's no way that Adams is going to be parted from her children for long, so they're meeting up somewhere in Europe, could be in Paris, or maybe Spain.

If we check the tapes for all the big Western European airports and the Eurostar at Gare du Nord Paris, we'll see her coming out at one of them."

Annette knew that she would never have made that leap, playing 'follow that cab' instead.

"Get onto the gendarmes, the Spanish police and Interpol, and bring them up to date. Now please, Davy. Then we're all going for a very well-earned lunch at The James."

****

The Lab.

Craig propped his feet up on John's desk and yawned.

"If you don't mind sitting through it again, I'll go with you tonight, John. But I can't promise to speak to her, and if I leave before the end I leave, and I don't want any grief from you. *And* we're sitting at the back."

John Winter was focussing on a microscope slide, just letting him talk. He said nothing until Craig had finished.

"It's a good play actually. I won't tell you the end but the death's pretty unexpected."

"What?"

"It's unexpected."

"I thought it was A Midsummer Night's Dream?

Where's the death in that?"

"Oh...no, that's only on Saturday and Sunday. They've been doing a Stephen Maray play since Wednesday. 'The Cold Stone'. Didn't you see it in London?"

"No, although I must be the only person who didn't."

Craig thought for a minute and then spoke again, hesitantly. "What ...?"

"Yes?"

"What role does she play?" She... as if mentioning Camille's name would suddenly make her appear.

"Camille plays the title role and she was very good. She ..."

Craig held a hand up to stop him.

"Thanks, but that comes under the heading of too much information. Any more and I may get the urge to work tonight instead. By the way, don't ever mention to my folks that I went, and for God's sake don't say that you went with me; Mum will shoot you as a collaborator. She won't even have her name mentioned; apparently she nearly strangled Dad after one syllable."

He lifted the dark-pine office chair and turned it around, slumping tiredly with his arms over its back. "This case is wearing everyone down."

He brought John up to date with Annette's and Davy's latest findings.

"Of course, they'll be long gone by now. I've said probably France or Spain, but they could be anywhere if they've got forged passports."

"Have they?"

"Definitely; good forgeries too. Our Fina Morales doesn't exist, and changing their names again won't be a major effort."

He was about to say something more but stopped himself. John knew exactly what it had been.

"You're thinking that if Jessica Adams will be dead soon anyway, and the kids are innocent, then why pursue them at all."

Craig nodded, as if actually saying it was a

complete betrayal of his training. Then he remembered the families of the dead, and he knew again why they couldn't leave it.

"We can't stop. It wouldn't be justice for the victims."

"I imagine that's what the McNamees thought when Lynsey Taylor got a five year sentence."

Craig nodded, conceding that it was the truth.

"What if Fiona McNamee had nothing to do with this, Marc, and it's just some woman that Adams is paying to be nanny to the kids? They could easily argue that she'd flown a nanny over to care for the kids, all above board."

"And exactly what did she use to pay this nanny? This nanny with a forged passport."

But John was on a roll so he ignored the question.

"OK then. Say Fiona McNamee held back some of the insurance money; there's no way she'd have spent two million pounds in four years, not unless she went to Vegas. Then, for all we know she could've found out about Jessica Adams' situation and just decided to gift her some money before she committed suicide. Then Adams decided to do this in return, in her memory?"

Craig looked at him, wryly. "When did you start writing fiction?" They both laughed.

"Fiona McNamee met Jessica Adams at the trial and liked her; that much we know. But to give her that amount of money for doing nothing, when she has two children of her own to provide for? No.

And no matter how much money Fiona McNamee might have left her; for Adams to kill and risk being caught, leaving her children at the mercy of the state when she died, when they'd almost certainly end up with her parents? No way, John. Fiona McNamee is alive, she's up to her eyes in these murders and we need to catch them both."

"Yes, but didn't Annette say that the McNamee kids will already get half a million and the house? So they're well provided for already. She *could* have just gifted the rest to Adams."

Craig rubbed his eyes hard with his knuckles, too

tired to keep arguing.

"You're wrecked, Marc. Are you sure you'll stay awake long enough to get to the theatre?"

Craig thought about it for a moment, sensing a way out, then he shook his head and stared at John with blood-shot eyes.

"Don't tempt me... but if I fall asleep during the performance, don't bother to wake me up either."

"I will if you snore. It disturbs the thespians."

****

The Italian Alps.

Jessie felt more alive than she had done in years, ever since the farm had started to go downhill. She closed her eyes to erase the painful memories. This wasn't a day for being sad; it was one of those special, perfect days that only came a few times in life.

She smiled and gazed over the cafe wall into the deep gorge below. The view was breath-taking. The steep slopes fell gently away to form an emerald-green chevron between the valley's walls, the grass dotted with white flowers, even in October. Tiny sheep grazed calmly miles below them, bored by the beauty of their surroundings, the business of eating much more important.

An open sandwich sat on the wall beside her, untouched. She had no time to waste eating, desperate to memorise everything around her. The fresh, cold air was quiet, broken only by the occasional clatter of plates and the loud whirr of camera-shutters, freezing the image to look back at in the years ahead. She didn't need a camera, and there would be no years ahead for her, only now.

Fiona reached over, poised to tap her on the shoulder but reluctant to disturb her dream. Jessie sensed her and turned around, smiling, her newly swollen face distorted by the grin.

"Did you ever think we'd get here, Fi?"

Fiona shook her head hard, setting her newly styled

bob swinging, "Never. Do you regret it?"

Jessie was emphatic in her reply. "No. You four are all that matter to me now."

She looked towards the table where the girls were sitting, helpfully covering Pia's face in food. The baby was laughing happily so she left them in peace. She ruffled her recently reddened hair playfully, fingering her newly full lips and laughing at Fiona's enhanced cheekbones and Botox-ed brow.

They looked nothing like the women who'd arrived in Paris two days before; one visit to a cosmetic doctor and hairdresser had ensured that. The only thing that had saddened her was cutting her daughters' beautiful hair, shorn into crops to match their boy disguises. They would become girls again when they were safe in their new home.

Jessie was glad that they'd chosen Italy to settle in; she and Michael had honeymooned there and she'd loved it instantly, the people's absolute love of 'bambinos' the final clincher. Fiona had begun studying Italian as soon as they'd made the choice, and she was almost fluent now. It was essential for the next stage of their plan.

Fiona peered up at the winter sun, thinking the unthinkable; Lynsey Taylor would have been freed this week, and she could never have lived with that. They'd *had* to kill them. She corrected herself quickly. Jessie had killed them, Jessie; reminding and convincing herself again that her denial wasn't cowardice, just her part of their bargain. If she ever confessed the girls would be lost, and it would all have been for nothing. All Jessie's sacrifice would have been in vain.

They stood for a moment longer watching the meandering sheep then they re-packed the bags and climbed into the car, ready for the final journey into the country that they both loved.

****

The ward sister stood with her arms folded, staring at Liam disapprovingly.

"Are you really sure you want him home, Mrs Cullen? He can be very noisy, you know."

Liam squeezed himself into the too–small wheelchair that they'd insisted on for his journey to the car, and gazed up at the three women balefully.

Annette was backing the sister up, enjoying teasing Liam while she could.

"Yes, are you sure, Danni? Because Jack Harris can find an empty cell for him at High Street. Just you say the word."

Liam squinted up at her, making a mental note to get back at her when he was better. "Just you wait till I'm back at work, Sergeant; you'll be making tea for a month."

Annette and Danni looked at each other and shook their heads. Then, without a word, they turned on their heels and walked off down the ward, waiting for the howl of indignation that would inevitably follow.

"Ah, come on, you know I was only kidding you. Take me home and..." Liam reached for some sacrifice that would convey the enormity of his gratitude. "I'll cook you dinner."

Danni swung around, astonished. "Hasn't there's been enough poisoning for one week?"

A student nurse who'd been watching the show laughed suddenly and Liam flashed her a smile, sensing support.

"Good to know we're entertaining the staff." He molded his best suck-up face. "Ah, come on now, girls, take me home...please?"

****

Craig liked her, but did he like her enough to take the risk again? Dinner could get messy and then they'd both lose out. But then life was messy, wasn't it? Except that he'd done a good job of keeping his life tidy for years. It was dull and it was lonely, but at least it was tidy, and tidy was good, wasn't it?

Maybe lunch would be better. There was less chance of misbehaving when alcohol wasn't involved, but then there was less chance of having fun as well. He turned the number over repeatedly in his hand, and stared hard at the phone, as if the solution would magically appear. God, he was too old for this crap.

Nicky's soft knock rescued him from the decision and he beckoned her in gratefully.

"What can I do for you?"

"Davy would like five minutes when you get time."

He nodded, smiling. Davy was still too shy to knock his door directly, using Nicky as a big-sister intermediary.

"Where's Annette?"

"Gone to help Danni get Liam home. She's got Erin and a six-month bump to carry as well."

Craig's hand flew to his forehead in realisation. "Of course, he gets out today. I would have collected him if Danni had said."

"She didn't like to bother you, what with the case. She wants this killer caught as much as we do. Anyway, don't worry; the two of them can nag him into submission."

He smiled. "OK, tell Davy I'll be there in five. I just need to make a quick call."

He picked up the receiver, suddenly decisive, and Nicky left, discreetly leaving the door open just a crack. Enough to hear his deep voice say hesitantly. "Hello...Julia, it's Marc, Marc Craig." Time for life to get messy again.

Chapter Twenty

Annette thumped in heavily, looking as if she'd suffered enough for ten women and Nicky laughed, knowing exactly why.

"How's Liam?"

The detective rolled her eyes meaningfully. "A hell of a lot better than we are. It nearly killed us getting him to go to bed when he got home. I had to threaten him with the Armed Response Unit, and even then he said that he'd beaten most of them at weights and to bring them on."

"I bet he has too."

"God knows what he'll be like when he's an old man. He's difficult enough now. Imagine trying to give him a bed-bath when he's ninety."

"Oh, thanks a lot, Annette. That picture will be in my head for days now."

Nicky laughed and shook her head, as if to remove the image. Just then, Craig emerged from his office, the smile on his face giving the P.A. all the information she needed.

He strolled over to Davy so casually that she could almost hear him whistle.

"Right Davy, what've you got for me?"

Davy was sitting in 'Emo World', a three-desk horseshoe of computers, each flashing with different colours and timings as if it had its own character. He pointed Craig to the screen on his left and clicked on a video file, opening it to show Jessica Adams and her baby emerging from the Eurostar terminal at Paris' Gare du Nord station. The time and date showed eight o'clock on Wednesday evening UK time.

He clicked again and she reappeared two minutes later, exiting on the Rue de Dunkerque heading onto Rue La Fayette, until she disappeared into the Metro at Magenta. A third click showed her leaving the Metro thirty minutes later at Rambuteau in the fourth arrondisement, before disappearing completely into the busy Marais district.

"I've been on the phone all afternoon trying to find more images. S...Sarkozy announced that he'd be installing extra cameras in Paris in two thousand and eight but most of them are in the eighteenth and nineteenth districts. My French is a bit rusty, but as far as I can make out Adams disappeared off the Rue Saint-Merri."

Craig nodded; it was exactly where he would have gone. There were far fewer cameras there, so she could walk through the side streets for ages without being picked up.

"Anything else in that area in the next few hours?"

"Only this. It was taken at nine pm UK time." Davy clicked again and showed Craig a few dark frames of two women walking with a pram and two small children wearing baseball caps, only to be lost again immediately.

"I've checked and that camera cut out just then and remained down all evening. Mechanical fault."

Craig put a hand on his shoulder, "Well done, Davy, that's excellent work." Davy blushed, embarrassed, and Nicky winked over at him, making it even deeper. The boss was in a very good mood.

Annette wandered across.

"But where does it actually leave us, sir? They could go anywhere from Paris. We know what they were called and looked like when they left the UK, but it wouldn't take much to change their looks and get new passports again, would it? They've obviously got the resources."

Her voice tailed off and she glanced down sadly. "And... Jessica Adams will be dead soon, so who do we pursue then?"

Craig nodded. "John and I had the same discussion earlier, Annette. But if Fiona McNamee was a willing partner then we have to pursue her."

Nicky stood up at her desk indignantly, "And leave those three babies alone in the world! Or even worse, with that paedophile of a grandfather. How can we, sir?"

At least she'd said 'we'. Its inclusivity somehow made Craig feel less of a villain. He looked at her kindly, but his voice was firm.

"We have to try, Nicky. They killed three people who also have families that loved them." She still looked defiant. "And remember, they nearly killed Liam." That burst her balloon and she sat down heavily in her seat.

Craig shrugged resignedly. "If it's any comfort, we have to look but I'm not sold on our chances of finding them. Interpol is unlikely to mount an expensive manhunt, and it would have to be huge – they could be anywhere in Europe or the East by now. It's a huge landmass with unfettered transit for EU members, so as long as they avoid airports and big cities we may never see them again."

Nicky allowed herself a small smile for the children.

"So let's start worrying about what happens when or if we actually find them. And that will get less likely by the day, especially when Jessica Adams ..."

He didn't need to finish.

South-East Italy.

They pulled the battered four-by-four hard-left off the country road, Fiona checking constantly in the rear-view mirror that they hadn't been followed. She'd been doing it since they left Paris, but Jessie was letting her guard drop slightly now. They were in a rural part of Puglia in South-East Italy, just off the Adriatic coast, and they hadn't seen a single car since the outskirts of Bari two hours before.

Fiona looked in the mirror again but Jessie realised this time she was actually staring at herself. She looked very different from the middle-aged woman who'd left Belfast. A short blonde bob had replaced her chin-length brown hair. And although her face was still swollen, with her new cheekbones and her lines smoothed and filled, she looked thirty-five again. Her face had been changed to suit the future they'd planned.

Jessie lifted a small mirror from the handbag at her feet to stare at her own reflection. She looked younger too. She smiled ironically; at least she'd be a pretty corpse.

The sun was setting behind them as they drove along the ever-bumpier roads, looking for a clearing. The girls bounced up and down in time with each bump, in a game Jessie had taught them years before on the farm's rough tracks. They squealed excitedly every time, the simple game never jading for them.

Finally, they found a small, square clearing; its worn earth surrounded by trees and its central heap of charred stones showing that it had once been a campsite. The car pulled to a halt and Jessie lifted the girls out one by one, each reaching eagerly for the fresh air and a chance to play tag amongst the leaves. Fiona motioned her to take the food, while she pitched the tent for the night. Their final destination was still fifty miles away and they all needed a rest, but a tent was a lot safer than some pensione landlady inconveniently asking for I.D.

The Italian evening was bright and balmy with none of the bone-cutting cold of a British winter, and Jessie felt well in a way that she hadn't done for months in the damp Ulster air. Maybe she had longer left than she thought. Just then, a searing pain behind one eye doubled her over and she set Pia on the ground quickly, turning away from the small group to be sick. Or maybe she hadn't.

Fiona put her arm around the younger woman, sitting her down on the rug that she'd just spread out. Eventually Jessie felt better and leaned over; opening the food basket that they'd packed before they'd left the city.

"Girls, come and have a drink. We have Orangina."

They ran around the trees one more time and then came screaming towards her, plonking themselves heavily on the tartan ground, each cuddling Pia as they sat. Then she poured the juice and spread the forest-feast in front of them, giving them each small, tin-foiled food parcels to unwrap as if they were Christmas presents and taking miniature toys and crackers out, so that the whole experience turned into more fun than they'd had in weeks.

They watched the sunset together before Jessie tucked them into a makeshift bed, then the two women drank wine and Jessie talked through the details of the girls' years ahead. Fiona taped each word for a dual purpose; to ensure she delivered Jessie's wishes as closely as possible, and to let the girls hear their mother's voice every night as they fell asleep.

****

The Grand Opera House, Belfast.

Belfast's Grand Opera House was appropriately named; it was large, ornate and ceremonial, in exactly the way opera houses and opera singers should be. It had survived Nazi bombs and thirty years of homespun terrorism, and through it all it had watched over Belfast, like a gilded, stone observer. Now it housed performances as diverse as King Lear and the Christmas Panto, and tonight it was housing The Cold Stone, with Camille Kennedy as the leading lady.

It was the first time Craig had left the office early in months, persuading his father to cover for his missed Friday dinner. Now here he was, waiting to see Camille perform for the first time in years and he was regretting it already.

He'd been drinking since six o'clock but he still wasn't drunk enough for this. He downed two whiskeys in the theatre-bar with two more waiting for the interval, while John stayed sober to curb the worst of his possible behaviour later that night.

There was no ignoring that Camille was in the play. Her face was on every poster outside and she had a special biography slot in the programme. "Camille Kennedy, a gifted American actress trained at RADA..." Blah, blah, blah.

Craig scowled at her photograph. She was still beautiful. Why couldn't she have at least gained weight? As if that could ever have killed his feelings for her. No hope; he was the fifty years married type, if he ever got that far, and he'd been closer ten years before than he would probably ever be again.

The performance bell rang and they took their seats, at the end of a row far back in the stalls; where he could see her but she couldn't see him. Not that Camille would have reacted while she was on stage anyway; she was far too professional ever to put real emotions before fake ones.

Suddenly the lights went down and she walked onto the stage. Slight, blonde and gorgeous, just as he remembered her. His eyes ran over her face and he stared into her soft blue eyes as if she could actually see him. His gaze resting on her lips; feeling their fullness pressing against his, as if it was only an hour ago.

He watched her walk to her mark and stand gracefully, to start the first of many speeches and dialogues that blurred into each other as his heart ached and he decided to drink himself deeper into numbness at the interval. All the time remembering her soft hair, and her soft skin, and her soft, soft words. And her lies.

By the interval, Craig was so drunk that he nearly missed John checking his phone. Except that he was never too drunk to see what was happening around him, or to avoid the meeting that he now knew Camille was trying to engineer.

He sat through the second act, already knowing who the murderer was, and then leaned over to John five minutes from the end, whispering very quietly "I'm leaving." He moved so quickly that John couldn't clamber out of his seat fast enough to catch him, before Craig had exited the plush, carpeted foyer into the cold night.

They reached the street and the chill air hit them both; Craig's slight unsteadiness the only sign that he'd drunk enough to sink the Titanic.

"Where are you going, Marc?"

"Home. I know exactly what she's planning, John.

Don't forget I know her too well. She sent you that text, the one that you thought I didn't see."

John stared at him with a mixture of surprise and shame.

"I didn't say that you would meet her, Marc. I told her I'd *ask* you, that's all. Just that I'd ask you."

"Asked and answered. OK? And the answer is no. And you can put it to her any way you like. No nicely, no way, no never..."

"Never? Really?"

"Never or for as long as I say. Whichever comes first."

Craig ended the conversation without a backward look, sprinting athletically across the road to a taxi beside the dark statue of Henry Cooke, which was known locally as the 'Black man'. Another politically incorrect Belfast term.

As he climbed into the cab and disappeared John turned back reluctantly towards the theatre, heading backstage to tell the leading lady that she wasn't getting her own way this time, or anytime soon. And that she would probably never get anything again from Marc Craig completely on her terms.

****

Limavady.

The sky above Julia was so clear that she couldn't remember ever seeing the stars like that before; each one shining separately, but all glowing together. She knew all the constellations: Orion, Sirius, the Big Dipper...an offshoot from her army navigation training, although she somehow doubted that the Chief of the Defence Staff would appreciate such romantic thoughts.

For a moment, she let herself wish on each of them, longing for someone to be there with her. Someone to point them out to, and kiss beneath them.

She chided herself to get a grip and reached into her pocket for her closest and most reliable companions, lighting one up and inhaling long and hard enough to blow smoke at the moon.

Chapter Twenty-One

Stranmillis. Saturday, 7 a.m.

Craig was woken at seven by his mobile and he groped urgently for the handset, knocking a glass of water off the table onto his varnished-wood bedroom floor. The liquid formed and broke like globules of mercury, and he muttered an expletive as he pressed answer, visualising the clean-up before he left for work.

"YES."

His hangover voice sounded rude even to him, and he glanced quickly at the screen; a private number. Realising he had no idea who was on the other end he swallowed and started again, more politely.

"D.C.I. Craig – can I help you?"

Silence followed, and his instinct told him that it was the silence of a woman. For one fleeting moment he thought it was Jessica Adams, then he immediately dismissed the idea. There was no way she could have found out his number. But any delusion that his mobile was beyond reach was squashed a second later.

"Hello, Marco..."

Craig was suddenly disoriented, as when you encounter someone in an unexpected place and don't recognise them for a moment. Then he realised that it was Camille. Her soft voice was instantly recognisable, its timbre and cadence unchanged by the passing years; although there were American inflections that he hadn't noticed on the stage. They would be Prick's influence.

How the hell had she got his number? John would never have given it to her. Why was she calling? And most important of all, what would he say?

He took the route of minimal response; a habit that his friends often said drove them mad. "Hello..." It was all left up to her to say. Why she had called, why she had left him, what was going through her mind.

"Marco...I need to see you. I need to talk to you and

explain, and..."

Suddenly she was babbling. Running randomly through the years, her sentences broken and streaming, like the water on his floor. She had spilt it and now she wanted him to mop it up, and say. "It's all OK." Except that it wasn't.

His anger surged and he wanted to shout at her, accuse her, and, a sudden realisation hit him and he was only half-ashamed of it, he wanted to hurt her. Really hurt her. Hurt her and break her in exactly the way she had broken him. His lips rushed to form the words, thinking up new and different tortures for her as she babbled on. But he couldn't.

The tears in her voice meant he couldn't, the memories they shared meant he couldn't, and his image of himself as a man meant he couldn't. So instead, he said nothing, waiting until she stopped. Sheltering in the silence behind her words until he had regained control. Then he hid again, as he always did, behind the job.

"Camille." He let the softness of her name hang there, asserting his authority through the silence that followed.

Until she broke it.

"Yes."

Another pause.

"Give me your number, Camille, and I promise I'll call you."

"But you didn't come backstage last night and..."

Her panic was immediate and urgent and he felt instantly guilty, but he wasn't playing games. He *would* call her, but only when he was ready. He needed time to find his feet.

His voice softened and he could hear her breathing calm as he spoke.

"I'll call you, I promise. It might not be today but I will call you."

His alibi became slightly brisker. "But it's ten-past-seven and I've got to get ready for work now; we've a big case on. Tell me how long you're here and give me your number... please." He could feel his control returning and with it his kindness, so he added. "It's good to hear from you."

Then he took her number and ended the call quickly with "Take care. Bye" before her softness could snake its way around his heart, as it had done for so many years.

He lay there for an hour, the weight of the love that had ruled him for almost a decade pressing down on him, threatening to break through the wall that he had built. He struggled as he felt it crumble.

Suddenly a dog barked outside and broke through his thoughts, saving him. And with one thrust, he propelled himself out of bed and into the shower, drowning his feelings. He stood there, letting the water run over his muscled back for minutes, until peace had finally descended. Then he stood for a moment longer, testing its strength. When he was certain, he dressed himself in the suit of professionalism; a façade that would fool everyone but him.

****

The C.C.U. 9.30 a.m.

"Sorry I'm late, Nicky. You knew I had that planning meeting, didn't you?"

The P.A. nodded in reply, puzzled. She knew that her boss was lying, but not about what. There were never routine meetings on a Saturday.

Craig smiled brightly. "OK, what have we got?"

"Nothing urgent, but Davy has some good news for you."

He dropped his briefcase beside her desk, something he never did, and she gazed at him curiously. There was definitely something off. He strode towards Davy, his gestures too ostentatiously macho for something not to have rattled his cage. And it was really none of her business, except that she cared.

"You wanted to see me, Davy?"

"I think we have s...something, chief. A party of two

women and three children heading out of Paris in a Blue Citroën... They lost them at the border, but the general direction of travel looked like S...Spain. I've asked the police to keep an eye out around Marbella, the place Fiona McNamee committed s...suicide."

"Or didn't." They smiled together at the irony.

"But if they head back to S...Spain then it makes it more likely that Fina Morales is Fiona McNamee—heading back to a place they know?"

"Correct. Great work, Davy. Update the Spanish police and Interpol and keep an eye on it, but...."

Craig paused, and his next comment shocked Davy so much that "Huh?" was all he could manage.

"Don't spend all your time on it."

Nicky and Annette heard his words as well, and the suddenness of him taking his foot off the case's throttle surprised them both. This wasn't like him; he was usually like a dog with a bone until he'd caught a killer.

Craig caught their glances and knew what they were thinking. That he was less than happy about pursuing a half-dead mother and her three small children, plus an older woman who may or may not have been innocent, half way across Europe. And they were right. But thankfully, a call he'd received thirty minutes before gave him the perfect smokescreen for his reluctance.

"We've caught a home invasion out in Sydenham. They got away clean and left two dead, so we'll have our work cut out for us today, especially with one man down."

Annette sat forward eagerly; with Liam away she could get a chance to lead. The ghoulishness of her excitement suddenly hit her, and she sat back, feigning dignity, until the eagerness in her voice gave her away.

"What needs to be done first, sir?"

Craig smiled, feeling on more solid ground than he had all week.

Chapter Twenty-Two

Howard Street, Belfast. Saturday, 10 p.m.

He had offered to drive to the country but Julia had insisted on Belfast, saying that she was owed some retail therapy, and adding "I've arranged to meet my friend Jenny for lunch and stay with her overnight", immediately removing the pressure on them both. Craig admired her gift for organisation, if not her seemingly absolute need for control.

So now, here they were on a Saturday evening, facing each other across the starched white tablecloth and polished cutlery of Deane's, one of Belfast's premiere restaurants. With her facing out and him facing in, just as his mother had taught him.

They'd covered the initial awkward silence and the confused air-kissing, and they'd talked and laughed their way surprisingly well through three courses and two coffees. Until there was nothing left to say that wouldn't hint at desperation, or the need to fill the silence, growing louder against the background of the waiters clearing the room.

So finally Craig paid the bill and asked for their coats, noticing again as Julia rose, how elegant she looked in her soft cream dress. Its fabric was draping and clinging to the curves beneath. Curves that her work outfit hadn't even hinted at.

Her hair was loose and long, with soft, undulating waves of red-gold that she fingered as she talked. Pushing them back and running her fingers through them constantly, releasing a perfume that he recognised but couldn't name. She was beautiful and sensuous and nothing like the professional he had argued with, bristled at, and eventually talked to sensibly about their cases. She was a woman and he was reacting to her just like a man, and that meant trouble.

Julia stared at him intently, as if she could read his

mind. And she could, just as he could read hers. As they walked onto the city street in the cool night air he reached for her, pulling her to him firmly and kissing her parted lips eagerly, the urgency of his own response surprising him. His pleasure was echoed in her fevered eyes, saying that it was the same for her.

He stroked her soft, bare shoulders, running his hands down her arms until he reached her shawl. He gripped it gently, pulling her closer. She could feel him drawing her in and she leaned hard against him; knowing that she could pull away but reluctant to move and break the moment, and the night.

Instead, she freed one hand and drew a finger softly across his face, tenderly running it along his brow and down his lean cheek, until it finally rested on his full, wide mouth. She reached forward to kiss him again and the heat that she felt shocked her, reminding her of long forgotten urges that were returned by Craig's body in quick reply.

He drew her by the hand into a nearby doorway, like an adolescent yearning to keep the moment safe. They stood there in their private world until the chatter of a passing couple broke the moment and pulled them back onto Howard Street.

Craig gazed into her bright blue eyes, seeing a softness that he hadn't noticed before. A frayed vulnerability that said. "You can hurt me."

It was the reality check that he needed to stop him taking the next step; the one that would lead them straight back to his apartment. Lead them to undress each other longingly and clasp each other's bodies in a night of sensual, hot movement. The step that could start a relationship...or a professional nightmare.

He stepped away from her slowly, putting air between them, then he dropped her hand gently, answering her quick, questioning look with a soft smile. His deep voice framed his next words carefully.

"I've had a wonderful evening, Julia."

"So have I. But... Marc?"

"There's no but. I want to see you again, but..."

"You said there was no but."

The words showed her pain and her eyes glistened dangerously. She glanced away to stop him seeing her sharp tears, but Craig had already seen them. He immediately wanted to smooth them away and he realised then that he was already too involved, so he stepped back even further, as if his physical distance would echo itself in what he felt.

"Julia..." He searched for the words to explain his confusion.

"I don't...We work in a small world..."

He looked at her hesitantly, begging for understanding. "I don't want to do anything that will damage anyone. Please try to understand that."

Then pleadingly, "I need to take this slowly... there's..."

She looked shocked; as if something had just occurred to her. Another woman, but of course... Why hadn't she guessed? He was handsome and talented; *of course* there was another woman. She could feel herself erecting the walls that she used at work, and quickly slipped her coat around her shoulders, covering her bare femininity. Mentally wrapping Julia the woman in the safe uniform of Julia the D.I.

He watched her, knowing exactly what she was doing, half-expecting her to tie her hair back as the final disguise. But it was too late; he'd already seen the woman and he knew that he wanted to see more of her.

"I see." But her tense voice said that she didn't see, not at all.

"No, you don't, and if you close this door you'll never see. All I'm asking for is time to sort out my head. I really want to see you again but I'm trying to be fair."

"Fair to who, Marc?" Her next words were almost yelled at him, clear in the cold, night air. "You're married, aren't you?"

Even as she said it, she knew that it wasn't true. But what then? A live-in girlfriend? Is that why he had wanted to end the evening now? He had someone waiting for him at home.

He half-laughed at the ridiculousness of her question. "No, I'm not married." He could see her next question forming. "And before you ask, I'm not living with anyone either."

What then? She looked confused and hurt and he knew that she deserved an explanation, but then that would mean understanding his feelings himself and he wasn't sure that he did. He struggled to form his next words.

"There was someone." He could hear his voice starting to break, but her vulnerable face meant that he couldn't stop now. "We were going to marry, but..."

But what? Camille's ambition was stronger than her love for me. Camille met someone she liked better. Camille met someone more useful to her career. Which was it? He didn't know, and in that split second he realised that he *needed* to know. He needed to understand, he needed to find out what was left between him and Camille and put it to rest one way or another, before it ruined what he could have with someone else. And before he hurt the woman standing in front of him, looking so beautiful and vulnerable in the winter night.

So he reached out a hand tentatively, hoping hard that Julia would take it. And she did. Then they drove the few miles to the ancient circle of the Giants Ring and sat in his warm car talking until the sun came up. He explained everything to her then asked if they could be friends until he had sorted out the mess in his head. Because if he didn't, he would make a mess of hers as well...

****

It was Sunday evening by the time Craig managed to call Liam, and after thirty seconds of small talk he got straight to the point, knowing that Liam hated phone conversations just as much as he did.

"When are you thinking of coming back?"

"Tomorrow, and for God's sake don't say no, boss! Danni is doing my head in. She follows me around like a minder. You'll be investigating her murder if I don't get back to work."

Craig laughed, imagining Danni fussing round him, with Liam swatting her away like a wasp. He'd intended to make him take another week, but he really needed him on the home invasion case.

"OK, we've a case and I need you. But you're only back on one condition."

"Anything. I swear to God if you asked me to sleep with Mrs Butler I'd say yes. Anything to get out of here."

"Funny you should say that..."

"Aye, right. What *is* the price then?"

"You're office bound for a week and Annette's working the lead."

Liam's immediate protest was predictable and Craig let him rant for a minute before interrupting.

"My terms or nothing, Liam. Think of it like this; you can have Danni fussing and Erin climbing all over you, or you can be desk bound in the office with Annette taking the lead. Entirely your choice."

There was complete silence at the other end of the line.

"I thought so. See you tomorrow."

****

The C.C.U. Monday morning.

By ten o'clock Liam was up to date on the home invasion, and they'd cracked every possible joke about his eating habits, chatting-up W.P.C.s and his superhuman powers of recovery. They would be rehashed for months to come whenever there was a slow day, or until something else appeared to give them better banter.

Craig had a week's freedom from Nicky's list, courtesy of her trip to Venice, and his temporary P.A. wasn't due in until eleven, so he had an hour to himself. He closed his office door, knowing exactly how he intended to use it.

He pulled his chair over to the window and gazed out. The day was so clear that he could see right past the H&W cranes, to catch a rare glimpse of Scrabo's historic tower in the distance. It had overlooked Newtownards since the mid nineteenth century, memorialising the third Marquis of Londonderry, Wellington's general in the Napoleonic Wars. Now it sat amongst the beautiful walks and parkland of Killynether Wood, with views that extended across Strangford Lough to the Mountains of Mourne and the Scottish coast.

Everything about the day seemed perfect, or as perfect as it could be when he knew that Jessica Adams and Fiona McNamee were still roaming around Europe, free from any comeback from their crimes.

But he was ready to do what he'd been putting off for days, and propping his feet on the window sill he lifted his mobile and dialled, hoping that the call would be answered quickly, before he had time to change his mind. He wasn't disappointed. Camille answered in two rings, as if she'd been waiting for him.

Her soft voice breathed his name gently. "Marco." The background tannoy of the airport departure lounge showed that he'd timed it exactly as intended.

"Camille, we need to meet." Then, cutting confidently across her next words. "In London, the weekend of the eighteenth... you choose where."

Chapter Twenty-Three

Lecce, Italy. November.

The girls were playing 'ring o' roses' in the villa's small shaded courtyard, as Fiona drank wine and watched them and Jessie fed Pia fresh peaches from the orchard on their three acres of land. A soft breeze blew Pia's baby curls across her face and Jessie stroked them back, marvelling that all of the girls had inherited Michael's golden waves and none of them her poker-straight brown hair. Although their brown eyes were all hers, especially Pia's.

She turned her face upwards to catch the last rays of the sun, as Fiona watched her protectively. She was so young and it was so wrong, but then, there was no 'deserving' death.

The breeze lifted suddenly, snatching a shutter that covered one of the villa's high windows, and Jessie looked up, catching a glimpse of the strange shapes the setting sun was throwing across the glass. For one second she saw Michael's kind face looking down, watching his girls, as he'd called them. Then the breeze settled and rested the shutter back, and he was gone.

She saw him more often now. A glimpse in the mirror as she turned, a shadow amongst the trees in the orchard, and every day in her children's faces. She knew it wouldn't be long before they were together again and she was at peace with it. Not welcoming it, for the girl's sake, but calmer now that she knew that they were safe. With the private adoption finally completed, making them the daughters of Signora Flavia Marino, Fiona McNamee had gone forever now too.

Fiona watched Jessie and remembered the day six months before when she had first contacted her. A day that had changed all of their lives. She'd recognised the kind girl who'd knocked at her lonely house in Glengormley from the jury of five years before. Jessie had been the only person to come and see her after the trial; expressing her sadness at Brian's death, and at how badly the legal system had handled Lynsey Taylor's sentencing.

Jessie had been different back then; fit and healthy, with the bloom that came from a happy marriage. Her joy had somehow hurt her own new widowhood, making it feel even rawer, but the young mother's kindness had prevented her pain turning to bitterness.

But the Jessie who had called at Glengormley months before had been a very different girl, worn down by grief and illness and afraid for the future. Not selfishly, but for her children. They had chatted and in their joint sadness they'd eventually struck a bargain that would give her and the children new life, and Jessie lasting peace.

Suddenly, Ruby pulled Fiona by the hand, out of her dream, while Anya took Jessie's, drawing them into their pretty game. Dancing clumsily around the small courtyard while Pia watched; again and again and again until they 'all fell down'.

An hour later, when the girls were in bed, Fiona brought out more wine and the blue folder that held the details of their futures. Then they started the preparations for Jessie's last journey, the saddest of all their lives.

****

Switzerland.

It had been the hardest decision of her life and Jessie knew that she would never leave the clinic. She would never see her beautiful daughters again, except in her mind's eye, but she was content.

She gazed around the small, still room, admiring the white sheets and walls, their soothing coolness enhanced by the view from her window over Lake Geneva.

Switzerland was famous for so many things: the Alps, priceless watches, scrumptious chocolate and...

Egress, the most famous euthanasia programme in the world.

She hadn't chosen her abusive childhood, she hadn't chosen her sudden widowhood, and she hadn't chosen the stranger that she had become, born of the mess inside her head. But she *had* chosen Michael and her children, and she could and would choose this, the way in which she died, rather than allow her children to watch her waste away, leaving them frightened and confused.

All the papers were secure now and the endless letters written, to be read at important times like birthdays and graduations and weddings. The little trinkets and small notes had been left wrapped in gift paper, to be opened when the girls cried too much or asked about their mum and dad. Pretty little things, to make them smile and give them answers. She trusted Fiona to make the decisions now, knowing that she loved her daughters nearly as much as she did. She would be a good mother to them.

They'd driven there yesterday, leaving the girls with their new nanny, and Fiona had recorded her final words, typing them up neatly. Now the final letter lay in front of her, just awaiting her signature.

In a moment, they would come and Fiona would hold her hand. No priest, no vicar, just the doctor and them, and then just them alone. Then finally, just the peace that would fall on the small room a few short minutes later. Giving them just long enough to say goodbye and then leaving Fiona in silence, but never alone again.

****

Monday, 12th November.

The home invasion had been wrapped up. The killers had turned out to be the couple's grandson and one of his friends, the disgust of the arrest stronger than any of them had felt before, as if there were no more taboos left to break.

Craig's relationship with Julia was simmering and she was giving him time. He couldn't use her to forget Camille and he couldn't forget Camille until they had met and dealt with the past between them. Their meeting was five days away now, still far enough away for him to cope.

Now he was looking out at the Lagan thinking, and really hoping that something would happen soon to stop him. He reached into his briefcase for a file and caught sight of his sports kit, abandoned in the corner weeks before and completely forgotten about. *That's* what he would do tonight. Time to get fit again, before his six-pack became a slab of toffee.

The sudden hard knock that shook his door could only have been Liam's, and Craig called him in without turning.

"Here, how'd you know it was me? My Chanel?"

The coy tone he used for the last two words made Craig laugh. "Hardly. Not unless Eau de Bricky is their new range."

Liam feigned offence, making to leave. "Ah now, is that any way to greet the bearer of interesting news? I'll just leave then, will I?"

Craig put out his hand for the sheet of paper he could see hidden behind Liam's back. "Give."

"I will, but I'll tell you what it is as well." He handed the page to Craig as he spoke.

"We've just had a call from the Swiss police. Hey, are they the ones who carry the poles?"

"You're thinking of the Swiss Guard at the Vatican. The Swiss police wear military uniform. Anyway, what did they want?"

Craig suddenly made the connection and lurched forward, urgently scanning the sheet. "Have they found Adams?"

"In a manner of speaking. She's dead."

"What? How? The tumour?"

Liam slumped in a chair.

"Nope. She did herself in. In that Egress clinic place, on Friday. They cremated her. She left instructions for a letter to be sent to us."

Egress... Exit

"Have we received it yet?"

"Not the original, they're transcribing and sending it over now. Apparently it's quite something, or 'Zut Alors' as yer man on the phone said."

"Was she alone when she did it?" The image of a living Fiona McNamee still haunted Craig.

"No, some old lady was with her. Grey hair. They said it was her grandmother, but she doesn't have one, does she?"

"I doubt it. It'll be Fiona McNamee in another disguise. Any details of the car they arrived in? Plane? Anything?"

"Davy's on it but it'll draw a blank. That pair have more passports than Jason Bourne."

Craig nodded. The note in front of him gave details of the call that Liam had just taken, and covered what they had just discussed. The two women had arrived without the children on November 8th, the day before the assisted suicide. In a Fiat; bought or hired, who knew? There would be no trail on it, he was sure of that. There'd been none for any of the other cars that they'd used.

"Who signed for her ashes?"

"Grandma. There's a photo of her coming through now. She looks like Mrs Santa Claus, only thinner. Name of Carola Brana."

"It might as well have been Mrs Claus for all the good it will do us. Let's see what the letter says."

The transcript had just been come through and Nicky brought them in two hot copies to match the drinks that Craig had already poured. They sat reading and drinking in complete silence for twenty minutes.

The letter started with 'I, Jessica Adams' and ended with her signature; faint and spidery, the way Craig remembered his grandmother's becoming near the end.

It was all there; every tiny detail of how she'd killed each of their victims. Maria Burton, Ian McCandless, Lynsey Taylor and Liam Cullen, then how she had killed herself and been cremated. Craig stared at Liam, smiling grimly.

"How does it feel to be on a list of the dead?"

"Bloody lucky, that's how it feels. Although if I could get my hands on her..."

"She'd run through your fingers..."

They nodded at the macabre truth of his words and continued reading. Everything was there: the wire, the bolt-gun and the deliberate fight in the nightclub. The remand and bail perfectly timed. The pure Heroin, her stint as a canteen worker using aconite from the farm's Monkshood to spice up Liam's chips, then the journey from Ireland to Europe, with Fina Morales, her supposed Spanish au pair.

Adams claimed that everything had been one hundred percent her plan, and one hundred percent her fault. She was fed up with the injustice of a world that had killed her husband at thirty and was killing her at twenty-seven. And she had never forgotten the treatment of Brian McNamee's family at all their hands.

She had outlined her father's abuse of her from the age of eleven to when she'd finally left home at fifteen, and how weak she thought the system was, accepting the word of a paedophile and his wife instead of the child's. The times, dates and details of the reports she made of his abuse to the school were all documented; every one of them ignored by the powers that be. Craig wondered if it might be enough to bring a case against her father and the school even now. He was damn sure that Jenny Archer in Child Protection would be keen to try.

Adams had thought of absolutely everything, even including a copy of the fake adoption papers making Fina Morales the children's legal guardian. Her name and address would be false of course: there would be another legal set in completely different names hidden elsewhere.

Craig wasn't sure that it mattered what the girls' new mother was called. Fina or Helga...or Fiona McNamee? Jessica Adams had loved her children and she'd described their new carer as a loving woman who would give them the best in life. They would pass the information to Interpol but Craig knew it would end up filed in a cupboard somewhere, unless the children came to their attention for some reason and they never would.

The two detectives read in silence until their cups were drained and longer, then they put the papers down, nodding at each other in agreement. There was no way that they'd get a conviction here. Jessica Adams had confessed to everything and she was dead. Even if they suspected that Fiona McNamee was still alive and had colluded in the murders, there would be no evidence to incriminate her. They'd been far too clever for that.

There hadn't been any money moved from Fiona McNamee's account since she'd 'died', or into Jessica Adams'. And without any evidence to link McNamee directly to the murders, what could they actually prosecute her for if they ever did find her? Falsifying her own death? Adopting while dead?

As Lucia would say. "Good luck with that one."

But Liam was one of their victims so Craig put it to him. "What do you think? Likely prosecution or not?"

Liam stared at him sombrely for a moment, until a small smile cracked his wide, pale face. Craig could hear a joke coming,

"I'm going to copy this and frame it. There's mileage to get from being dead, you know. It could get me all sorts of sympathy, maybe even a few free pints."

Craig smiled wryly. "Maybe... but I wouldn't hold your breath." They both realised what he'd said and laughed. Liam shrugged.

"Aye well, at the end of the day, what's the hope of finding them? A snowball's in hell. And what happens to the kids if we do? They've already lost two parents; they don't need to lose another one, do they, and end up with a paedo granddad? Even if we managed to prove their new mother *is* Fiona McNamee, we don't have anything to tie her to the killings or even paying Adams to commit them. No money passed between them. Everything we have: prints, photos, confession, everything proves Adams did it."

He linked his hands behind his head, rocking back on his chair precariously.

"I say let her rest, and that's what I'll be saying to the rest of the victims' families with your OK? We already have a dead killer, and not a hope in hell of punishing anyone except those kids in future, and that wouldn't be any sort of justice. Let it go, boss."

Craig nodded in agreement. "OK. You speak to the families and I'll do the report for the public prosecutors and Interpol. We'll file it under no further action unless they say otherwise, but somehow I don't think they will."

"What about the McNamee kids? Do we even hint that we think their mum's still alive?"

Craig shook his head. "On what evidence? All we have is conjecture and we could start them searching for a ghost. They've suffered enough, Liam. Let's leave it alone."

"OK. I'll tell Annette then, just in case she gets the urge to confess all."

Then he grinned broadly and Craig knew that grin was going to cost him money. He was right; it morphed seamlessly into Liam's best martyred look.

"It fair works up a thirst being dead you know... but I'd say four or five pints should sort it out..."

****

On a late November evening in Lecce, three little girls sat chatting and crying in the evening sunshine, as a kind woman told them all about their mother who had loved them very, very much. She played recordings of her voice, she sprayed her perfume on them so that they could smell her again, and she showed them a video of them all laughing. As often as they wanted her to, until one by one they fell asleep in her arms.

Fiona would never stop telling them a sanitised version of how Jessie had given up everything, including her own life, to make sure that they would be safe forever. And it wasn't a lie, it was just a fairy story; to hide the realities of an unjust world that they were too young to understand.

THE END

Core Characters in the Craig Crime Novels

D.C.I. Marc (Marco) Craig: Craig is a sophisticated, single, forty-two-year-old. Born in Northern Ireland, he is of Northern Irish/Italian extraction, from a mixed religious background but agnostic. An ex-grammar schoolboy and Queen's University Law graduate, he went to London to join The Met (The Metropolitan Police) at twenty-two, rising in rank through its High Potential Development Training Scheme. He returned to Belfast in two-thousand and eight after more than fifteen years away.

He is a driven, compassionate, workaholic, with an unfortunate temper that he struggles to control and a tendency to respond to situations with his fists, something that almost resulted in him going to prison when he was in his teens. He loves the sea, sails when he has the time and is generally very sporty. He plays the piano, loves music and sport. He lives alone in a modern apartment block in Stranmillis, near the university area of Belfast.

His parents, his extrovert mother Mirella (an Italian pianist) and his quiet father Tom (an ex-university lecturer in Physics), both in their late sixties, live in Holywood town, six miles away. His rebellious sister, Lucia, his junior by ten years, works in a local charity and also lives in Belfast.

Craig is a Detective Chief Inspector heading up Belfast's Murder Squad, based in the Co-ordinated Crime Unit (C.C.U.) building in Pilot Street, in the Sailortown area of Belfast's Docklands. He loves the sea, sails when he has the time and is generally very sporty. He plays the piano, loves music by Snow Patrol and follows Manchester United and Northern Ireland football teams, and the Ulster Rugby team.

D.I. Liam Cullen: Craig's Detective Inspector. Liam is a forty-seven-year-old former RUC officer from Crossgar in Northern Ireland, who transferred into the PSNI in two-thousand and one following the Patton Reforms. He has lived and worked in Northern Ireland all his life and has spent almost thirty years in the police force, twenty of them policing Belfast, including during The Troubles.

He is married to the thirty-seven-year-old, long suffering Danielle (Danni), a part-time nursery nurse, and they have a one-year-old daughter Erin and are expecting their second child. Liam is unsophisticated, indiscreet and hopelessly non-PC, but he's a hard worker with a great knowledge of the streets and has a sense of humour that makes everyone, even the Chief Constable, laugh.

D.S. Annette McElroy: Annette is Craig's detective sergeant and has lived and worked in Northern Ireland all her life. She is a forty-three-year-old ex-nurse who, including her nursing degree, worked as a nurse for thirteen years then, after a career break, retrained and has now been in the police for an equal length of time. She's is married to Pete, a P.E teacher at a state secondary school and they have two children, a boy and a girl (Jordan and Amy), both young teenagers. Annette is kind and conscientious with an especially good eye for detail. She also has very good people skills but can be a bit of a goody-two-shoes.

Nicky Morris: Nicky Morris is Craig's thirty-seven-year-old personal assistant. She used to be P.A. to Detective Chief Superintendent (D.C.S.) Terry *'Teflon'* Harrison. Nicky is a glamorous Belfast mum, married to Gary, who owns a small garage, and the mother of a young son, Jonny. She comes from a solidly working class area in East Belfast, just ten minutes' drive from Docklands.

She is bossy, motherly and street-wise and manages to organise a reluctantly-organised Craig very effectively. She has a very eclectic sense of style, and there is an ongoing innocent office flirtation between her and Liam.

Davy Walsh: The Murder Squad's twenty-four-year-old computer analyst. A brilliant but shy EMO, Davy's confidence has grown during his time on the team, making his lifelong stutter on 's' and 'w' diminish, unless he's under stress.

His father is deceased and Davy lives at home in Belfast with his mother and grandmother. He has an older sister, Emmie, who studied English at university.

Dr John Winter: John is the forty-one-year-old Director of Pathology for Northern Ireland, one of the youngest ever appointed. He's brilliant, eccentric, gentlemanly, and really likes the ladies.

He was Craig's best friend at school and university and remained in Northern Ireland to build his medical career when Craig left. He is now internationally respected in his field. John persuaded Craig that the newly peaceful Northern Ireland was a good place to return to and assists Craig's team with cases whenever he can. He is obsessed with crime in general and US police shows in particular.

D.C.S. Terry (Teflon) Harrison: Craig's boss. The fifty-three-year-old Detective Chief Superintendent is based half-time at the C.C.U., where he has an office on the twelfth floor, and half-time at the Headquarters building in Limavady in the North-West Irish countryside. He shares a converted farm house at Toomebridge with his homemaker wife Mandy and their daughter Sian, a marketing consultant. He has had a trail of mistresses, often younger than his daughter.

Harrison is tolerable as a boss as long as everything's going well, but he is acutely politically aware and a bit of a snob, and very quick to pass on any blame to his subordinates (hence the Teflon nickname). He sees Craig as a useful employee but resents his friendship with John Winter, who wields a great deal of power in Northern Ireland.

Key Background Locations

The majority of locations referenced in the book are real, with some exceptions.

Northern Ireland (real): Set in the northeast of the island of Ireland, Northern Ireland was created in nineteen-twenty-one by an act of British parliament. It forms part of the United Kingdom of Great Britain and Northern Ireland and shares a border to the south and west with the Republic of Ireland. The Northern Ireland Assembly holds responsibility for a range of devolved policy matters. It was established by the Northern Ireland Act 1998 as part of the Good Friday Agreement.

Belfast (real): Belfast is the capital and largest city of Northern Ireland, set on the flood plain of the River Lagan. The seventeenth largest city in the United Kingdom and the second largest in Ireland, it is the seat of the Northern Ireland Assembly.

The Dockland's Co-ordinated Crime Unit (The C.C.U. - fictitious): The modern high-rise headquarters building is situated in Pilot Street in Sailortown, a section of Belfast between the M1 and M2 undergoing massive investment and re-development. The C.C.U. hosts the police murder, gang crimes, vice and drug squad offices, amongst others.

Sailortown (real): An historic area of Belfast on the River Lagan that was a thriving area between the sixteenth and twentieth Centuries. Many large businesses developed in the area, ships docked for loading and unloading and their crews from far flung places such as China and Russia mixed with a local Belfast population of ship's captains, chandlers, seamen and their families.

Sailortown was a lively area where churches and bars fought for the souls and attendance of the residents and where many languages were spoken each day. The basement of the Rotterdam Bar, at the bottom of Clarendon Dock, acted as the overnight lock-up to prisoners being deported to the Antipodes on boats the next morning, and the stocks which held the prisoners could still be seen until the nineteen-nineties.

During the years of World War Two the area was the most bombed area of the UK outside Central London, as the Germans tried to destroy Belfast's ship building capacity. Sadly the area fell into disrepair in the nineteen-seventies and eighties when the motorway extension led to compulsory purchases of many homes and businesses, and decimated the Sailortown community. The rebuilding of the community has now begun, with new families moving into starter homes and professionals into expensive dockside flats.

The Pathology Labs (fictitious): The labs, set on Belfast's Saintfield Road as part of a large science park, are where Dr John Winter, Northern Ireland's Head of Pathology, and his co-worker, Dr Des Marsham, Head of Forensic Science, carry out the post-mortem and forensic examinations that help Craig's team solve their cases.

St Mary's Healthcare Trust (fictitious): St Mary's is one of the largest hospital trusts in the UK. It is spread over several hospital sites across Belfast, including the main Royal St Mary's Hospital site off the motorway and the Maternity, Paediatric and Endocrine (M.P.E.) unit, a stand-alone site on Belfast's Lisburn Road, in the University Quarter of the city.

Printed in Great Britain
by Amazon